SNOW VILLAIN

MICHAEL P BLATTENBERGER

ISBN: 978-1-0880-7201-1

Printed in the United States of America

Published by Book Marketeers.com

DEDICATION

I dedicate this work first to my father, Del who taught me the love of our language; to my mother, Dolores who showed me the importance of understanding humanity, to my sister Karen who showed me how to love unconditionally and especially to my lovely bride, Catherine, who continues to inspire me every day to be a better man.

ACKNOWLEDGMENT

THANK YOU TO ALL MY FAMILY AND FRIENDS WHO HAVE HELPED SHAPE ME AND HELPED ME BECOME THE BEST VERSION OF ME.

Table Of Contents

PART ONE

She was short in stature with jet-black curly hair, but she carried herself with an air of confidence. She was the managing partner in her own law firm, Mahern, Miller and Associates, so she had come a long way to achieving all her goals. She was always working on major cases surrounding public anti-trust or politically based litigation. Her partner, Wilson Miller, was a great researcher and focused on jury selection, background detail, and forensics. She was the litigator. She had always loved the debate and the English language's ability to lead one through a discussion by using just the right verbiage to make a point or win an argument. This week had been exhausting and she had promised herself that she would leave early to beat the traffic at the end of the day. Sadly, it was almost six o'clock by the time she shut the lights and locked up the office in the new Bank Building at Delaware and West Mohawk St. in downtown Buffalo, New York, and began her journey home.

Christie Mahern got into her new red Ford Mustang sports coup and began the long drive home in weather that could only be described as a "Buffalo Winter". It was cold, 24 degrees, with the wind chill at about 10 degrees, making standing outside a challenge even walking into the basement parking lot 30 feet from the elevator was bone-chilling. As she pulled out of the parking lot, she was trying not to think of the three cases she was working on. It was Friday after all. She needed to clear her head. She needed to pay closer attention to the road as all the crazy maniacs she traveled beside each day were headed out on the cross-town 190 to their little hovels of safety. It was dark now this winter night and beginning to snow more heavily again as she passed through the toll heading to the Thruway.

She cursed herself for not leaving earlier but the telephone was ringing off the hook continuously after lunch as she returned to the office from court today. She reviewed her three cases.

Her largest case was Private Sector Providers vs. New York State. A class action suit against the state was brought by a group of local private companies providing educational, residential, therapeutic, vocational, and support services to the developmentally disabled population. That one centered around funding losses over the years that New York has deferred into its own system based upon its control over the decisions in the State's Division of Budget regarding federal apportionment.

Then there was the VASCO vs. The City of Buffalo case. She represented Victor A. Sinclair's company in a case that centered around the issue of where the new Peace Bridge was to be located. Should it be placed in what many thought were the most ideal and fiscally feasible spot owned by Mr. Sinclair or the property owned by the City of Buffalo which would mean millions of dollars going into the City's coffers, lower taxes, and many more jobs for a declining local economy, was the question. In the later scenario, it was suspected that Mayor Johnny Galway would somehow divert the major cash flow into the City's suspected system of graft which he controlled for both political and financial gain. Christie's final case was the initial preparations for the Sorrento Cheese Co. vs. Perrier Incorporated in a buy-out attempt by the French company. The car phone rang. Christie answered with her headset still on. It was Mickey Symans from the Mayor's office.

He was the head engineer. He was calling about getting the exact specifications for VASCO's land on the waterfront that would be purchased by the Peace Bridge Consortium. "Christie, Symans here. I was just wondering if you have the land specs for VASCO's property on the waterfront?" Christie replied, "Hey Mickey, I just looked at them before I left the office. Do you have a pen ready? I'll give them to you now."

As she had just looked at those documents before leaving the office, she gave him the reference page in her preparation document for the court proceedings in a few weeks.

Mickey was impressed with her ability to answer his pointed question with such accuracy while driving home from the office. Her scan of the documents late in the day worked to her advantage though it cost her time getting out of town before the heavy weekend traffic began.

As she hung up the phone with a hearty thank you from Mickey, she focused again out the window and realized the snow began to fall a bit harder and the wipers were automatically activated. She loved the new Ford Mustang she drove and the power she felt driving it. As the Mustang was purring through the evening traffic, Christie realized she was already at the 190 South - Thruway (90) merge. Traffic here was slowed, especially on Friday night. She merged South driving on the 90 toward the exit to the 400 on her way to East Aurora. It was a bit easier as the right lane merged into the upcoming exit rather smoothly.

She would be home in twenty minutes after getting on the 400 east if traffic moved normally. Her mother thought she was crazy to live so far out in the country away from where she worked in downtown Buffalo, but Christie loved the quiet of the country in contrast to the hectic pace of her everyday work life in town.

She noticed the snow was coming down more steadily and there was so much left from Wednesday's big storm, you couldn't tell how much new snow had already fallen. It just all began to blend into a blur of a sheet of white wool covering the area with a billowy softness. As everyone said in town, "it's pretty to look at but hell to drive in."

She was now on the 400 and began to think about Perry. That was Perry Kline. The detective in the downtown Police Precinct 3. They had been dating on and off for some time now. He kept saying the relationship they had must stay casual as he was still reeling from his recent separation and divorce from his wife, Donna. He said to her that it wasn't fair to Christie to get really, serious as this was his "rebound" relationship.

He didn't think he was ready to move to a serious relationship yet. That was disheartening to Christie because she knew the sex was the best either of them had ever experienced, she was ready for this to be a long-term thing, and sadly frowning she thought that maybe his feelings toward her were not focused on the long term and his recent divorce was a crutch he was leaning on to avoid commitment. As she looked up past the flapping windshield wipers, she saw the oil tanker just ahead with the bright yellow letters VASCO OIL on the back of the truck. She knew she was too close, so she began to slow down. Too late; the tanker was now breaking as she could clearly see the brake light flashing red very brightly. The tanker began fishtailing back and forth across the road as she applied her brakes.

The second time she pumped the brakes was much too forceful as she felt the Mustang begin to spin on the ice. In the dullness of the early evening's darkness lit brightly by the falling snow across her windshield, she saw only a black blur through her windshield. She could feel the car's spinning increasing speed and the next sensation she felt was a sudden jolt.

Then there was only blackness and an eerie quiet. She couldn't see. In the silence, she only heard her heart beating. She was still alive so that was something. Christie opened her eyes and still saw nothing but blackness. She began to panic a little…wondering. As her eyes became adjusted to the darkness, she first realized that she was not seriously injured. She was clearly shaken. She felt for the door handle and tried to open it. It wouldn't budge.

She leaned over to the passenger side and that door seem jammed as well. She was able to crack the window down about an inch and the snow began to fall in the car. She realized she was in a snowbank. She lifted the door handle and began shouldering the door and got it to move an inch or two. Her 105 lb. body was no match for the snowbank.

Christie removed her seat belt and was able to turn in her seat with her feet on the door. She just kicked with both feet on the door, and it began to move to the point where she had to get her bottom closer to continue. After about what seemed like hours but was only ten minutes, she had the door opened enough to begin to crawl out.

She could see just over the snow pile that off in the distance, the tanker truck with his flashers on stood at the side of the road about 50 yards up the road. The night air was brisk; the snow was still falling but just barely now. She leaned over to crawl out of the car with her purse in hand as she saw no other movement around. She looked down to see where to place her foot in the snow and she felt herself SCREAM!! She didn't really hear a sound. She just felt the ringing in her ears. The image she was looking at was unimaginable. All she could see was a face looking straight up at her with their eyes wide open as if in surprise but a stillness that was freaking her out. It was a man; his face was blue like he had been there a while. He seemed to be buried beneath the snow and he was dead. The most frightening part was that she recognized him. There was no doubt about it; it was Buffalo Mayor Johnny Galway.

The next thing she knew, she was walking toward Route 400 slowly as the snow was deep; now aware she was about twenty yards from her car as she stepped onto the shoulder of the highway. As she turned to her left, she saw a police squad car approach her on the shoulder very slowly with its flashing lights illuminating the night. Christie began talking to the West Seneca Patrol officer as he exited his vehicle and began to approach her on foot. She felt like she was screaming as she explained what she had seen when she got out of her car. He calmed her and asked if she was hurt. She shook her head no and she was suddenly very tired. He grabbed her around the waist as her legs began to fail her. She leaned on the young officer, and he spoke into his shoulder-mounted radio, "Central, this is car 41, Wilson, calling. We have a car off the 400 at mile marker six and a possible victim. Send back up and the ambulance. Over.

They walked to his cruiser, and he sat her in the back seat on the passenger side with the door open. Minutes later, there were police everywhere. A black Chevy sedan with a red flashing light on its dashboard pulled up behind the patrol car she sat in. She could see two detectives exit the vehicle. It was Perry Kline and his partner Paul Gorci from Buffalo Police Department Headquarters. Perry nodded to her as he walked by. Paul politely did say, "Hello." Within minutes, Perry was back at her side. He said, "What happened?" Christie replied, "Well, Detective, I've already given a statement to the first officer on the scene from West Seneca and explained everything I could to that officer," as she nodded toward the young patrolman standing next to Perry and looking young enough to be her son. Perry barked, startling her, "Well Ma'am, I guess you're just gonna have to repeat it again to me."

The look on the face of the young officer from West Seneca made Perry almost burst out in laughter. Even Christie thought it was very funny, as she did most things this man said. Perry nonchalantly said to the patrolman, "She's an old friend, we've worked a couple dozen cases together.

Maybe he meant cases of wine she thought because she hardly ever encountered him in a professional capacity. Perry was pulling her off to the side and talking in much gentler tones, "Are you okay?" "Yes, Detective, thank you" was all she could come up with and, of course, her brightest smile.

She could see off in the distance that pictures of the scene were beginning and the digging out of His Honor, Mr. Johnny Galway, was about to start. Within a matter of thirty minutes or so, they had the body completely uncovered and she watched as Perry stood over the body as he watched the coroner do a quick observation to make some pronouncement that was, of course, redundant at this point. No amount of thawing out would bring any more life back to Johnny Galway. The Mayor of the Queen City was quite deceased. Perry supervised the area being cordoned off so that the investigation could commence, however, he knew in his mind that they may have to wait until spring to find any real clues which might be easily accessible.

So, the scene's integrity had to be preserved. As Perry turned to walk back toward the highway, he passed the body of the mayor just as the coroner's team was getting ready to bag the body. Perry noticed a large hole on the back right side of the mayor's neck which was previously hidden.

Oddly, there were no signs of blood, so Perry quickly ran his trained eyes over the body and noticed something sticking out of the mayor's vest pocket. He said to the Asst. Coroner, Ted Zack, "Hey Ted, what is that in his vest pocket?

Grab it for me will you, I don't have any gloves on." As Ted Zack pulled his gloved hand away from the pocket, he turned and opened his hand flat so Perry could see.

It was a key. It was a heavy gold key with a red plastic tag that said—HYATT HOTEL 220.

Perry watched as Ted place the key in an evidence bag then he returned to the road where he found his boss, Parker Clark talking to Christie. They were talking about how she would get home. Christie hoped that she could shag a ride with Perry, but Parker was insistent that he be the one to drive her home as Perry would need to continue working the scene. Parker said, "Perry, you finish up here; I'll take Miss Mahern home and I'll meet you back in the office." "Okay Chief", was Perry's only response. As he walked back toward his car to talk to Paul Gorci, he thought he would have really liked to have taken Christie home so he could ensure she was okay but realized it was better if he got back to working the scene.

This would probably be the case of the century in Buffalo, New York and he was right in the middle of it. It would be bigger that even he knew at that moment but as the days passed, it would become more evident to everyone the significance of the case and the Department's ability to solve this. Parker and Christie walked to his unmarked vehicle as she watched Perry rejoin his partner Paul at the group of forensic people already gathered at the site. It was five minutes before seven and they all knew it would be a long night. The family had to be notified. There would be countless strategy meetings to sit through on how to deal with the press and delegate the tasks involved in completing this investigation.

Then there was the key to the Hyatt Hotel room found in the mayor's vest pocket. Perry thought the hotel would be the first place to start. He told Paul as much and added that Paul should probably start at City Hall to find out the mayor's activities that day, who was the last to see him, and trace his activities in the past few days with the mayor's aides. At that point, they jumped in the car and headed back downtown.

Meanwhile, Parker turned down the police radio volume in his car so he and Christie could talk. He knew Christie was seeing Perry on and off but he himself always had been attracted to her and as always, he would be the consummate professional; taking extra care to not reveal those thoughts. He wanted to get a sense from Christie, what she had been working on, what her relationship with the mayor was, and more importantly how much she knew about her brother Matt Fogelberg's feeling toward mayor Galway after just losing the election to him, but he'd have to tread softly as she was a pretty shrewd lawyer and would be aware of his intentions if he was too eager.

Christie broke the silence in the car after ten minutes or so by saying, "Parker, who do you think did that to the mayor?" The mayor had been shot in the back of the head at what looked like close range. The conditions around the body didn't show signs of blood or a struggle according to the forensic team. She thought to herself who she thought had murdered the mayor while waiting for The Chief's response.

Parker thought a second then replied, "Well Counselor, the mayor had many friends, and being a politician from South Buffalo for as many years as he was; he probably had almost as many enemies. There is no telling who could have gotten that close to perpetrate an act like that." Christie probed further, "How well did you know Johnny, Parker?" Without thinking, Parker replied, "Johnny and I go way back, and frankly I liked him an awful lot. There were times when his lifestyle and some of the things that came out of his mouth really left a bad taste in my craw. What about you?"

Christie thought quickly about her gut feelings and then parried with, "I knew him from several City Hall committees, a real estate case I am working on, and very casually at police functions over the years. After the last hard-fought election, I can think of three or four people who would have loved to see him being carried out of that snow crypt-like he was tonight." Parker snapped back, "Yeah; and who might those people be do you suppose?"

Christie carefully said, "Oh, no one I would want to blurt out to the Chief of Police Detectives at this point without having a chance to think these things through as I am still a bit shaken. Besides, would being angry at someone necessarily drive a person to kill them?" They both sat in silence…thinking. Christie reviewed the names in her head, knowing it was best to keep her mouth shut at this point in front of the Chief of Detectives for God's sake. Parker just wondered. They were pulling into Christie's driveway at that moment in mid-thought she realized Parker was never at her house. How did he know where it was?

Hmmm, she wondered. In her mind, she had been a thousand places since the conversation in the car had ceased. It surprised her that she was home. She realized she had left her briefcase in her car but said nothing about it. She instead said, "Parker, thank you so much for the ride home. Will the Department have my car towed or should I call a mechanic?" Parker simply replied, "You're welcome for the ride, and don't worry about the car as I already ordered it towed to Colello's here in the village. They will call you after they check it over and when it's ready, they will drop it off for you."

Christie smiled broadly and said, "Thanks, Chief. Good night." "Good night, Christie, I'll wait here until you get into the house," said Parker.

With that, she pushed open the door, jumped out, and turned to leave pushing the door closed. She ran to the house and as her door opened, she waved to Parker as he began backing up to leave out of the driveway.

Her telephone began ringing before she put down her purse or took off her coat. She ran to the kitchen and grabbed the receiver.

"Hello." It was Perry Kline. "Hi Christie, just checking to make sure you got home okay." "Yes, I did, Detective just walked in the door. I am pouring myself a glass of wine and falling into bed. By the way, I am glad you called, thanks. I need a huge favor. I left my briefcase in the backseat of my car. I have a bushel of work to get done over the weekend. I know you are busy right now but how soon can you have someone drop it off here for me?" Perry thought a moment then answered, "Well, I just dropped Paul off at headquarters and I am headed to the ... he paused; he was going to say the Hyatt but instead said; I have one stop to make first then I can swing by Colello's in about an hour if you need it tonight.

Or if you want, I can wait until first thing in the morning to swing by your place. Your call." Christie thought a second and said, "If it's not too much trouble, I would love it delivered tonight. Thanks." She didn't want too many folks possibly rummaging through her papers that contained some very confidential notes about all the cases she was working on. She wouldn't sleep until she had it back and silently cursed herself for not remembering it at the scene. She guessed she was still a bit flabbergasted at what she had seen. Perry called her name again, "Christie!" She came out of her reverie. "Yes," she muttered. "Twice I said that I would be there tonight, and you didn't respond. Are you sure you're alright?" "Sorry," Christie replied quickly. "I was just thinking about all that happened tonight. I'll let you go. Thanks." Perry sighed in relief, "I will bring over an extra big bottle of your favorite wine when I bring your briefcase later. See ya." Then the phone went silent.

Christie sat in her favorite chair and looked out at the night and sipped her glass of wine. She kept flashing back to seeing the face of Johnny Galway looking up at her in the snow. She shuddered. She began to run down the list of people she was thinking about while riding in the police car with Parker Clark.

She breathed a sigh of relief that she had kept her wits about her at that moment and not said a word. Frank Galway was the first name on her list. He was the mayor's younger brother. Frank was always a champion for his brother Johnny in public, but in the quiet backroom with close friends, he admitted to being quite jealous of Johnny, envious of his women, his political success, his business savvy, and all his good fortune. She remembered down at Mulligan's Bar in the Allentown district of Buffalo, Johnny and Frank had gotten into fisticuffs on two separate occasions while drinking and arguing over women. Christie asked herself, would a brother kill a brother?

Maybe not she finally concluded but the motive was certainly there. The next name on her list was Victor Sinclair, the real estate mogul, and minor sports team owner. He was the majority shareholder in the Buffalo Stallions Soccer team. Rumor had it that he was first trying to buy the Bisons' AAA baseball team and then he was mentioned as a potential buyer for the Bills National Football League team from Ralph Wilson. Victor was quite the ladies' man as his tall, thin, athletic Greek body made him the most eligible bachelor in town years back. Christie represented Victor in his real estate battle against the City of Buffalo and Mayor Johnny Galway over the placement of the new stadium for the Bisons Baseball team in its efforts to get a bid from Major League Baseball as well as the new Peace Bridge site location.

Christie felt a headache coming on as she thought of the next name on her list. It was, Matt Fogelburg. He was an up-and-coming young politician who had won the Councilman post in the old First Ward four years ago as a Republican and most recently lost the Mayoral election in September to Johnny Galway by a very slim margin. He was also her baby brother. Suddenly, she got very tired. She had another name on the list to consider but she needed a shower. She knew Perry would be stopping by to drop off her briefcase later and she wanted to have cleared her mind when he arrived.

She ran the water to get it to temperature for her shower, got undressed, and stepped into the water. Within 15 minutes, she was done, in her robe downstairs on the couch with another glass of wine. She turned on the television to see if the events of the evening had made the news yet.

Christie, being a good lawyer and mulling over the case that she knew was ahead, wondered if people would put her on the suspect list in their minds. She had gone out with Johnny Galway after his divorce; she was representing Victor Sinclair, Galway's current opponent in a high-profile real estate court case over the placement of the Peace Bridge and Johnny had just beaten her brother in the recent mayoral race. She knew of another scenario but didn't let herself even think about it. She laughed at the thought. The next thing she knew, she had fallen asleep and was dreaming that someone was banging on her door trying to get into her house.

Perry Kline had just dropped his partner Paul Gorci off at Headquarters and was headed down Church Street toward the Hyatt Hotel. He was there in 5 minutes, pulled up at the front door under the overhang, parked, and walked past the doorman, Reggie, waved and went to the front desk. There behind the counter was Jackie Cuffaletto, an old friend of his from the neighborhood. She smiled broadly as he approached the desk. Perry smiled back and said, "Hi Jackie. How are you? You sure are looking great as usual." Jackie, of course, blushed and replied, "Well Charmer, is this a business or pleasure visit?" Now it was Perry's turn to feel redness begin to appear on his face. "Unfortunately, it is business, Jackie. I need to know who was registered in Room 220 for the last two weeks." Jackie tried not to show any signs of alarm on her face, but she knew that was their missing key and she knew who she thought did not return it.

Perry watched her closely as he finished his question for any signs of a response. Jackie was keeping it pretty close to the vest and held a deadpanned expression then asked, "Anyone, in particular, you're looking for?" Perry cautiously responded, "No one in particular, but we found the key on an investigation, so we are tracking leads. You know, routine stuff." Jackie just nodded and went to the end of the desk to the computer. She tapped on the keys for a couple of minutes and said, "The report will be up in a minute or two, Perry." She walked down to where the printer sat on the back table. As she approached it, the machine began to hum with activity. Jackie grabbed the copy from the tray. It was a one-page printout that she scanned then handed to Perry.

Perry scanned the list quickly and his eyes went quickly to 12-10 Wednesday night.

Hyatt	Hotel		BFLO DT			Auto	Days
Month	Date	Day	Guest	CITY	ST	Plate	Days
DEC	1	Mon	J. Maltry	Erie	PA	JD6-1777	1
	2	Tues	Dr. J. Steinberg	Denver	CO	DDS-25531	1
	3	Wed	P. Celinas	Dallas	TX	VP 8-450 F	1
	4	Thurs	E. Volsier	Reno	NV	12-LI-3445	1
	5	Fri	P. Corectt	Philadelphia	PA	DIR-4545	2
	6	Sat	P. Corectt	Philadelphia	PA	DIR-4545	-
	7	Sun	S. Mills	Denver	CO	None	2
	8	Mon	S. Mills	Denver	CO	None	-
	9	Tues	C.M. Fuda	Keene	NH	815-BBG-9	1
	10	Wed	M. Keen	New York	NY	None	7
	11	Thurs	M. Keen	New York	NY	None	6
	12	Fri	M. Keen				5
	13	Sat	M. Keen				4
	14	Sun	M. Keen				3

"That's interesting!" Perry said out loud. Jackie asked, "What?" Perry just shrugged his shoulders and said, "Oh, nothing. Just looking at the names".

To himself, he wondered if the M. Keen on the list was the clue he was looking for or not. "Jackie, Thank you so much. This is very helpful and if this helps as much as I think it might, I owe you a dinner at Salvatore's. He then turned on his heel and left as quickly as possible, not waiting for a response from Jackie. I will probably be back in the morning to speak to you and the manager (he said over his shoulder). He would ask them questions later when he confirmed his suspicions about M. Keen.

Jackie wondered to herself how M. Keen had been entered in the computer on her shift without her knowledge. She thought of the people with access to the computer and ran the names in her head. She wrote down a list as she knew it might come back to her if the police were asking questions about that week. She put the list in her pocket.

Perry stopped into Headquarters to talk to Paul Gorci. As he got off the elevator on the second floor, he saw Paul talking to someone in Parker's office. Minutes before Perry entered, Paul was sitting in Parker's office having returned from City Hall. They heard him first before they saw him. Frank Galway, stormed across the outer office floor from the elevator bellowing about needing to see the Chief. As he got to Parker's office, Perry exited the elevator. Frank was yelling, "What are you guys doing to find out who killed my brother?" Parker began in his calm Norwegian manner, "Well Frank, just like in every investigation…" Frank didn't let him finish and bellowed again, "This is NOT like any other case. This is my brother and the Mayor of Buffalo!!" Parker now stood behind his desk trying to remain calm but as Perry approached closer, the conversation got more interesting. It also got much more heated. Perry went to his cubicle to listen.

The strain in Parker's voice could be heard, "Now Frank, I know how you must feel…" Again, he was interrupted by Frank yelling, "NO. I DON'T THINK YOU HAVE ANY FRIGGIN' IDEA HOW I AM FEELING!! MY BROTHER'S BEEN MURDERED AND…" It was now Parker who yelled in a booming voice that may have shaken the windows on the floor, "FRANK, CALM DOWN. Get a hold of yourself. We will have every available person on this case and stop your yelling. I am not deaf, and it is getting us nowhere." Frank spun on his heel and headed to the elevator, "I'll go as high as I have to in order to get the manpower needed to find who killed my brother!!" He was gone as quickly as he entered.

Perry walked into Parker's office. Paul had a stunned look on his face but was jotting notes. Parker was now sitting back in his large black padded swivel chair and addressed both Paul and Perry. "Perry, close the door, please. What do you guys have so far?" Perry began first, "Chief, I went to the Hyatt and got the list of names of those in room 220. That's the number of the key found on the mayor tonight." He laid the sheet down on the Chief's desk. Parker scanned it quickly.

He looked at Perry, "Thoughts?" Perry said, "Look at yesterday's entry. M. Keen. I am wondering if it was registered to Johnny or his wife, Margie. It's her maiden name. I have a meeting with the Manager and desk clerk at 8 am to get the details. I thought I would make a quick trip to question Margie tonight to get a statement from her. And what did you make of Frank's performance?" Parker responded with, "After I dropped Ms. Mahern off at her house, I made a personal visit to see Margie before I came back here.

She took it very hard. I know they were apart, but they spent many years together. My gut is that her reaction was legit. I got the sense that she was genuinely startled to learn of the news and immediately broke down emotionally." "Great Chief. Did you ask her about the key or making a visit to the Hyatt?" asked Perry. Parker quickly responded, "I asked her when the last time was that she saw Johnny and she said two weeks ago. I asked her if she was seeing anyone and had she ever rendezvoused at the Hyatt in the last two weeks. She gave me a funny look," paused, and said, "If I want to meet with anyone Mr. Clark, I am free to have them to my home. I don't need to sneak around at some hotel!" Paul said, "WOW! I'll bet that was awkward boss! Didn't you and Margie date after her and Johnny split?"

Parker just shot Paul a dirty look and said, "So do you have anything to add to this conversation?" Perry made a mental note to get some background on Parker's involvement with Margie Galway before he spoke with her tomorrow. Paul thought a second; realizing he had hit a nerve with his boss and began, "Well Chief, there was not much activity tonight at City Hall when I got there. A few committee meetings but not many of the mayor's staff. I did run into Mickey Symans going home when I was leaving. I asked him when the last time he saw Mayor Galway. He said that he had not seen Johnny since Monday night at the closed meeting on the Waterfront real estate case.

I asked him who was there. He hesitated a minute and said, Johnny, Denis Schinto, his counsel, Dean Coretti, Councilman of Lower West Side, James Maltry, Councilman of BlackRock, Neal Seagle, Councilman West Side, Rev. Charley Woodman, Real estate Purchasing for the City and Karen Maltry, Galway's Assistant, and him.

I figured that would give me a list of folks to follow up with tomorrow." Parker then said, "Okay, follow those up, Paul." To Perry, "Set up a meeting of the team tomorrow at 11 am and we'll share info and strategize then. Now, Perry, hand me that chalkboard behind you." Perry handed the Chief the 2 ft. by 3 ft. whiteboard with an attached dry erase marker. Parker started writing while at the same time Paul and Perry made quick lists of suspects in their heads. Parker said, "OK, does anyone want to start with a suspect list?" Paul, wanting to make amends for blurting out to the Chief about dating Margie, "I am thinking those with motives are Margie Galway, Victor Sinclair, and maybe Matt Fogelburg."

Perry quickly added, "I was thinking about anyone else that could gain from Galway being gone. His brother Frank came to mind. Then I wondered if we should be thinking about all the women he has dated since and maybe before splitting up with Margie. That's a long list so we may need a larger whiteboard." He quickly thought in his head-Linda Carnello, Joni Wilsco, Catie Fuda, Mel Barstow; and oh yeah, Christie Mahern. Parker turned the whiteboard around not having added anything since he asked the initial question. In bold black letters, it said: FRANK G. - MARGIE G. - VICTOR S. – MATT F. – JONI W.

The list had no real surprises. Parker began, "Frank has been quite vocal of late in some of his late-night haunts about how his brother always got the women, the jobs, and the attention that Frank has also sought. Margie has been embarrassed by Galway's running around, womanizing, and misusing her political clout to become so successful in politics but never acknowledging her ever. Matt had some terrible arguments with Galway in as many bars as you can name over the past seven months of the last election.

Then there is Joni Wilsco. She was really in love with Johnny to hear her tell it and was elated to have the chance to be with him after the Galways' split. I guess she dated him right after high school then lost him to Margie and then once they reconvened their tryst, Johnny humiliates her by bringing Linda Carnello to the Policeman's Ball that year. Anyone else for the initial list?" Paul and Perry both sat there in silence thinking about those they wanted to add but wanted to wait. Interestingly, they both thought about Parker Clark. They both said in unison, "That's a pretty good list to start, Chief." Parker stood and said, "Okay, you guys will take the lead on this. Perry, you handle the press. Perry why don't you handle Frank, Margie, and Victor. Paul, you can focus on Matt, Joni, and me." Silence. Parker continued, "Yes, I know you both were probably thinking of me anyway; I want you to investigate me just so we can say we covered all the bases." Both Paul and Perry began to speak but Parker held up his hand and said, "Off you go, see you back here at 11 am. Good night!"

Paul and Perry shuffled out of the office and met back in their cubicle. Neither said much until Paul said, "Wanna switch?" They both laughed. "No way," said Perry, "I'm going to head out. Call me if you need me, otherwise, I'll see you at 7 am for coffee at Botz's on Elmwood" Paul replied, "7 it is!"

Perry headed out the door to his cruiser. He headed toward East Aurora. As he drove out of town, he called Colello's Garage in town. Mark Colello answered, "Hello, Colello's." "Hey Mark, it's Perry Kline. How late will you be there?" Mark replied, "A couple of hours, I am checking out that car that uncovered the mayor just off the 400 tonight." "Okay Mark, Thanks. I am going to swing by in the next hour to look at it with you." They hung up.

As his car sped along the route to East Aurora, he made a mental note to pick up some wine. Perry then began to think about Christie and how they met. Although they were three years apart in age, Christie and Perry had gone to the same high school together in Valley Stream, New York (a typical middle-income community of Long Island located more than an hour's drive from Manhattan). He left before his senior year to move to Buffalo. Then moved to be with his then love interest Donna Foster who he would later marry in Syracuse New York. Christie left after graduation to go to law school at the University of Buffalo. It was ironic because they knew each other casually in school as he played basketball, and she was a cheerleader.

Perry went to the Police Academy in Syracuse then moved to Buffalo after his first year as a patrolman to take a position in the Internal Investigation Unit in Buffalo. This was recommended by his Academy classmate, Paul Gorci who knew the Department was looking for someone with no ties to the City of Buffalo's current criminal and political elements as there had been quite the shake-up of personnel after an internal drug problem became a scandal during Paul's first year. Luckily, he avoided that crowd and was able to work toward his goal of becoming a detective along with Parker Clark. Neither Perry nor Christie knew the other was in Buffalo. Five years later they reunited. As he remembered the circumstances, it brought a smile to his face as he drove.

It happened 5 years ago now at, of all places, the Policeman's Ball. It was held at the Center for Tomorrow on the Amherst Campus of the University of Buffalo. It was a beautiful venue that Perry had been to once before.

He attended the wedding of his cousin Joe Dobrowsky. Perry remembered walking in the door sporting his newly acquired Versace tuxedo from The Tuxedo Junction in the Main Place Mall. It fit well and his 6'2" 210 lb. frame made quite an impression on those in attendance as he sauntered into the festivities without a date. A lot of guys took dates to the Ball, but he felt he wanted to keep his options open at the time. He stood at the bar drinking his

CC on the rocks with a splash of "7" while carrying on the perfunctory idle conversation with a few of his fellow officers, Johnny Pacetti and Lenny Rommunski. They were soon joined by Parker Clark, Paul Gorci and Donna Smith a then Report Technician who had recently passed the Detective's exam and was starting her training. Perry became bored with the shop talk, and he wandered to the other side of the bar.

He casually gazed at two women sitting at the bar just to his left. The older of the two was seemingly chewing the ear off the cute brunette who listened very intently facing away from him. He had just ordered a refill when the brunette turned and shot Perry a quick glance looking directly into his eyes. He froze. He felt his knees weaken and a chill raced through him stopping at his loins. He had to turn away. He took a deep breath and thought, "What the hell was that?" As he reached for his fresh drink, he glanced over toward the ladies again only to find the brunette staring directly into his eyes again. He felt more vulnerable than ever before. He looked away again. He thought, "what was it about this woman's eyes?" He felt almost giddy. His mind raced. How could the town Casanova be affected like this by a mere glance? It wasn't a mere glance though and he knew it. The third time he looked, she was staring back at him again.

This time he had to physically move away attempting to gaze around the rest of the festivities. More truthfully, he was trying to collect his composure. He chanced another glance and this time she was again facing away toward her friend. He could now better size her up and relax. He was able to focus on her and liked what he saw. Pretty, sophisticated but dressed rather conservatively in a black sports coat with a white silk blouse. Strait-laced in a pantsuit he thought. He noticed a gold broach on the lapel of her coat and tried to decipher what it was so he could use it to make an opening move.

She quickly spun her whole body around and said, "What are you looking at?" Being in his mind quite the bon-vivant, his matter-of-fact response was, "Your chest!" He heard himself say this and he could feel the blood rush to his face and neck. He really felt HOT! What on earth was he thinking? He had met hundreds if not thousands of women and this was the best retort he could come up with? He instinctively approached her and closed the twenty feet between them in seconds. As he reached her, she spun completely around on the bar stool.

She spoke firmly over his feeble attempt at an apology, "Well. Here they Are- take a good look!" With that, she opened her sports coat with a hand on each lapel and smiled. Perry felt that chill then the heat from more blushing, almost to the point of dizziness. He saw quite the figure beneath the silk blouse and realized quickly that she wore a skirt below the jacket with a rather revealing slit up the side exposing a great set of legs. He stammered, "I'm really, very sorry. I was taken by your eyes when you looked at me and when I had a chance to look, saw the broach and wanted to make a humorous remark to begin a conversation.

I don't usually have my foot in my mouth when I do that." "Don't be sorry, she said, eyes twinkling again, "I thought it was funny and you're here, aren't you?" "Yes, Yes, I am." Perry offered trying to be calm. Let me introduce myself, I'm Perry Kline." She said, "No, that can't be. Now you're going to try to tell me you went to school on Long Island?" He was speechless!! Who was this girl? All he could do was stare into the penetrating eyes. Perry had never been down this road before nor this quickly. He was flabbergasted to say the least.

She began calmly, "My name is Christie Mahern. It used to be Fogelburg in school. I did go to school in Long Island with a Perry Kline. Are you that Perry Kline?" He laughed and she laughed as well. The night took on a completely different life after that. Instead of the party he dreaded every year where he looked for the first opportunity to make a quick exit, this promised to be quite different. It was like they were the only two in the room. The evening flew by as he remembered. There was a lot of touching through dinner. They tried to be discreet, but the excitement got the best of them both. Almost like the inevitability of a runaway train. They spoke of so many things that night: old friends, school, jobs they had held, and people they jointly knew, being just a few of the topics. Time really flew by.

During the awards portion of the evening's ceremonies, someone had to hit him twice to cue him to go on stage to the podium to receive his award. He had no clue what award he was accepting as he had obviously been distracted. He began by saying, "Thanks to all my fellow officers for their support which makes my job a pleasure to go to each and every day." He began to lose track of what he was saying as he looked over to his table and made eye contact again with the vision he was sitting with at dinner.

He glanced down at the plaque he held and realized it said he was being recognized for his legendary Community Service. He then added, "Without the support and efforts from all of you, the work being done and projects being successful for our local youth would never be realized. So, on behalf of them, Thanks to All of YOU!" He had spent countless hours working at the South Buffalo YMCA, coaching as well as organizing programs like the Professional Pals Project which teamed local business leaders with a group of young people interested in similar hobbies and activities. Everything from sports, Arts & Crafts to Public Speaking and

Community Volunteering. He thoroughly enjoyed his time at the center, but his speech ended abruptly as he was still lacking focus which brought out a quick blush while he scurried back to the table to Christie's side. He was always much better at public speaking than most as he reveled in the attention and a chance to talk about his work with local youth. He slid into the chair next to Christie, with a nod to each other.

As the awards were ending and staff was making room on the floor for the dancing to begin, they chose, to leave separately as planned. Their plan was to meet at the Holiday Inn on Niagara Falls Boulevard near the exit off the 290. It was quiet there most nights and was close. She lived in East Aurora, and he lived in this great old mansion on Richmond Avenue near Porter Avenue (a stone's throw across the traffic circle from Kleinhan's Music Hall). Both locations were too far away. She walked in and he was already sitting at the bar. He had already ordered her a cabernet. They quickly kissed as she sat down. She thanked him for the drink and said, "Do you have a room here?" "No," he said, "it was the first place I thought of to come to that was this quiet and close to where we were."

As a three-piece combo called, Cruisin' Fusion began to start up after their break, Perry said, "Sit tight, I'll be right back."

He walked back to the bar before the band began the first song in the set. It had taken all of four minutes. Christie knew because she looked at her watch when he left and when he returned. "Oh, by the way", he said, "I have a room here. Would you like to join me there?"

They walked toward the elevator with Christie's hand around Perry's arm. He looked at her in the mirror when they arrived at the elevator in the lobby. She was quite the looker and in great shape. He noticed the muscles in her legs which meant she worked out or probably ran. She had a white satin blouse on under her black blazer with the broach on the lapel which he first noticed but still hadn't identified. They rode in the elevator in silence and the bell signaling the floor rang, and they both exited quickly moving right down the hall to Room 201. Once inside, Christie turned to Perry, and they kissed. It was electric. Garments began flying in different directions and as he freed her bra, he admired her firm full breasts for a moment before he felt his trousers sliding to the floor. He stepped out of them and his shoes and was as naked as she was now. They embraced and fell on the bed. Their lovemaking was extraordinary. There was no hesitation from either. There seemed to be an unusual amount of familiarity even though it was their first sexual encounter. They rested then began again. She had as much stamina as he and they seemed to want to learn every nuance of this physical tryst as they both knew it was something very special. They lost count of their crescendos.

Christie looked at the alarm clock on the nightstand and the red numbers read, 5:22 A.M. As their breathing calmed once again, Perry said, "Wow, thank goodness I didn't find out how good you were in high school!" Christie looked at him quizzically, "Huh?" He replied, "We'd never have graduated!! Let's shower and I'll take you for breakfast." The shower was long enough to run out of hot water. They dressed and left. She followed him. They ate at Bruno's on Elmwood Avenue. What a memory.

He realized that he had reached downtown East Aurora, so he quickly began looking for Colello's Garage. It had been a while since he had been out this way. He saw it at the next light.

He parked in front of the office and walked in. He saw Mark Colello out in the closest bay working on the red Ford Mustang that he recognized as Christie's. Mark saw him and waved one finger in the air. He began to lower the car from the elevated lift. Once down, Mark walked into the office.

"Hey Perry, how's it going?" said Mark. "Crazy night, Mark. Anything wrong with the car? Did the murderer's weapon get caught underneath?", Perry laughed. "Well, Sir. Maybe and maybe not. I found this when I lifted it up to check brakes and pipes."

Mark threw him a plastic bag. In it, Perry saw one blue winter glove. It looked like police issue, but he couldn't be sure. The size made it seem like a man's glove. Perry asked, "Does it belong to the mayor?" Mark answered, "Hell if I know. I was going to ask you the same question. It does seem to have blood on it. I unhooked it with a set of pliers and placed it in the bag and sealed it." Perry said, "Nice work Colello, you might have solved the case. I need to get Christie's briefcase out of the car as I am on my way to her place.

I am going over to ask her some additional questions. Will you guys have time to bring her car to her tomorrow or is there something that would cause it to be impounded do you think?" Mark replied, "I'll have my older brother Dickie run it to her with one of the guys early tomorrow. Does that work for you?" "Perfect, Thank you!" Perry shot back. "Have a good night, sir." Perry picked up wine at Reed's liquor store next door to Colello's then drove his cruiser several minutes to Christie's on Olean Rd. to drop off her briefcase. He rang the bell three times without a response.

He banged on the door and waited. He was just about ready to use the key he knew was under the potted plant next to the door when he saw movement inside. Christie walked sleepy-eyed across the kitchen and opened the door. "Hi, Perry, I fell asleep after I had a bath and two glasses of wine, sorry I didn't hear the bell." Perry smiled and said, "No worries, Doll. Can I come in for a minute?" She stepped back and swept her arm motioning him to enter. Perry handed her the briefcase and a bottle of her favorite Cabernet. "I really can't stay Christie as I have a hundred things to get to before morning.

I just wanted to give you the case and let you know that Mark at Colello's checked over the car and it has no issues. I will get the ok from Parker to release it back to you in the morning. They will drop it off early. How are you?" Perry asked with a worried look. "I think I am fine. You really can't stay for a glass of wine?" Christie said hoping he would. "As long as you are alright, Doll, I think it's best if you get some sleep. I am sure the press will be after you in the morning for interviews and I know if I have one drink, you'll talk me into staying as I shouldn't drive after drinking, and wouldn't it be nice to cuddle, etc. And yes, that would be great, but Parker is going to be expecting me to solve this thing in a day or two and I have some leads I need to chase down so I hope I can get a rain check Miss Mahern?"

"Oh, OK, Detective Kline.", she said with a sigh, "I will look forward to cashing in the raincheck sometime soon, and thanks for getting the briefcase and the wine for me. I owe you two." They said good night, kissed and Perry left heading to headquarters.

As Perry drove, he thought about Johnny Galway. He had been a typical Irish lad from South Buffalo, New York. He attended Timon High School, playing three sports, baseball, basketball, and football. Baseball was his professed favorite. He also excelled in the classroom and was captain of the debate team.

He was quite the ladies' man the stories herald. He dated plenty of girls from the Mount (Mt. Mercy Academy) as well as OLV (Our Lady of Victory Academy) both all-girl schools and LHS (Lackawanna High School). The last two were four blocks apart on Ridge Road in Lackawanna. One of his favorite hangouts was the SouthRidge Restaurant. It was on the corner of Ridge Road and South Park diagonally across from Our Lady of Victory Basilica.

After graduating from Canisius College in Buffalo, he met and married, Margaret Keen.

Margie seemed to settle Johnny down as he began his political career. She was certainly an asset to him as her family was an old well-known name in Western New York politics. They were together for twenty years and had just divorced four years ago, just as he was finished his second term as mayor ended. He would never finish his third.

When Perry's partner Paul had done his initial City Hall interviews, most folks assumed Johnny had gone down to Myrtle Beach on one of his usual winter jaunts to visit his older brother Tommy who was a former Erie County Executive, and Johnny Galway's closest advisor. Tom had a four-bedroom condo right on the water next to the Whispering Pines Golf Course. Tommy and Johnny used to golf down there regularly.

He and Johnny would visit and play several rounds as they discussed the questions Johnny brought to him. The latest surely would have been the battle with Victor Sinclair over the placement of the new Peace Bridge and ultimately the new Waterfront stadium. Last year, Margie Keen was out of town the same week as the mayor and the rumors flew that they were meeting down there to rekindle the relationship. There were stories that both Johnny and Margie had strayed often from their marital bed over the past ten years, but everyone knew they loved each other dearly. Or so it seemed.

One of the stories around City Hall of late was that Charmaine Sinclair, Victor's wife, had set her claws into Johnny and they were having a torrid affair. Rumor was and history had shown that Mayor Johnny Galway had a difficult time resisting the charms of a beautiful, rich woman and Charmaine was both. The fact that she was the estranged wife of his archenemy would have certainly sealed the deal. Victor was much older than Charmaine and she was as rich as he was, so she had always been independent financially and they had an iron-clad pre-nuptial agreement.

Charmaine's wealth had come from her family's business back in Syracuse, New York. The Soledad family owned both a motor-freight trucking company and a coffee company for over forty years. The Sinclairs kept up pretenses for the public. Those close to them knew Victor had been running around with other women for years while Charmaine kept up the image of the dutiful wife chairing fundraising events for worthy causes championing the needy. Her circle of donors were those in Buffalo's elite communities. Generally, in public together, the Sinclairs were the model couple, however, at more intimate gatherings of close friends, Victor could be seen often being verbally abusive to Charmaine and openly flirting with other women.

The question was, Did Victor kill Johnny Galway? Was this the love triangle that went bad?

Perry was now back at Police headquarters downtown. He was hungry so he asked Paul if he wanted to order out from Chef's. Paul just picked up the phone and put in their usual order. Each got a cup of pasta Fagioli, Caesar salad, and a small portion of Spaghetti Parmesan. Perry's mouth began to water as Paul called in the order. It would be delivered within 20 minutes in the downtown district. Paul hung up and he and Perry went to the conference room.

Paul began, "OK, they said 20 to 25 minutes because it's Friday night. I set up meetings with Parker for tomorrow, as well as Matt Fogelburg. Joni Wilsco is also coming in on Saturday after work at 4:30 ish". Perry was quiet for a second. He then tossed the plastic bag on the table. "Colello's found this under Christie's car when they checked it out tonight. Mark put it in the plastic bag so maybe we can get a print or two. I spoke with Margie Keen saying that I would be visiting her at 9:00 am tomorrow. She sounded like she had been crying. I left a message for Victor at his office as I got his Company answering machine. Frank Galway will be harder to catch up with, but I thought I would let him calm down first before I interview him. Maybe I'll invite him to lunch someplace quiet.

By the way, Paul, what did you think of his tirade today here at HQ?" Paul thought for a moment and said, "Well, Partner, if I was a betting man, I would lay down a chunk of my hard-earned cash that Mr. Frank Galway could either have done it, ordered it, or knew it was coming. The public display of outrage certainly seemed out of character for Frank. We all know he was not the favorite of the Galway brothers, but it seemed like an over-the-top Broadway performance.

Tommy and Johnny were always close. Frank seemed to be the one left behind. He struggled in school; wasn't very athletic and lost all the women he wanted to mostly Johnny and a few to Tommy who was also a player. The more I thought about it, I generated five reasons he would be our top suspect. For one, he was always jealous of Johnny getting all those women. I think he had an eye for Linda Carnello who Johnny dated. A friend of mine who runs the bar at the South Shore Golf Course said that he heard Frank telling his golf foursome one Saturday that he was really peeved at his brother because he wanted a chance to date Charmaine Sinclair. Then there is the politics. Frank wanted to be Councilman and Johnny got it. Frank wanted to be Mayor and Johnny got it.

I think Frank has mentioned he will run for County Executive next election so he can have more jurisdiction than Johnny. Let us not forget his falling out with his brother Tommy the ex-County Executive. I heard they fought over money in a shady money laundering deal around city contracts and Tommy wouldn't help him run for County Exec because of their money quarrels. There have been rumors of his drug involvement and he's been seen with members of the Utica, New York organized crime family. The only thing that Frank seemed to bring to the brothers was his muscle. He stood six foot six inches and even in his younger days, he was a very fit 230 lbs. Frank never lost a fist fight.

Even though his brothers seemed to shun him, he believed that family came first; no one ever challenged Johnny or Tommy even though Frank was a few years younger. He was known as short-tempered and impulsive, not to mention strong as an ox and some said a bit crazy. Perry listened intently and said, "Seems like you have given this some thought Paul." "I was always paired against him in Phys. Ed. Classes in school even though I was four inches shorter and twenty-five pounds lighter," said Paul.

I was always, wrestling, blocking, or just teamed against him. Luckily, we got along just fine, and he and I had a healthy respect for one another, I would always try to stay on his good side. He was just too damn strong not to." Perry then stood and accepted the food that was being delivered by his favorite Chef's waitress, Marie Vendetti. "Hey, Marie, nice to see you. Doing deliveries is a surprise." Marie smiled, "I took the order from Paul on the phone and couldn't resist seeing that cute face of his. Also, it has been crazy all night and all the drivers were out on runs."

The person that Johnny Galway went to see at the Hyatt Hotel that day was an old friend. His old friend had left an envelope for Johnny at the front desk that just said -JOHN G- on it. Johnny asked for the envelope and the young blonde clerk gave it to him and waited but Johnny just turned and left saying a quick, "Thank you." He walked to the elevators.

In the envelope, he found the room key for Room 220 with a note that said, "Let yourself in, I'll be waiting."

Johnny put the envelope in the breast pocket of his suit's vest. He had a small bag over his shoulder with a bottle of Tequila, limes, and a saltshaker. It was their favorite drink when getting together after any long separation. They hadn't seen each other in over three years. This, he thought, figured to be one of those rowdy drunken reunions. He slipped into the elevator pretty much unnoticed as 8 pm on a wintery Wednesday was not really a busy time in the downtown hotels. He had told his secretary, Karen Maltry, he was going to a long meeting tomorrow then maybe taking a long weekend. He told his driver, Richie Moyers that he had brought his own car today and wouldn't need him. "Take the rest of the week off Richie, I've got some personal business from now until Monday." He had left City Hall leaving his car in its parking spot and took a cab.

The elevator bell dinged on the second floor and Johnny walked out. He headed left to Room 220. None of the maids appeared to be on the floor as it was late at night. He entered the room with the key. Only one lamp was lit. The curtains were drawn. Johnny smiled. He heard the water running in the shower as its door was ajar. He looked at his watch. 8:05 pm. It was time to drink, and he wanted to be ready like he needed a reason, and grinned. He set his bag on the couch table in front of the window took off his coat, unpacked the glasses, Tequila, and cut-up limes. He took two ice cubes out of the bucket on the table and poured two drinks. He drank one quickly. It burned but tasted good. He refilled his shot glass and opened the curtain slightly.

He gazed out the window to look out at his city. It continued to snow that evening which made his view look like one of the small globes with the winter scenes. It was a Buffalo winter, they said there would be five to ten inches again overnight. As he let the curtain close back up, he downed the second shot in one gulp still hearing the shower running. He saw the lights flash and the room went dark. He fell to the floor with a heavy thud.

He had tasted his last Tequila. He never saw or heard the killer fire two small caliber bullets into the back of his head. Johnny was dead.

His body was dragged into the bathroom and slumped over the tub. The water still running. His shirt and tie were cut off as he bled into the tub. When the blood stopped, he was dressed in a clean shirt and tie and his coat. He was rolled into a laundry cart retrieved from the hall earlier. He was covered with several large blankets and comforters. The bathroom was checked for any blood residue. Clean. 10:30 saw the killer push the cart onto the elevator and hit G for the garage. He quickly checked the garage; it was empty. The cart was rolled to where the van was parked at the loading dock. The hatch opened and the cart rolled smoothly into the vehicle. The killer jumped down off the dock and got in.

The van was started and driven into the evening's white wonderland. The van sped quietly up Church Street to Elm Street. It turned left and headed out the Route 33 Expressway toward the Thruway. The van then headed south and got off the exit to East Aurora. Because of the impending blizzard forecasted, there was literally no traffic to be seen. Off on the Aurora Expressway 400, the van stopped over a slight hill. Lights off. A long plastic sled was extracted from the vehicle and the body rolled onto it. The sled was dragged easily across the fresh snow like an Olympic toboggan. It stopped well off the road into a previously dug-out trench; four by seven feet square and two feet deep. The body was dumped off the sled face up and quickly covered with snow. The person delivering Johnny to his new resting place smiled as the snow kept blowing and further concealing him in what would be his frozen crypt. He might be there past spring or so it seemed to his killer a "villain in the snow". The dark grey van sped east on the 400 exiting at Transit Road then disappeared into the night.

On that Saturday morning, Perry stopped into the Hyatt very early to speak to George Stepanovic. He and Perry had been in school together here in town. George's Dad used to own a restaurant at the foot of Gates Avenue in Lackawanna during the heyday of Bethlehem Steel Corporation which could be seen across the back of his restaurant across Route 5 toward Lake Erie. George was in his office behind the front desk as Perry walked in.

He was out front in a flash with a beaming smile as this expected visitor, his old friend, approached the desk. Perry flashed the missing key to Room 220. George was stunned, "Where the heck did you get that?" "Well partner," Perry replied, "I was hoping you could tell me. Can you tell me who used that room last?" George stepped quickly behind the desk to the computer. He said, "well let's get a print-out for you, my friend. It shouldn't take but a few minutes." Perry asked, "Boks, how often do you work the desk?" He used his childhood nickname given to him by his brother.

George said, "Every Monday so I can check out the weekend's tallies and I make the schedule on this computer as well." Perry continued, "How many people have access to the computer here?" George replied, "That's a fluid number, I will have to think about that one and get back to you but probably no more than eight to ten folks." The machine George stood in front of started making a humming sound as the processor searched for the answer. George took a quick peak to make sure there was sufficient paper in the tray. Soon the printer began to spit out the report George had ordered. Jackie Cuffaletto the desk clerk handed the printout to George who scanned it the same way Perry had the night before. George could see that there was an obvious patron that the police might be interested in on the printout. He looked at the name signed in on Wednesday night then handed the printout to Perry saying, "Well Perry. I can see from the names on this sheet that you might be interested in one of them very much. I can see there are some errors in the data. Anyway, Perry, take a look at this."

Hyatt	Hotel		BFLO DT		St	Auto Plate	Days
Month	Date	Day	Guest	CITY	ST	Auto Plate	Days
DEC	1	Mon	J. Maltry	Erie	PA	JD6-1777	1
	2	Tues	Dr J. Steinberg	Denver	CO	DDS-25531	1
	3	Wed	P. Celinas	Dallas	TX	VP 6660	1
	4	Thurs	E. Volsier	Reno	NV	12-LI-445	1
	5	Fri	P. Corectt	Philadelphia	PA	IR-4545	2
	6	Sat	P. Corectt	Philadelphia	PA	DIR-4545	-
	7	Sun	S. Mills	Denver	CO	None	2
	8	Mon	S. Mills	Denver	CO	None	-
	9	Tues	C.M. Fuda	Keene	NH	815-BBG-9	1
	10	Wed	M. Keen	New York	NY	None	7
	11	Thurs	M. Keen	New York	NY	None	6
	12	Fri	M. Keen	New York	NY	None	5
	13	Sat	M. Keen	New York	NY	None	4
	14	Sun	M. Keen	New York	NY	None	3

"Well Perry", said George, "It seems that the room was signed out to a M. Keen for the week from the tenth to the sixteenth. It says NYC with no plate number. Could this be Margie Keen, Johnny Galway's ex-wife?" George spoke to Jackie on the desk, "Jackie, could you check to see who checked in M. Keen for the 10th thru the 17th, please?" Jackie began typing into the computer. She looked at George then Perry and then frowned, "it says that I checked her in from an internet request. It also says I checked her in Wednesday morning in person with two keys. I never took the order, nor did I check anyone in on Wednesday. I distinctly remember because we had that major snowstorm; we didn't even check anybody in or out as the roads were bad and the airport was closed." "Thanks Jackie," said George.

George continued, "Looks like we are going to have to have a staff meeting today with all the folks that have access to the computer to nail down what happened." Jackie quickly went back to the computer to email the staff. "3:30 pm today, OK for this, Boss?" "Great thanks," George replied.

Perry then asked if they could see the room. George walked out from behind the desk motioning Perry to follow., "Sure, follow me."

On the elevator, George asked him, "Where did you get the key, Perry?" Perry looked straight into George's eyes hoping for 'some reaction', "It was in the vest pocket of Johnny Galway. We found him dead; buried in the snow last night in a shallow grave about fifty feet off the 400." The look on George's face told Perry everything he needed to know. George was in shock. Knowing him for as long as he had, Perry was sure it was the first time he had conjured the thought. They were now in the second-floor hallway. They walked toward Room 220. It had yellow police crime tape across the doorway. George said, "What the hell is that?" Perry calmly said, "I put that up last night when I came to talk to Jackie at the desk about the registration list."

George pulled his key ring out unlocking the door. "There is a uniformed officer inside George so don't be alarmed. I didn't want anyone disturbing the evidence. I think this may have been where Johnny was whacked." George pushed open the door cautiously. Sure enough, there sat Officer Scott Layman in a desk chair at the window so he could see people enter before they saw him. He stood, "Good Morning, Detective." Perry looked at him and held his hands open as if to ask, "Anything to report". "Not even a mouse was stirring here all night, Perry." Layman answered and sat back down writing something on the clip board. "George, sorry for all this subterfuge but I can't miss anything on this case. I wanted to be able to clear you immediately so you can help. No one is to know there is a cop in the room. Whoever used the room may have another key and return to check to see if they forgot anything. Forensics will be here in twenty minutes to go through the place. Layman is here to insure they are not surprised during their investigation. It will be interesting to see if anyone shows up."

George looked pale. He began, "Perry, I am so glad you didn't tell me last night. I would have never slept. Thanks. I will keep this close to the vest.

When I meet with my staff this afternoon, I will tell them that an old woman died in here and no one is to enter. I will also freeze the computer so only three people will have historical access till further notice." "That is perfect Boks," said Perry using George's high school nickname again. As they left the room, the forensic team headed by Ted Zak appeared ready to enter the room. "It's all yours Ted," said Perry as he walked past the team with George. Ted just nodded and ushered his team into the room. They heard one of the technicians say, "Wow nice place. Hey Layman, how's it going. Touch anything?" They both laughed. Layman held up his gloved hands as if he was under arrest showing nothing was touched.

The room was indeed quite lavish. It had a large king-size bed in the center of the wall directly opposite the window to the right of the door. There were two walk-in closets in the room and a door straight ahead to the ensuite bathroom. In front of the window to the left was a couch table. Just in front of that were two swiveling rocking chairs in between them a square coffee table with a couch facing the window and the large TV hanging in the upper right corner next to the window. To the left of the window up against the walk-in closet wall was a small bar, refrigerator, and coffee station. Through the door to the bath, they found to the right a 10 by 10- ft. walk-in shower with three shower heads including a rain spray. The enclosed water closet to the left then side by side vanities with large mirrors. Next to the shower was a large four-person jacuzzi. The forensic team began its work. Officer Layman now sat out in the hall.

Tommy Lafleur from forensics was in the bathroom when he called out, "Hey, Ted. Come in here a minute." Ted came in with his camera around his neck. Tommy pointed to a red dot on the wall just above the jacuzzi about four inches above the faucets. Ted took four or five pictures and said, "Nice work, Lafleur, get that sample and double check for others." "Maybe we got lucky, and they didn't clean as well as we do", said Tommy. Three hours later, the team left Room 220 and Officer Layman went back into his post inside the room next to the window.

Ted found a shot glass on the floor under the curtain at the front window of the sitting area. It had a great set of fingerprints which would be run through NCIC as soon as he returned to HQ. The prints and the spot lifted from the bathroom were the only things found in the room. Whoever used the room had done a pretty good job of cleaning up; but these two items may have been their fatal flaw.

Scott Layman watched the Forensic Team leave after three hours. He wondered if what they found would lead to anything. He also wondered if anyone would reenter the room. They had established a coded knock that only the police and the manager knew. The hotel staff was told not to enter the room but not given the code. He heard the coded knock. He still got ready and had his hand on his revolver just in case. The door opened. It was George the manager, "Officer, it is almost lunchtime. Did you want me to order you something from the kitchen?" "No thank you sir" he replied, "I should be relieved shortly but I appreciate the offer." George left.

That afternoon, George had all the staff meet in the conference room. The people from the front desk, bell captains, housekeeping, kitchen staff, and the sales team. He had Jackie Cuffaletto take attendance and notes so he could hand them to the police later. He thought of a video tape but decided against it. In the room besides George, the manager and Jackie were Reggie Braxton (Bell Capt.), Dennis Shooda (desk), Kirt Leoz (sales), Mary Fine (desk) Evie Burks (Housekeeping), Cindy Deeps (Desk), Patty Evenly (Housekeeping), Don Hitchcock (Security), Joanne Kaz, (Desk), Lillie Mae Mason (Sales), Sandi Mehilyk, (Housekeeping), Thomas Kenneth (Maintenance), Missy Walker (Desk), Claudette Rivers (Desk), Carol Warlis (Desk), Carol Charles (Housekeeping) and Sara Eve Maltry (Desk).

George began by saying that there was a police investigation going on regarding the death of an older woman. It was possible that the Hyatt was the sight of the incident. He stated, "As you can see, Room 220 has been restricted and has police crime scene tape over the door. No ONE is to enter the room for any reason until further notice. Police have requested no one enter to avoid your fingerprints being found when you had no reason to be in the room. Now we have two important situations that I need to clear up today.

The first is the keys for Room 220. We have two remaining. They are now locked in my desk. We are missing two. If anyone has one, please drop it in the key return. No questions asked." George said that last part just like Parker and Perry had instructed. There was a new hidden video camera on the drop box so anyone dropping a key would be clearly identified. He continued, "The second situation is no one remembers checking in the person for Room 220 on Wednesday, December 10th. Does anyone remember checking someone in that day for Room 220?" He waited and there were folks looking around shaking their heads, but no one offered anything. "My second question is", said George, "does anyone remember what that person in Room 220 looked like? Reggie Braxton said from the back of the room, "Is that the tall, well dress fella I told you about, George?" George answered, "Exactly Reggie. They must have been seen at some point walking in the lobby or the hall by one of us. We have them on video, however, the clip we have of them at the desk was not identifiable." George waited and still nothing, "We had a lady die in 220 last night so that room is off limits to everyone."

He watched intently the faces of the folks in the room for any sign of guilt or suspicious behavior. Unbeknownst to George or anyone else, Micah Blair had installed a closed-circuit pencil camera in the conference room so that Perry, Parker, and George could review the meeting. "Any questions?" said George. He got nothing from them. "Thank you all. Have a good day." He dismissed them.

George was back in his office and the phone rang. It was Perry Kline, "How did the meeting go George?" George replied, "I just got done Perry and it was so silent you could have heard a mouse burp. I told them about not going into the room and about dropping the key to 220 in the drop box if they had one. No questions asked. Just like you said. I looked around the room and didn't see anyone flinch when I said a woman had died in the room. No one asked who found her or any other questions. They were not a very responsive group. Sorry." Perry said, "No worries. Thanks for having the meeting. Keep your eyes open for our tall, well-dressed man. See ya."

The day of the funeral, it was a bitter cold day. Our Lady of Victory Basilica at Ridge Road and South Park Avenue was overflowing with mourners. There were 1000 people in the church and that was with many standing in the aisles. There were some family members, police and fire officials, politicians, and many friends. The event was being video recorded by Micah Blair. He was a professional photographer who did excellent work and was also a licensed Private Investigator and an old friend of Perry Kline.

Micah had set up in of all places the confessional which had a perfect hidden view of those in attendance coming and going but also provided secrecy that video was being taken. Perry figured that with as large a crowd as was expected, maybe the killer may somehow be in the crowd. It was a long shot but as Parker said, "Cover all our bases and DON'T MISS ANYTHING!"

Micah set up miniature cameras at each entrance as well as a long one on a tripod hidden in the sacristy which had a one-way window in it so the priest or anyone at the window could clearly see everyone in the church. Micah's intent was NOT to MISS ANYONE who attended. He had gotten to the church at 7:30 am to set up everything. He had even brought some snacks to eat while waiting for the event to begin. He activated the cameras at 9 am. People began arriving at 9:30 am.

The procession began a mile or so down South Park Avenue at Colonial Chapels. The hearse was loaded after a short prayer led by Monsignor Stanley. It drove up South Park Avenue to Ridge Road with a police escort and made the right-hand turn onto Ridge to park forty feet from the corner; directly in front of the Basilica's front door. There was an honor guard of fifty police, firemen, and State troopers on either side of the walkway to the church from the street. The funeral director got out of the car and opened the rear door while the pallbearers exited the vehicle behind the hearse to assemble at the rear of the hearse. He quickly gave instructions, turned, and slid the casket halfway out, and then instructed the six men to begin the removal and watched them walk to the front door.

He encouraged them to move a bit quicker so they and the 50-man escort could get out of the bitter wind and cold quickly. They moved a bit quicker, and the process took 1 minute 30 seconds to get into the church but seemed like forever to those who stood at attention along the way. As the casket entered the church, they all quietly groaned a sigh of relief.

The director then had them pause to ensure the Monsignor had arrived at the front hall to lead the procession down the center aisle to the place in front of the main altar. It was over 150 feet from where they stood. He had placed the rolling carrier under the casket so they could all rest a few minutes while they waited for the Monsignor. The side door to the front hall opened and the altar boys carrying four-foot candles entered followed by folks carrying the Bible and the sacraments followed by altar boys carrying burning globes of incense with them entered. They were followed by four assistant officiants who then covered the casket in silk cloths and held buckets of holy water which the monsignor would use to Bless the congregation during the procession. At the back of the group, the Monsignor signaled them to begin with the candle carriers.

Silently, the candle carriers began the procession, and almost magically the organ music which had been playing quietly began a processional march which those in attendance immediately recognized as their cue to stand. The casket was rolled by the pallbearers and the walk down the aisle began. People along the aisle could be seen most generally crying or with saddened faces lowered as they watch Johnny Galway's casket approach the altar for the last time. Monsignor Stanley wore a portable microphone so those in attendance could hear him through the Basilica's sound system. The service went quickly. It was a solemn hour which was appointed by the homily of Monsignor Stanley who was a long-time friend of Johnny Galway.

Monsignor spoke of their friendship, Johnny's many family members and friends who would miss his humor, dedication to the community, and advisement and counsel to many; even himself. It was such an impassioned talk, that it left few dry eyes among the congregation. He then led the recession; followed by the mass' officiants and altar boys then pallbearers once again rolling the casket to the hearse. The eight men loaded Johnny in the hearse.

They would drive the three blocks east on Ridge Road almost to Woyshner's Flower Shop to the north entrance of Holy Cross Cemetery. It had been announced that on the family's wishes, only invited guests were allowed to follow the hearse for the interment.

As the weather conditions had worsened since the funeral began, the authorities had advised that only the immediate family would stand at the grave site. With the Police escort, there were still over 100 vehicles most of which would observe the internment from their vehicles.

The hearse arrived at the grave site, the casket was carried forward, the immediate family quickly gathered in the small shielding tent and Monsignor arrived in a black limousine which the family provided. He said the final prayer and the casket was lowered. The Monsignor was driven away, the family said its goodbyes, and left the green shielding tent erected above the final resting place of John G. Galway.

Perry and Paul were in their office conference room with Parker Clark and Micah Blair. They were busy identifying the many people that had gathered to pay their last respects to the fallen mayor. Perry had a hunch they would find the killer somewhere in the video. They had listed 1,150 people already and had to call three senior officers to assist with the identifications. They had snapped pictures of 40 or so people that they could not identify. Parker thanked Mr. Blair for his comprehensive work and putting together a composite video of all the events.

Paul Gorci was given the unenviable task of completing the naming of all the mystery attendees. Perry headed back to the Hyatt Hotel to continue the interviews of the staff. At the Hyatt, the young desk clerk, Sara Eve Maltry, who Perry had questioned the Tuesday after the murder, was at the front desk. She motioned him over and said, "You know, I was thinking. When you asked me the other day if I knew the man who I gave the envelope to, I said I did not. Well, after reading all the newspapers and seeing the TV reports about the murder; I can now confirm it was Johnny Galway.

Being from the South towns, I didn't immediately make the connection, but it was absolutely, the mayor." Perry's heart lept in his chest. The first solid lead. "Now Sara Eve", he began, "how did you get the envelope again?"

Sara Eve replied, "Mary from Maid Services gave it to me when I came on that morning at 8 am. She said it was left in room 220 on the dresser with a nice tip. All the note on it said was 'Mary- leave this at the desk for me, Thanks'. Neither Sara Eve nor Mary Fine remembered seeing who was in room 220 that day but the register said it was M. Keen. Mary had told him that day that so many people come and go, it was hard to remember everyone.

Perry began to sadly walk away when he looked up to the mezzanine level above the desk and saw the closed-circuit camera pointed down toward the desk. Holy jeepers! Perry thought to himself. How could I have been so dumb? He spun on his heel and headed straight for the Manager's office. He knocked, heard "Come In" and walked inside. The cook from the kitchen was just getting up from his chair and leaving. Perry waited for him to leave and said, "Boks, how long do you save the videos from the front desk cameras?" George looked at him and said, "We run them on a four-month cycle, why?" Perry asked pleadingly, "Please tell me you have the video for the week of the murder still on file"?

"Well Mr. Kline, I believe we do", George said smiling, "How dumb of me not to think of that first". Perry was on the phone with Parker. "Hey Chief, can you run down to the Hyatt right away, I think we may have the murderer on video!" Parker hung up without a word and grabbed his overcoat; and hurried out of the office. He took the stairs not wanting to even wait for the elevator. He shouted to the desk technician, Donna Smith, "I'll be at the Hyatt." He was out the door, jumped into his car parked right in front, and made a U-turn on Church Street to the Hyatt in two minutes after he left his office.

He used his flashing light but no siren. He never even thought about a gosh darn video at the Hyatt. He screeched to a halt five minutes after he hung up with Perry. He walked into the hotel and Perry was at the front desk.

"Hey Chief, George is setting up in the conference room, follow me," said Perry as he walked past George's office. George was already viewing the video, "I just started. I thought we'd start with Wednesday a.m." Perry and Parker sat quickly with eyes glued to the screen. About 20 minutes into the recording, it showed 9:30 am on the clock behind the desk. They saw a slender tall man approach the desk. He had a wide-brimmed Stetson hat that obscured his face. Perry looked at his shoes. Very expensive and spotless. The crease in his trousers looked like it could cut like a knife. He had gloves on. You could not hear his voice on the tape. Sarah was not at the desk. The only one there was a bell captain, Reggie Braxton. He asked the guy if he could help. The man said something that the camera didn't pick up. Reggie turned and pulled a key out of the drawer and handed it to the man. The man gave him a thumbs up and flashed a bill that Reggie took with a loud, "Thank you!"

As Perry, Parker, and George watched the man turn and walk away from the camera. George said, "Wait!" when Perry and Parker rose to their feet. "Let's see if we can see what car drives past the front door." They waited. Two minutes passed. A white late model Cadillac sped by. "Can you freeze frame the car, George?" said Parker. He did just that and all you could see was the hat. George said into his intercom, "Sarah Eve, send Reggie into the conference room ASAP please." They could hear her reply, "Yes Sir, right away." Three minutes later, a knock on the door to the conference room came. "Come in!", yelled George. In walked Reggie Braxton. "Yes sir, you wanted to see me?" he asked.

Parker responded, "Mr. Braxton, you gave a key to a gentleman on the morning of Wednesday the 10th at around 9:30 am. Reggie put his hand to his jaw and said, "Gee Mr. S, I hand out lots of keys when whoever is on the desk steps away for coffee or a break." Parker looked at George and he pointed to the screen that already had a shot of the man and Reggie handing off the key. "Oh yeah," said Reggie, "I remember that guy alright. He tipped me twenty bucks. He looked, how do you say it, somewhat effeminate. I noticed his shoes were Ferragamo's, the hat was a Belissimo Fox Fedora, and the overcoat was a Dior cashmere."

Being the fashion plate that Reggie was when out of his Hyatt uniform, he noticed these types of things and said, "this guy had certainly not shopped in our lovely city for that outfit. Probably New York, LA, or Miami is what I'd guess." Parker was impressed and asked, "Did you get a good look at his face?" "Naw", said Reggie, "The brim was covering most of his face and he had his head down." Perry then added, "Do you remember how he asked for the key?" Reggie thought a minute, "I think he just said something like, 'I think I left my key in the room, can I get the key for 220, please'.

I saw there was one key in the slot, so I gave it to him." "Anything else, gentlemen?", said George. Perry and Parker shook their heads. "Thank you, Reggie. That'll be all", George concluded his visit.

Parker said, "Well I guess we are going to have to scan the video a bit more closely now. Perry, I will see you back at HQ." Perry thanked him for coming down and replied, "I am gonna look at the rest of what George has. I'll see if I can spot this guy again. Sorry for the false alarm." "No worries, nice work," said Parker as he left. Perry sat back down. George ordered two black coffees from the kitchen.

After two hours of rewatching the videos from the entire week, they had no luck finding another sighting of the thin man. Perry then thanked George and returned to Headquarters. No one was around and it was close to 5 pm so Perry decided to head home for a shower and then grab some dinner. On the way to Richmond Avenue, he called Christie at her office. No answer.

He then caught her on her cell phone. "Hi Christie, have you made plans for dinner tonight?" Christie replied sadly, "Well I am sitting having drinks before dinner with Linda Carnello. She is spending a few weeks in town. Can I get a rain check?"

Perry said, "No worries, Doll, it was just a shot in the dark as I took a break after a long day. I will give you a call later if that's okay?" "Talk to you soon then, Thanks," was her reply. Perry sat at the kitchen table and went through his mail.

There were the usual bills, junk mail, and a letter from the Police Benevolent Association (asking for this year's donations, he guessed), and a postcard from Ronnie Olsen reminding him he had volunteered to help decorate the hall for the Lackawanna High School Class Reunion this Saturday.

The committee would meet Friday night, that's in three days he thought at 7 p.m. at the VFW Post 63 on South Park Avenue in Lackawanna. Perry had transferred to Lackawanna for his last year of high school here in Western New York and got pretty involved in the social activities as he had finished most of his required credits and thus had a lot of free time. This was one of his favorite committees as it brought old friends together for a happy occasion. Ah, the Reunion, he thought. It must be the 15th. He always had a great time at these, but this was not the time to be off doing this kind of activity with the amount of work still to do on the Galway case.

He thought about giving Ronnie a call to let her know he was just slammed and didn't think he could break away. "Hey, Ronnie, Perry Kline here. How are you?" Ronnie was happy to hear from him, "Great Perry, we're all set for the big bash and the turnout looks like another success. I am just tying up a few loose ends." "Ronnie, the reason I'm calling is to let you know I don't think I can make Friday to decorate with this case I am working on," Perry said sadly. Ronnie quickly replied, "No worries, Perry, I think Joni, Tina, Ron, Dennis, George, and I can handle all that. Just make sure you stop in for a visit as there are many people looking to see you again if you know what I mean." "Okay, Ronnie, I sure will try. Thanks for understanding. Talk to you soon," then Perry hung up.

He felt better that he had called. He really liked Ronnie and her husband Ron. He jumped into the shower as he was thinking of going back into the office to look at the funeral video again to see if he could find the tall thin man from the Hyatt. As he stepped from the shower, his cell phone rang. It was Paul Gorci. "Hey, Paul, what's up?" said Perry.

"I am just on my way to the Ace of Clubs to grab some dinner. How far away are you?" Perry responded, "I just got out of the shower. I can be there in twenty minutes." Perry and Paul walked into the Ace of Clubs within minutes of each other. Melanie Barstow seated them at their favorite table. It had a great view of those coming and going and they could see the TV. Mel was their favorite server. She took their drinks and dinner order and left.

Paul began the conversation as he watched Mel strut into the kitchen to place their order. "I have been reviewing the videos again from the funeral since 10 am. There are only two people unidentified. A man and a woman. They didn't seem to be together," said Paul, as he slid two stills of the man and woman. Perry looked at them, but nothing registered. The female did look familiar, but he could not place her.

Melanie brought the drinks. She leaned over Perry's shoulder and said, "Why do you have a picture of those two?" Perry asked, "Why, do you know them?" "Yeah," said Mel, "the woman is Linda Carnello. I don't know what her married name is now but that's her!" "But this woman is blonde and…." Perry's voice trailed off as he stared at the picture. He wouldn't have recognized her in a million years as a blonde. Her make-up was different, and her hair was down. They had dated in school. She was then a dark brunette and wore her hair in a beehive. Perry remembered going to a drive-in on a double date with Linda Charles and Jake Green. Perry and Linda were in the back seat, necked a bit until Linda Charles found some sort of wrapped chocolate in the glove box that Jake said was laced with marijuana and the girls began wrestling over it as his date Linda leaned over the seat to try to get some. A crazy, fun night but he had Jake drive them back to Linda Carnello's house shortly after 11 p.m. as her father gave him a look as he picked her up asking what time they would be home.

Perry had heard the rumors that her father was an alleged underboss of the Magellan Family out of Utica, New York but they had no confirmation. He wasn't taking any chances. Perry began again, "Melanie, I would never have recognized her, and we went out in high school. I suppose you know who the other guy is too?" Melanie laughed, "You know him too. It is Dickie Moyers. I think he is a cousin to Johnny Galway on his mother's side. He used to sing at Jacobi's on Abbott in Lackawanna for years with the Keller twins." "Wow", said Perry, "You have got quite the memory. Maybe we should use you at HQ when we have those lineups!" Now it was his turn to laugh. Melanie continued, "The other woman in the picture is Catie Fuda. She is a few years younger than us and is originally from Syracuse, New York. She is dating Micah Blair, I think. She was married but came to Buffalo for a job in insurance.

Perry thought he had seen her around but didn't ever meet her. He noticed her beautiful blue eyes and her great legs. He was brought out of his thoughts by hearing Paul say to Melanie, "Hey Mel, have you worked undercover before, or is your knowing everyone from waitressing all over Buffalo been the key?" Melanie shot back, "You're lucky Gorci, I thought you were gonna say I was old and saw everyone grow up or something smart-ass like your usual comments. Don't forget who is serving your meal to you tonight, Detective!" Paul held both hands in the air as if being held at gunpoint and replied, "Madam, I would never tell anyone as adorable as you that they were old." They all laughed. Mel left, returning to the bar.

Perry then related to Paul how the day went at the Hyatt. He and George interviewed the maid staff and desk clerks. He showed him a picture of the guy that Reggie Braxton gave the key to last Wednesday for Room 220. Paul commented how unlucky they were to not get a good view of his face. They ate dinner in silence until Micah Blair came into the restaurant and stopped at their table.

Micah said, "Did you ever get a good look at the man from 220?" Perry was a bit shocked but remembered that Blair was a former cop and now a private gumshoe, so he was obviously working on the biggest news story of the century as well. Perry commented, "By the way Micah, did you get a picture of him from George at the Hyatt?" He nodded affirmatively. "Well, see if you can match him up from the videos you shot at the funeral." Micah said, "I was going to tell you that is in fact just what I was going to do this evening after I grab a bite." He walked off toward Melanie at the bar before either of them at the table could respond. Micah Blair sat at the end of the bar and ordered dinner from Melanie, who stood one barstool away at the waitress' station at the end of the bar. Big Mike Chides was behind the bar and brought Blair his usual drink, Grey Goose on the rocks with a splash of soda and a twist of lime. Blair laid down a twenty-dollar bill and Chides asked, "Does Mel have you on a tab with dinner?" Micah said, "Let's keep it separate so I can tip both of you." "OK", said Chides as he was known since high school. He rang up the drink and left his change on the bar.

Blair pushed a five-dollar bill into the trough of the bar which Chides grabbed and thanked him by ringing the tip bell over the register. Mel brought Micah his dinner as Perry and Paul left.

It was Saturday and Perry had worked all day reviewing the videos with Micah Blair at his office in the Ellicott Square Building. They spotted a thin guy dressed to the nines that slightly resembled the man from the Hyatt but in both cases, his face was obscured by a large, brimmed hat. The hat was different from the one they saw him wearing at the Hyatt and his overcoat was different as well. Micah mentioned as did Reggie at the Hyatt that this guy whoever he was, shopped at some exclusive stores and was meticulous with his attire.

Perry left at 4:00 p.m. He called Christie wondering if she was at his house. She answered on the first ring, "Mr. Kline, how can I help you?" Perry said quickly, "Are you at my house yet?" "Yes, Mr. Kline, just as you requested. I am so excited that you are taking some time away from your busy investigation to escort me to the reunion tonight." Perry chuckled. He had asked her to meet him at his house so they could drive together to the reunion. This would alleviate him having to drive to East Aurora to pick her up then drive back to Lackawanna. He assumed she would stay at his place after the event. Her car would be at his house so he could go to work in the morning, then she could drive herself home.

As he pulled into his driveway, he saw Christie's red sports car parked in the visitor's spot in front of the garage. She greeted him in a long silk robe as he entered his house through the garage. It was a rose, wine color, and went to the floor. It clung to her very shapely body like a second skin. Perry said, "Are we staying in tonight, Miss Mahern? Or are you wearing that lovely number to the reunion?" She smiled and offered him a beer, "Well, no Mr. Kline. This outfit was to entice you to spend some time with me before you had to get dressed and leave for the reunion. IF YOU HAVE TIME." She lingered on the last four words. He grabbed the drink, clinked her glass of champagne, and swallowed half the bottle. He set it down and stepped toward her lifting her up and carrying her into the bedroom. It was then twenty of five. They stepped out of the shower together at 6:05 p.m. She said,

"That was the exact amount of attention I needed from you Mr. Kline; however, we will now be fashionably late for our event." Perry just smiled. The lovemaking was as spectacular as always and they both wished they could just return to bed and catch up on their time together, but they were both excited to see many of their friends.

They arrived at the V.F.W. on South Park in Lackawanna at 7:05 p.m. They made great time. Jackie Cuffaletto was at the door just finishing a cigarette as they drove by the door. They parked not too far away so they walked in from the car. They noticed Dennis Shooda plowing the driveway as they approached the door. He was pushing the evening's snow up into a pile he had been stacking for weeks now. As he pulled away from the pile, he stopped. He jumped out of the tractor and bent down and retrieved something from the ground. It was a man's winter glove. Dennis looked up as Perry and Christie approached and said, "Not surprised to find one of these in the pile." Perry was about to retort as they entered the foyer; Dennis had just tossed the glove to the girl working the coatroom saying, "Put this in the lost and found box, I just found it in the snow pile. See if anyone claims it." The coatroom girl was Ellen Niche who screeched, "Dennis, there's blood all over this glove!" Perry took out his pen and lifted the glove. He said, "Dennis, you're not bleeding, are you?" Dennis checked and wasn't. Perry said, "Dennis, do me a favor and grab a plastic bag out of the kitchen. Ellen didn't touch it and Dennis has gloves on so there may be prints on this." Dennis returned in seconds from the sign-in desk just inside the door, "Ronnie Olsen had a plastic bag with her at the check-in desk." Perry placed the glove in the bag and called Lackawanna Police. He then said, "Christie, you go ahead in while I wait for LAPD."

She walked into the hall and Dennis went back outside. He came back in two minutes later and said, "Perry, you're gonna wanna see this." Dennis went back out the door. Perry followed with the glove in the bag, "Did you find the other glove?" Dennis had walked to the snow pile and pointed to the middle of the pile.

There were two bloody fingers poking out of the pile of snow. "Holy Moly, did you touch anything, Den?" Dennis replied, "No Sir, I was looking around before I got back in the tractor to see if I could find the other glove." Just then, the police arrived.

Out of the cruiser stepped, Captain Joel Budzinski. "Perry, what have you got?" "Well Joel, I thought I had a bloody glove; but it looks like Dennis has discovered something else with the snowplowing." Perry pointed to the fingers in the pile. Captain Budzinski got on his radio and called for two more cars and forensics. He then began to yellow tape off the area. He said to Dennis, "Do you have a small shovel handy?" Dennis pulled one off the tractor and handed it to him. Captain Joel approached the pile as the other two cruisers arrived.

Joel carefully slid the shovel into the pile about six inches under the fingers. He met resistance. He then went to the right of the fingers six inches and met resistance again. At that moment, forensics arrived. Three officers stepped out of the vehicle. They were already gloved as they approached the pile of snow. The older one said, "We'll take it from here, Captain." Perry didn't know him. His name badge said, "PORTER". Perry watched as the three men from forensics carefully began to remove the snow around the fingers. They were attached to a hand and then an arm. Then they realized the man was face down in the pile. As they removed a large chunk of snow to the right, a head appeared. Perry gasped out loud. He recognized the man. It was Frank Galway. There was a bullet hole in the back of his head. In thirty minutes, they had him completely uncovered. The other officers from LAPD had erected a three-panel, plastic shield to isolate the excavation.

As Perry looked behind him, he saw a slew of police cars. Surprisingly, two cars were from Buffalo PD. Out of the closest one stepped, Parker Clark. Perry said as he approached, "I was just about to call you, Chief. We just found Frank Galway buried in the snow pile the plow guy was adding to from today's storm. He had found a bloody glove and I grabbed it for evidence.

He was searching for the other glove and saw two bloody fingers sticking out of the pile. I called LAPD. They are pulling Frank out onto a stretcher now." Parker walked toward the paneled area as he said to Perry, "OK, Thanks Perry. What's going on inside?" "High school reunion," said Perry.

They both watched as forensics placed Mr. Galway on the stretcher. They both said it at the same time. "OH, NO!" They had both seen it. It was a red tag in the breast pocket of Frank's shirt. Parker said to the tall forensic guy, "Porter, grab that red tag in his top pocket. Officer Porter pulled the tag out of Frank's pocket with a pair of tweezers. He slid it into a plastic bag and held it up for Parker. He turned it around so they could see. They both said, "Oh No!" again. The tag said 'Hyatt Hotel 220' there was no key with it. Perry said, "No Key!!" Parker looked at him and said, "This is getting weirder by the day. So, the killer is using the room key as their signature but this time they kept the key." Parker called dispatch at Buffalo PD, "Hi, Donna. It's Parker. Who is working the room at the Hyatt tonight?" He waited. "Layman, thanks, patch me through to him." Parker spoke into his radio, "Layman? Parker Clark. Any activity today?" He listened. Officer Layman had told him nothing to report. "Stay alert and pass the word to the next shift. We found another key tag but without a key at this point." Layman said, OK, Chief. I'll pass on this info. Thanks."

Frank Galway was frozen solid. The coroner, Ted Zak, said he'd probably been there two to five days, but it was hard to say exactly. Parker and Perry went into the VFW and sought out Ronnie Olsen. Ronnie was the organizer of the Reunion. He asked her to make an announcement that the side door to the parking lot was closed tonight for a police investigation. There would be a desk set up at the back door to either make or schedule a statement for the police regarding the current investigation. No reason for alarm but it should not take more than 10-15 minutes at most. LAPD would be at the rear exit. If there were more than five people in the line, folks could take a number for when to return. People began to drift over to the door and to set up a line to give statements. The LAPD was getting their IDs and asked them a few questions about being in town in the last two weeks, their relationship, if any, to the Galways, and their current employment.

This information could give them a clue about who was there and how to contact them. There were four officers present there. Three were taking statements and the fourth was taking pictures. You could not leave until you had received a wrist stamp from them.

As the night wore on, Christie was looking more beautiful than Perry could remember. He had an opportunity to dance a couple of numbers with her. He wanted to leave but all the statements had not been completed. He knew it would be a late night. How could this be? He asked himself, "Were the two prominent brothers from Buffalo murdered by the same killer?" The band wrapped up at 1 P. M. He walked over to the bar where Paul Gorci was talking to a couple of firemen from just a block away on South Park. Perry pulled him aside and let him know when they were clear of everyone; what they had found. Frank was buried in snow with a Hyatt tag but no key. Paul looked shocked but thought a minute and said, "I guess that means we should restructure the list, huh?" Perry said, "I was thinking the same thing partner. I am going to offer the guys from LAPD a break at the desk. If they don't need me, I am going to take Christie home. We'll get a fresh start early in the morning.

Maybe we can meet for breakfast." Paul replied, "I just told Parker I would stay and clean up anything the Lackawanna Police needed help with. Parker is finished outside and as you can see the crowd is dwindling down to about thirty people or so. Why don't you check out now? I'll meet you at the office at 8 am with breakfast." "You are the man, Brother," said Perry, as he slapped Paul on the back, "I'll check in with Parker before I leave as I have got some ideas on our next strategy. Thanks."

Perry walked outside and motioned to Parker. Parker stepped under the crime tape and said to Perry, "I just checked with LAPD. They have finished all the statements inside. We are done out here as you can see, we plowed everything to make sure we didn't miss anything. So, we are going to wrap it up. I'll leave one unit from LAPD and one from ours to clear out the building. You should probably take your lady home and we'll start fresh first thing in the morning. Oh, by the way, the room key was in his coat pocket when Ted pulled him out." "Okay, Chief", said Perry, "see you in the morning."

Perry brought Christie's coat to her as she stood seeing him approach. She was sitting with Ron and Ronnie Olsen saying goodnight. "Are you ready to leave Ms. Mahern?", He said with a grin. "Yes, Detective, are we going for breakfast, or are you taking me straight home?" "We could stop at the Wayside up the street if you'd like," said Perry as he watched her smile and nod. He said goodnight to the Olsens thanking them for their efforts as well as praising the great job they had done, once again. They walked out the side door as it was closer to his car. As they got into the car, she realized it was running as Perry had asked one of the guys from Buffalo PD to start it up for him as he was getting ready to leave. Perry stated, "We don't have to go to the Wayside for breakfast. We could stop at the Towne at Allen Street and Elmwood Avenue if you would prefer. It is totally your call."

Christie knew he would be busy all day tomorrow so she said, "Maybe we can go straight to your place, and I'll make you some coffee and eggs there. I know you'll be up at the crack of dawn in a few hours." Perry smiled and hung a left turn at South Park and Ridge to head to Route 5 and the quickest way to the 190. "You're the best Ms. Mahern. Sorry about the craziness tonight. I hope to make it up to you after breakfast. 10 minutes later, they were exiting the 190 at Porter Avenue and headed east to Richmond Avenue. He lived right at Symphony Circle across from Kleinhan's Music Hall. "By the way, he began, "Can you do me a favor?" "Depends!", she threw back. He chuckled, "Can you make a list of ladies who dated both Johnny and Frank Galway? That might give us a link to find our murderer or at least a motive maybe!" "Let me think about that one for a minute," Christie said beginning to make a list in her head. She knew the best person to call would be Ronnie Olsen. She was in contact with so many people in the Lackawanna/South Buffalo area that it would be silly not to call her. She pulled out her cell phone. "Hey, Ronnie. It's Christie. I just got home and was wondering if you could put your thinking cap on. Tell me who dated both Galway brothers. I'll call you in the morning. Thanks."

Minutes later, they were rounding the circle and pulling into his driveway. He dropped her at the back door then turned into the garage. Christie knew where the key was; she entered the house and got busy. She was in the kitchen pouring water for the coffee when Perry came in from the garage.

They were both glad to be back out of the cold. Perry went into the family room to make a fire as Christie began making eggs. She used six eggs with three yolks. They both always watched what they ate. She popped a bagel into the toaster as Perry walked back into the kitchen with her robe. She smiled and began to undress right before him. She turned so he could finish unzipping her dress which she let fall to the floor.

He picked it up and hung it over his arm. She then undid her bra and let that slide down her arms. As she had her back to him, she flung it over her shoulder and turned to grab the robe. His eye sparkled as she donned her robe and she smiled back saying, "Thank you kind Sir. The eggs are close to done. Could you pour the coffee and I'll do the bagel? Light cream cheese?" "Yes, please" was his response. "By the way, Doll, thanks for calling Ronnie tonight. We'll see if her list is different than ours." Then they ate. After a quick clean-up, they retired to the family room and sat next to each other before the roaring fire.

Christie had wine in her hand while Perry was working on another cup of coffee. He didn't figure to get too much shut eye tonight as the morning would come very quickly. Perry leaned over and kissed her. "Thanks for a great evening. I really enjoyed our two slow dances!" They both burst out laughing. Christie said, "I think we said about ten words to each other tonight. I was taking furious notes after ending a conversation with small little groups. I tried to get a sense from those conversations whether the murderer was in the room. I have got a couple of hunches, but I'll keep those under wraps until I can do some snooping around City Hall next week." Perry looked at this vision next to him and said, "Just for shits and giggles, what the hell do you think is going on, Counselor?" Christie leaned closer, kissed Perry very passionately and said, "Put another log on the fire and let's go to bed and talk."

Christie got up and walked into the room off the family room which was the master. Perry quickly threw a log on the fire, stoked it a bit, and followed within seconds. All he could now think about was the fire burning inside him as he watched the raven-haired beauty slip naked under the covers as he threw off his own lounging pajamas.

They didn't have a word about the case, the murders, or what either of them thought was going on in their adopted city of Buffalo, New York. They looked into each other's eyes and were swept into the frenzied physicality of their longing for one another.

Once again, they made love like a symphony was playing an old standard from the fifties. The kind your Grandparents listened to after visiting guests for dinner had left and the kids were in bed. It was amazing for both her and him. They lost track of time and held each other as sleep enveloped them.

Perry awoke from what felt like a 5-minute nap only to find it was really four hours later. It was 7:30 a.m. He slipped out of bed and looked back to gaze at this young woman who had touched his heart so deeply. It made him wonder if he was really in love again. He showered in the guest bath so as not to wake Christie. He quietly dressed. She still hadn't stirred. He would let her sleep. He decided to head to work but before he did, he left her a note.

It read: 'Hope you slept well. Glad I didn't wake you. You look very beautiful when you sleep. It was hard to leave and go into the office. I can still smell you as I stand here writing this. Stay if you'd like but if you go home text me. Oh, by the way, I think I'd like another chance at a great evening so I would like to have dinner together tonight. I know it's your preparation for cases time but last night was not how we should spend a Saturday night. XXX, P.'

PART TWO

It was 7:55 a.m. when Perry walked into Headquarters. Ted Zak was in his office as Perry walked down toward the bullpen as they called it. It was a group of desks scattered around the middle of a large room with cubicles separated by five-foot panels. There were 12 private offices up against the walls surrounding the bullpen. His partner Paul was sitting in the cubicle next to his, already on the phone. He handed him a cup of Dunkin' Donuts black coffee and a bag with two of his favorite glazed donuts. He waved but said nothing. Perry set his coffee and Danish on his desk, took off his coat; and headed to Ted's office.

As Perry entered, Ted was talking into a recorder to edit his notes from the autopsy he had attended in Lackawanna last night with the county coroner, Kathy Pantella. Perry sat in the visitor's chair and waited. Two minutes later, Ted took off his headset and said, "Well, Perry, it was the same gun and almost the exact same place for bullet entry. Quick and effective into the rear left of the Occipital lobe downward through the Medulla in the brain stem. It literally killed him instantly. Almost as if someone took a scalpel and severed the brain stem to stop all involuntary functions like his heartbeat and breathing. Either the murderer was lucky both times; or more likely, this was a professional hit." "Good morning, Ted!", said Perry Kline in his best serious voice. Ted laughed, "Good morning, Perry. Sorry, could you tell I have not been to bed yet?"

Perry just waved at him as he got up and left the office, "No worries, Ted. You just solved the case." They both laughed as Ted handed him a report.

When Perry got to his desk. He found Parker sitting on his desk with Paul in the cubicle with his chair and Micah Blair sitting on Perry's plush rolling brown leather couch. Or so it seemed as it could almost fit two and had a high back that molded around Perry's six-foot-three-inch frame.

"Sit!", said Perry as he saw Micah getting up, "Good morning, everyone. You guys looked like you were in a heavy discussion about something. Don't let me interrupt." Parker laughed and said, "We were arguing about whether the Bills would ever win a Superbowl." Paul said, "We gotta get there first, Chief." Perry laughed and said, "Shall we begin by restructuring our list?"

He continued, "I just spoke with Ted. I have his reports here (Holding up the folder he just received). I'll give you the Reader's Digest version. Both Galway brothers were killed with a 32-caliber gun. The entry angle on each was such that they died instantly. He went on to say that they were both bruised but that could have been either from a struggle or being moved directly after the shoot. He commented that both men had something under their fingernails. He is checking to see if they match. The cut on the mayor's neck when Ms. Mahern unearthed him was caused by the car's underside. I asked about the no blood factor, and he said there was little blood left and what was left was frozen. He said that neither man had blood on their clothes. When I asked why, he replied, 'They were either redressed in fresh clothes or they were naked when they were shot.'"

The cubicle was silent as everyone processed this information. Parker said, "Both of these guys were legendary ladies' men. Could it be that we're not looking for just a female but a couple?" Perry said, "We need to look at suspects first then see if they would have had an accomplice. If we could identify a solid motive, then we might have better success identifying a suspect or suspects." Paul Gorci said, "OK, Chief, let's go through our lists like Perry mentioned. You guys can reel off names and I will jot them down. If we run out of suspects, we'll talk about motives like Perry mentioned as I have a couple of ideas. Ok, I am ready. Fire away."

He pulled up his 2-by-2 whiteboard and began to write. "I'll make two columns. One for single suspects and the other for couples.

Suspects: <u>Single</u>	Suspects: <u>Couples</u>
Margie (Keen) Galway	Victor & Charmaine Sinclair
Linda Carnello	Matt F. & sister Christie M.
Joni Wilsco	Any combination of two or more
Mel Barstow	of those from the single's list.
Christie Mahern	
Matt Fogelburg	
Victor Sinclair	

He turned the board around so the others could see it. He said, "I left Parker off the list as I think we can discount the Chief. I also left Frank off the first list as he is now deceased. Any thoughts?" Perry had several but never voiced them. Parker said, "Thanks for taking me off the list. We don't seem to be any further ahead than we were. Let's redouble our efforts."

Perry picked up the phone and dialed Christie at her home as it was Sunday morning. She picked up the phone and said, "Hello." Perry said, "Where have you been all night? It sounds like you just walked in the door." The reply was, "May I ask who is calling?" Perry laughed, "You are not only sexy but very funny, Ms. Mahern. How are you? Did you think about a list? Did you hear from Ronnie Olsen?" Christie was putting on her robe; she set the phone down for a second. When she held it to her ear, she heard, "Christie, are you there? Christie, are you there?" "Oh Mr. Kline, I didn't recognize your voice at first. I was just donning my robe after a leisurely morning shower. How was your night?" She smiled to herself remembering the torrid love scene they created at his house the night before. "It was wonderful, did you hear my questions?", Perry asked sounding a bit agitated. "Mr. Kline, you sound very busy this morning, are you working on a Sunday?" Christie shot back as she sorted through her desk for the list she put together.

She didn't let him answer as she found the list, "Well Perry, I thought about it and just got off the phone with Ronnie Olsen before I stepped into the shower. Our lists matched." She looked down at her list for ladies that dated both of Galways, "Got a pen? I'll read it to you."

Christie read: Catie Fuda, Linda Carnello, Joni Wilsco, Melanie Barstow, Tina Oliver, Charmaine Sinclair, and Christie Mahern. I was thinking about it. If it was a female like we thought, how would they move Frank's body alone. I thought maybe it's more than one person doing this, so I thought my brother Matt and I could be suspects. Then I thought of the Sinclairs, Jim Maltry and his mom Karen Maltry, Joni Wilsco, and Dennis Shooda, and Eric Volsier and his wife Kris Volsier from Reno, Nevada."

Perry was taking notes furiously, "Ok, Christie, I have some follow-up questions. Who the heck is Catie Fuda?" "Well, she is dating Micah Blair. She is from Syracuse originally but has spent the last few years in Keene, New Hampshire doing some insurance investigations. I think she works for the Feds. I am not sure in what capacity. Ronnie is pretty sure Catie Fuda dated Johnny Galway too; but it was short-lived."

Perry was writing non-stop and getting a hand cramp, "Ok, so why Jimmy and Karen Maltry?" "Christie answered, "Well, Jimmy ran against Johnny in a councilman race and lost through some alleged voter fraud. Jimmy could never prove it and changed parties. His mom shortly thereafter was hired as Johnny's personal administrator. She has been there throughout his reign." Perry couldn't make the connection but wrote things down, "I know Joni and Dennis. Why them?" Christie poured herself another cup of tea, knowing this would be a longer conversation.

She continued, "Joni Wilsco dated Johnny and Frank as well as Dennis Shooda. She and Dennis were great friends at school, and they still see each other. Dennis ran a limousine service for years and had dealings with both Frank and Johnny as both liked to impress with being escorted in those limos." Perry then reset, "Christie, I appreciate all this information. Is it okay if we reconvene? I have a few more questions and I know you like to prepare cases on Sundays."

She smiled and responded, "Thank you, Perry. That was very thoughtful of you. When you do things like this, I really feel close to you and appreciate what a great guy you are. Hey, by the way, you haven't told me whether you've crossed me off the suspect's list, yet?"

Now it was Perry's turn to smile. He had a sixth sense sometimes when dealing with females. Even sharp ones like this attorney he was dating. Some said he was just too smooth when he dealt with the women around him, which of course, made him more appealing. He continued his questions, "I didn't know Linda Carnello dated, both brothers. Are you sure? and why Mel Barstow?" Christie thought to herself, this should shake him up a bit and she noted he still hadn't dismissed her from the list, "Well, I got this from Ronnie. Mel dated both Frank and Johnny. It was rumored that Frank got physical with her, so that ended poorly.

She is currently dating a guy from North Buffalo named, Freddy Gilroy. He has had some dealings with Frank and the Utica mob. Those dealings didn't go so well. He also began dating Mel right after she split from Frank. Maybe he was harboring some ill will for Frank. Now not many people knew about Frank and Linda because Frank knew Johnny would put a stop to that and make a huge scene for them both. Only a few folks knew like Ronnie Olsen, Karen Maltry and I think maybe Donna Smith from your

Department." Perry then asked, "Tina Oliver?" Christie looked again at her list for the notes she had written, "Tina was Johnny's secretary when he was a councilman. She dated Frank during that time. She left him quickly. She dated Johnny secretly maybe while he was still with Margie or right after their split. It didn't go well as she wouldn't tolerate his running around. It got ugly at the end during his first mayoral run to the point where she left him and the job as his secretary."

"Wow!", Perry still taking notes, "Amazing. Now you have Charmaine Sinclair. I didn't know she dated Frank." Christie thought this'll be an eye opener for you Mr. Kline, "It was not widely known but she dated Frank at the same time she was still seeing Johnny Galway. I don't know that Johnny ever knew but there was a handful of people who heard but no one ever said for sure. The real reason was conjectured that she had Victor's permission to date them so she could get information from them for Victor to use against them." She heard his pen drop. "Counselor, you have given me more information in twenty minutes than I have unearthed in weeks. Thank you so much. I gotta go but can we have dinner tonight?" She replied, "Dinner at my place 8 o'clock. See you then." The call ended. Perry had four pages of notes and more questions that he would address that evening.

He motioned for Paul to follow him. He walked into the conference room. "Partner, we need to get Micah Blair over here without Parker and go through some things. Maybe we should meet for lunch outside the office." Paul said, "Why, what's up?" "Let's drive over to Chef's and use their back room" replied Perry walking back out of the conference room. Paul followed but his mouth never opened as he knew that Perry had dug something up that could be very explosive; he just followed, grabbed his keys, and headed out the door to his vehicle. Perry was calling the restaurant to see if the room was available. Paul called Micah.

The ten-minute drive was quiet. Paul parked and they both walked into Chef's. Marie Vendetti greeted them at the door. "Follow me." is all she said. It was Sunday morning at 10 a.m. Too early for the crazy lunch crowd to be there. Perry had figured that being a regular. Marie said, "Coffees?" setting down two menus in the small intimate room with three small tables for two. They both nodded and she left, closing the door behind her. Paul waited for Perry to speak. He began, "I just got off the phone with Christie. I had asked her to give me a list of people that went out with both Galway brothers." He continued, "I'll jot down the names and then we can discuss each of them. Let's look to see what they said in their interview and look at whether they have a motive, opportunity; and ability to pull this off." Just then Micah walked in.

Perry said, "Paul, I think this case is bigger than we even know at this point. The information keeps coming in and it is getting stranger by the day. I have a cramp in my hand from taking notes while talking to Christie for fifteen minutes.

He wrote: Linda Carnello. Perry said. "Did you know that Linda dated Frank also?" Paul shook his head no. Perry continued, "He supposedly dated her the same time as Frank. I knew Linda from high school. She was a model with that killer body. Everyone wanted a date with her. I double-dated with her once. I heard her father was connected to the mob or so people said. She was always on a higher plane than the rest of us. She had much bigger fish to fry it seemed. I did a bit of checking into her past. She has lived in Las Vegas, started as a showgirl. She moved to Los Angeles and did five or six films as well as one rumored to be somewhat pornographic. She was mainly a fashion model.

I couldn't corroborate that X-rated one; but it could have been with her looks. Then her life seems to have dropped off the planet for five years and now she has reappeared here in town a week or so ago. She has been traveling alone while here and doesn't seem to have the strength to kill Frank alone nor does she seem to have a close relationship here that we know of. As far as motives, nothing jumps out at me. Thoughts?" Paul looked somewhat overwhelmed with the information but added, "I didn't know she dated Frank; it's not surprising. I heard she was hurt by Johnny as she fell hard for him, and he kicked her to the curb publicly. Her dating Frank makes sense when you look at the big picture.

Micah said after he walked into the room taking off his coat, "I was there the night at Smitty's Tavern on Abbott when he announced he was running for Councilman the first time. He made the announcement that he and Margie Keen were going to be married. Linda Carnello was there and obviously didn't even know she was being dumped. She stormed out of there even knocking a few people over in the process. So that could have been her motive." Perry wrote on his notes putting a plus mark behind Linda's name for motive. He also wrote that Linda must be further researched. There seemed to be more about her they didn't know than the information they did know. "Now, we have to link her motives to include Frank", Perry noted.

Next: Melanie "Mel" Barstow. Perry began again with his notes from Christie. Mel dated Johnny first. That ended with her catching him out with another woman. She later went out with Frank. Then it's rumored that he got physical with her and hurt her badly one night. Her current man, Freddy Gilroy worked as a bartender around town but was thought to be linked to the mob but no one could confirm that. He grew up in North Buffalo but lived in South Buffalo for years. He knows the Galways and the fact that Frank got rough with his girl might give him a motive. I think I remember he has a sister Rosa Ebert who is very politically active in the South Buffalo area." Paul interjected, "I knew him from my senior year of High School baseball. He was a tough customer back in the day and it would not surprise me that he had a connection to the Utica underworld. He may even have his own group in town. I will see if I can get anywhere with that lead."

Next up: <u>Tina Oliver</u>. Perry again began. From what my sources tell me, Tina was the administrator for Johnny Galway's Council office. She worked for him during his three terms as Councilman. During that time, she dated Frank Galway. It ended very abruptly; she just outclassed him, and it became a stumbling block for their relationship. It was rumored she dated Johnny secretly. No one knows if it was while he was still married to Margie or just after they separated. That relationship ended quickly as well. Either due to the secrecy affecting them or him running around with his 'stable of lady admirers'. She is very closed-mouthed about either Galway. She works for the Party. Micah offered, "I knew Tina when she was married; her husband treated her poorly which eventually caused their breakup. She vowed then to never allow a man to mistreat her in any way, shape, or form."

Then he wrote: <u>Christie Mahern</u>. Perry said, "Paul, you did some digging about her. I am a bit too close to be objective. What did you find?" Paul pulled out a large, folded pile of yellow pad pages and began, "Well, I used several sources on this one and it turned out to be more difficult than I had expected. She was married a while ago and has two children. Michael and Lexi. Michael just graduated and is headed to Harvard Law School next June and is working as a clerk for Judge John Roberts of Buffalo. Her daughter Lexi is in her third year of study at the Julliard School of Music in New York City. Tuition there is over $40k a year so

Christie and her ex must be doing ok financially. Word has it that Lexi is quite the violinist and has given several concerts around the country already. Christie dated both Frank and Johnny who both got one date. Those two encounters were insignificant as they were both at the Policeman's ball and neither date lasted the entire night. She left both events as the brothers were up to their usual misogynistic behavior and Christie was not standing for it one minute. She has been vocal to her inner circle of friends that she was quite upset with Johnny when her brother Matt lost the mayoral election to him under the blanket of suspicious political behavior."

Perry thought for a moment then added, "Nice work Paul. I didn't know she dated both brothers as we've never gotten into the past relationship's conversation. I am thinking that she has too much to lose to jeopardize her career, the kids, or her life to vindicate her brother's allegations concerning his election loss. I'll have to remind myself to talk to her about it." Perry was thinking he must call her right after this meeting to let her know she was off the list. It just dawned on him that he had forgotten to do that when Christie was relating the information on the suspects that he was now sharing with Paul and Micah.

Then Micah said, "Perry, you and she have been seeing each other casually for how long? You have not talked about passed lovers?" Perry just shrugged saying, "Never came up."

Now came: <u>Charmaine Sinclair</u>. She was originally from Syracuse, New York. She was married to Victor Sinclair for about 12 years when they split as their quest for power caused too much strife as one person described it. She had her own money from her family's coffee business using imported beans from Venezuela. She sold that business for $70 million and moved to Western New York with an alleged female partner but no one seems to know who that was. Shortly after her arrival, she began dating Victor and they quickly married. After they parted empires, she dated many powerful men from in and around Buffalo. She is reported to have been running a cocaine operation in the area but has always been one step ahead of the police. She has dated Johnny Galway, Micah Blair, Frank Galway as we just recently learned, Matt Fogelburg. I know of no motives but that she dated these guys and may have been treated poorly but could that have led to her becoming a serial murderer?" Micah added, "We dated for two months and had fun but that's all.

Finally, he wrote: <u>Catie Fuda</u>. Perry began, "There is not a lot of information on her as she was allegedly married before, but we couldn't find the name of her former spouse." "I can help a bit here," said Micah, "She was married to Edgar Weinberg who was an assistant golf pro somewhere in the Finger Lakes area of central New York. She has a son, Christopher Weinberg, who lives on the West Coast and has his own business. She has a background in Insurance Fraud Investigation and moved to Buffalo when she started dating Micah Blair. She currently has her own company called WIFI (World Insurance Fraud Investigation). I just recently heard she bought a restaurant downtown somewhere as she is quite a gourmet chef." Perry said, "Thanks Micah. Do you know if she ever dated the Galways?" Micah replied, "I don't think I've heard that, but I will double check. Can we discuss the possible males now?" Perry drew a line under the females and began with the males.

<u>Matt Fogelburg</u>: He has been a political opponent of Johnny Galway for several years. He is also Christie's brother." Paul interjected, "Has he dated anyone of our female suspects?" Shrugs were expressed around the room. Perry said, "We know Charmaine, that's it." Micah offered, "I will check into this one." Not much else was said.

Next Perry wrote: <u>Parker Clark</u>. Silence filled the room for minutes when he began, "We know Parker has dated all the women on the list. His ex-wife is now Jennifer Steinberg and is a dentist, has remarried, and lives in Denver Colorado. He really had a thing for her, but they grew apart. He dated Margie Galway, but I think that's over." Micah jumped in, "Do we have a solid motive for him to jeopardize his career to kill Johnny and Frank Galway?" Paul stood and walked to the board, "If these murders are about a love triangle, what would Parker gain from killing either of the Galways? Also, why is he not here?"

Perry said, "I just have a hunch that he is dirty. Some of the things he has done lately don't make sense. Why would he have us investigate him? What has he hidden so well we couldn't find it? I wouldn't be surprised if he walked in here after eavesdropping our talk in the conference room earlier." Paul marked the board with yes/no Motive. He wrote a YES after Parker's name saying, "Parker really had no motive. Neither Galway was a threat to him. He dated the same women as the Galways but his history with them ended amicably." Perry said, "I have no evidence on him yet." Paul then erased the YES."

Perry then wrote: <u>Victor Sinclair</u>. He again took the lead in the discussion, "Victor has verbally declared he would love to eliminate Johnny and Frank from his world on several occasions. With the Galways out of the picture, he would highly likely control the property purchase for the Peace Bridge and the downtown stadium. He knows Johnny dated Charmaine. I don't know if he knew about Frank unless she told him herself to just throw one in his face as he had thrown so many women in her face." Paul wrote a YES behind Victor's name on the board. He sat back down at the table. The three detectives were quiet for a minute then the door opened. In walked Parker Clark. "Hey guys, I stopped in for lunch and one of the waitresses asked if I was looking for you all, so here I am." He quickly scanned the board. "Damn, did I miss the discussion about me?"

Paul slid a chair to him and said, "Well Chief, you said to 'look at you as a suspect', to cover our bases and I was given that assignment as you remember. You had so many skeletons in the closet. We thought you were crazy to take a chance on giving anybody an opportunity to look at you. Also, we could not come up with a solid motive unless you can suggest one?" Everyone laughed including Parker. Parker said, "Thanks, guys. If anyone volunteers to be investigated, I typically dig harder. I thought you, Paul, would find anything if it was there. I am guessing you found I was clean. Did you all come up with a prime suspect yet with a solid motive?" Perry rose and pointed to Victor's YES after his name. "It looks like Victor would have the most to gain from removing both these men from "His world" as he has been heard to say several times."

Parker responded, "Does it strike you as odd that he would have made these pronouncements prior to committing this double murder?" The room became silent again. Micah spoke, "Hey, did we forget to discuss Joni Wilsco?" Perry quickly grabbed the marker and wrote:

Joni Wilsco went on the board. Micah asked, "Isn't she friends with Linda Carnello and Christie as well as most of the folks in your class Perry?" Perry who was thinking about Parker was interrupted by the question, "Joni is a good friend of the Olsens. She was very well-liked by everyone I know. She hangs out at the Ace of Clubs with Mel Barstow. She has been dating Rick Moyers lately. He is singing at the Ace of Clubs this month. She has also been dating Dennis Shooda of late." Micah said, "Let me check on her further."

As they adjourned, Perry wrote Erik & Kim Volsier and Freddy Gilroy on his pad but kept them to himself.

Paul and Perry drove back to headquarters. Paul said, "Perry, who do you think did the murders. You've been tight-lipped around the office on naming a prime suspect." Perry spun in his chair to check the room and said, "You know Paul, it really could have been anyone. Maybe someone different than we are even aware of at this moment." Perry continued, "The victims were both liked but had many enemies they had stepped on over the years. I have a hunch that it's someone closer than we think but I will keep a lid on that as I might shoot myself in the foot if I'm wrong."

Frank Galway had come into the Hyatt differently than his brother had. He had been sent a key in a large, padded envelope with a simple note which read, "Hey Buddy. Some old friends are meeting at the Hyatt tonight to discuss finding your brother's murderer. The cops don't seem to have a clue. We saw the whole thing go down so we would like your help bringing them to justice. See you at 8 p.m." It was signed, "An Old Friend."

Frank walked into the hotel from the south side parking lot entrance door. It was 8:00 sharp when he pushed the button for the South end elevator. No one was in the hall when he reached the third floor. He used the key for Room 320. The room was dimly lit. The shower was running; a low, voice said, "You are the first one here. Make yourself a drink." He looked to his left and saw the library table in front of the window with a bottle of Tequila and an ice bucket. He went over to the table, poured himself a stiff shot without ice, and chugged it down in one gulp. Then the lights went out. He hit the floor with a thud. He was a big man, but the walls and floors were sturdy enough to cushion the sound. What happened to his brother, had now happened to him. He was rolled into the laundry cart with a towel wrapped around his head where the bullets had entered. After the room had been wiped clean, his murderer placed extra blankets over the body and rolled him to the elevator.

In the basement, he was rolled into a small van that was marked Home Depot on the side. The driver closed the rear hatch, jumped into the driver's seat. They drove out of the garage exiting the Hotel grounds making a right turn onto the Skyway going south on Route 5. The van exited at the Lackawanna exit and made a left heading east on Ridge Road. The van turned right at South Park. It had snowed heavily that day, but the Lackawanna Department of Public Works had the pavement just wet as always. The van pulled into the parking lot of the VFW. No cars were there. The van drove to the back of the lot. It parked along the south side of the building about 40 feet from the side door. The rear latch was open, the body was slid out, into the snow. A shovel from the back of the van was used to cover the body. It was snowing so hard at that point, after five minutes, it looked like the rest of the snow piles in the parking lot. As the van was leaving the VFW parking lot, the driver looked back seeing the van's wheel marks were now covered over. It drove out of the lot like it was never there.

The van rolled out of the dark VFW parking lot and turned right heading south toward Blasdell. As the van passed in front of the Fire House next to the stadium, a snowplow passed headed north and the driver watched it turn into the VFW to begin plowing. The driver chuckled. Old Frank would be piled under some large plow drifts. The van continued to Lake Avenue where it turned left heading east. It entered the Thruway heading toward the south towns.

The van exited at the Hamburg exit Rte. 75 and went west then turned into the gigantic Leisureland Bowling Alley parking lot. It parked next to a white Cadillac. The driver locked the van after wiping the insides down and entered the Cadillac. The shiny white Cadillac covered in snow had the windows brushed off in two minutes and the car now warmed. It drove back onto Rte. 75 and reentered the Thruway headed South toward ski country.

Matt Fogelburg was one of the suspects identified by the detective group in the Chef's restaurant meeting. He was one of the three major shareholders in the Hyatt Hotel downtown on the waterfront. He was quickly moving up the ranks going from Committeeman to the Councilman followed by a run, albeit unsuccessful, for Mayor against Johnny Galway. The campaign was very aggressive. No one remembers what specifically set this trend but by the end, both camps had pulled out all the stops. It became the ugliest campaign for mayor in years.

It had separated the city of Buffalo almost in half. The election of that year saw the largest turnout for a November election in a non-Presidential year. It saw 76% of registered voters go to the polls. Of the 300,000 or so people in the city, there were 228,000 votes cast. The final totals were said to be closer than reported by the Buffalo Evening News. They reported the final totals as 115,130 for Galway and 112, 870 for Fogelburg. Matt had not planned to go to the collective high school reunion; he told his secretary he was going out of town after the Council session broke for the year-end holidays. He said he would not take any calls but to text him if there was an emergency. Matt packed his skis and some bourbon and headed for Kissing Bridge.

Matthew had a small cottage a half mile away from which he could even ski to the lodge. He got there on a Friday night around 6:30 p.m. He unloaded his white Cadillac of the supplies he had purchased; TV dinners, eggs, bacon, and bread for breakfast, milk for coffee, and of course the three bottles of Jack Daniels' bourbon. He showered, had a drink, then headed to the KB Lodge. He was surprised that his dentist, Jennifer Steinberg was at the bar. They had a drink, exchanged pleasantries and she left after an hour. She had been to a conference in town and got in some skiing. He was sad when she said she was engaged. She had moved to Denver. He had always thought dating her would be extra special. He had one more drink, left the bar, then headed over to the chair lift. He saw that the South trail had the lights off and he thought that looked romantic. He got off alone and noticed no one behind him on the lift. He never saw the 'Trail Closed' sign covered in snow. He skillfully entered the trail and noticed how quiet it was back here. You could see the lights from the lodge in the distance. As he skied, he noticed the dark spot in the snow, too late. His skis stuck in the mud, and he flew out of his skis into a tree. He slammed into it with his shoulder and head then the lights went out.

Linda Carnello loved coming back to Western New York. She went to school here and left for the west coast for fame and fortune right after graduation. She was married to an actor and a director. Both marriages were short as both had died sudden deaths within a year of the marriage. The actor was a stuntman and was killed when his parachute failed to open in a scene done over Palm Canyon just north of San Diego.

The director she married was 20 years her senior and was killed in a small plane crash in Montana where he planned to retire. She was left with both her husband's significant inheritances. As a result, Linda no longer had to work but she invested in property in Western New York as she frequently visited her father, Stan, and her brothers. She loved to ski so she had invested in Kissing Bridge heavily and was majority owner within a few years. She had a small villa built adjacent to the KB property.

As Linda headed up the hill late on that Friday, she noticed that the Devil's Funnel Trail's lights were out. She loved that trail and knew that meant it was probably under some repair. She jumped off the chair lift and headed straight to the Funnel as natives called it. She would just be extra careful. Halfway down she noticed a patch of ice followed by a dark mud strip ten feet wide and almost all the way across the trail. As she slowed approaching it, she noticed a yellow jacket at the base of a tree off to the left. As she traversed the slope, it became apparent that it was a person. She stopped and realized it was Matt Fogelburg. He was unconscious. Being as familiar with the grounds as she was, she knew not twenty yards up the hill was the Ski Patrol Station. There would be a snowmobile and backboard there. She undid her skis and ran back up to the station and grabbed the sled. Back down the hill now, she rolled Matt onto the sled and packed their skis as well; then traversed the hill down toward her property just about 200 yards to the right. It took her minutes to reach the villa.

With all the snow of late, she was able to steer the sled onto her front porch and she then was easily able to drag him into the large front room. She thought for a minute and decided to take him to the guest room at the front just off the entry foyer. She was able to see the large goose egg on his head as she took off his jacket. He began to show signs of waking as she began lifting him onto the bed. Matt was able to help her get him off the sled onto the bed. He looked at her and reached for his head and passed out again. Linda wrestled with him for ten minutes getting his boots and pants off. She rolled him under the covers and retrieved an ice bag from the kitchen. She spent the rest of the evening attending to him.

Back in the day, Matt Fogelburg was a good student and enjoyed student government, the yearbook club, and debate teams much more so than sports. He was asked by the coach of the baseball team in junior year to come out and he did under pressure from his dad, who he lived with in Buffalo after his parents' divorce.

Not only did he make the team, but he was also spotted as a potential pitcher and really took to the position. He became all-state in his senior year and had seven offers from big league clubs. He also wanted to go to law school, so he chose to go to the University of Buffalo, whose law department was touted as one of the best in the state. This was a controversial decision within the household as his dad and stepmom thought baseball would have been a great opportunity for him.

Matt knew in his own head that he didn't have the drive it took to commit to the rigorous training it would have taken to gain the next level and frankly, he loved the law more. As Matt finished law school, he worked as a clerk for a year at his sister's firm, Mahern, Miller, and Associates; however, he left after one year to run for office in North Buffalo as a committeeman with eyes on Councilman then Mayor. Matt's long-term goal was to represent New York as a Senator in Washington. He was on track so far. He had purchased property near the BlackRock Canal and envisioned building up that location in the same fashion as the small boat harbor off Fuhrman Boulevard. He would create a waterside extravaganza not unlike the Baltimore Waterfront which had major hotels, shoppes and was near the Orioles ballpark. This project was in direct opposition to that of Mayor Johnny Galway and his brother Frank who saw the new Peace Bridge from Canada; just south of the BlackRock toll barrier on 190; which would also be the new home of the Bisons baseball park.

The Friendship Bridge which was the new Peace Bridge Project was also in the plans of Victor Sinclair. He planned on using the site of the Naval Park, as the best scenario for the citizens of Buffalo which, of course, he owned. This made Matt a very unpopular fellow in the real estate world. This became an unfavorable issue used against him in the recent mayoral election.

Matt had gotten a call from his sister, Christie that Friday morning. She said, "Hello Councilor." Matt replied, "Hello Counselor." It was their running joke with each other. She continued, "Matt don't take this the wrong way; but did you kill Johnny and Frank Galway?"

Matt was silent building the drama, then said with a laugh, "From your lips to God's ears, Sis. Why, am I a suspect?" Christie replied, "As a matter-of-fact little brother, you are indeed considered a possible suspect. I think you should lie low for a spell."

Matt really began to laugh and said, "Sis, there is no way anyone can prove I did something that bad. I really wouldn't ever consider the risk; nor did I hate either of them enough to try anything that stupid. There are plenty of others that hold a stronger hatred for those boys than did I! Sure, I felt like killing them both after they stole the election from me last month and the things that he was quoted to have said about me afterward, they were untrue and angered me.

There was also the abuse of power Johnny used to sway the Department of City Planning to propose his plans for the waterfront instead of mine." Christie's heart lept into her throat, "My God, Matthew. Are you out of your skull? Please don't ever repeat those words again. It sounded like a confession to me, your sister, the lawyer. What do you think it would sound like in front of the Police or even worse, a jury?" "No need to worry Sis, but thanks. I have too much work I want to accomplish. Maybe, we can have dinner and talk soon. Got to hang up now!" Matt didn't wait for her goodbye. He hung up and made a call to his secretary telling her he would be unable to be reached until Monday. He thought for a moment about what his sister had said. He decided to put together a timeline of his activities during the days surrounding the murders, just in case. He packed his bags, skis, and some bourbon and headed to the slopes.

Meanwhile, Paul was checking the prints of Matt Fogelburg to see if they matched the partial prints that were found in Room 220 on the shot glass. He had been asking around and found at least ten people who independently corroborated the fact that Matt had said 'he would like to see the Galways eliminated'. Paul called Perry and told him of this. Perry said, "Maybe it's time we brought Mr. Fogelburg in for questioning. I'll call Christie in ten minutes before we serve him to give her a heads up. She'll probably represent him." Paul added, "I also found four people who told me without any provocation that Matt said, 'Now if we are talking about Victor Sinclair, him I would personally like to have a hand in his demise.'

"Wow", said Perry, "He has really been shooting off his mouth. In all our years on the beat Paul, have you ever heard of a murderer pronounce his wanting to kill someone; then going ahead and doing it?" Paul quietly said, "Not that I can remember partner. He is a law school graduate. You'd think he would be smart enough to keep his comments like this in his back pocket." "Paul, get the address of his office, I will call Christie; then we'll pay a visit to Mr. Fogelburg." Perry made a call to Christie's office. She was in court said the receptionist. He then called her cell, but it went to voicemail. He struggled with leaving a message but said, "Christie, Perry. I am on my way to talk to your brother. Just wanted to give you a heads up."

Paul got up and said, "I spoke with Matt's secretary, she said he is gone for the weekend and is not reachable on his phone."

Linda felt movement before she opened her eyes. Her bedmate grunted and she looked at him. He was holding his head. She softly spoke, "Well good afternoon, Councilor. How is your head?" He was startled. He turned his head looking at her as his eyes began to focus. "Where am I and more importantly, is that you Miss Carnello?" Linda grinned and was impressed that he remembered her saying, "Matt, yes, it is Linda. You are in my villa next to Kissing Bridge. You took a spill last night and just woke up." Matt still groggy said, "How long did you say I was here?"

"Since yesterday" was her reply, "you have been in and out of sleep since I found you on the trail. Do you remember what happened?" Matt laid his head back down on the pillow as his head began to clear and said, "I was out on my first run after a drink at the lodge on Friday. I took the Palm Canyon trail and realized too late that the lights were off because it was under repair. If I remember I was looking at the lodge lights when I hit a patch of ice and sped up almost losing control; then I hit a dark patch which I now realize was probably mud. I remember flying out of my skis into some branches then the lights went out." Linda interrupted, "How many fingers do you see". He opened his eyes and saw three long slender digits, "Three. Right? By the way, what are we doing in bed together?"

He noticed the top of her negligee above the sheet and blanket. He felt down his body and he was naked. He said, "Hey, I'm naked under here!? Linda laughed, "Well, when I cleaned you up last night, I wanted to check you over to make sure you were not injured. It was also easier to give you a sponge bath without clothes. You haven't spoken since very early this morning when you awoke, looked at me and said, 'Jeez, you're more beautiful than I remember. Can we have sex now?' Then you rolled on your side and went back to sleep. I knew you were fine, so I let you sleep. I figured you'd wake up when you were ready.

I am here in bed with you because, first, I love sleeping against such a fabulous body; and secondly, I wanted to be here to check on you if anything went wrong. I also wanted to be here when you were finally awake so I could tell you where you were and not have you panic in these unfamiliar surroundings."

Matt looked again at her chest peeking out from the sheets and her ample bosom, "I have been working non-stop for the last month since the election loss; I guess I needed to catch up on my rest and the blow to the head just put me into quite the sleep mode." Linda again interrupted, "Are you hungry? You must be famished." Matt thought for a minute, "Yeah, I guess I am. I need to drain my bladder first then I could really use a cup of coffee and a real hot shower. My bones feel like I tackled a tree." They both laughed.

She threw the covers back and got out of bed. Matt watched intently as her body appeared in the pale purple negligee which hid very little on her exquisite body. Her long legs and voluptuous curves made his body tremble. She walked around to his side of the bed and handed him a beige robe that had been lying at the foot of the bed. Linda said, "Here put this on if you're shy. Follow me to the shower." Matt knew he was aroused and would be somewhat embarrassed by his hardening member at the sight of this magnificent creature and truth be told, he was a bit shy anyway. He slowly swung his feet over the side of the bed and rose slowly putting on his robe. Linda seeing that he was steady afoot, walked toward the ensuite bath. She reached into the shower and turned on the hot water.

When she turned, Matt was right behind her smiling. She laughed and said, "You seem to be in a good mood. How does it feel to walk?" He couldn't stop looking at those beautiful breasts almost in full view beneath the pale purple, "I feel okay and will probably be better after a shower." She smiled and said, "I can stay and help to make sure you don't tumble in the shower if you want. I'd hate to see you reinjure yourself after that nasty spill you had." Matt blushed. "Well, I, I, I," he stammered, don't have my sea legs quite yet. I need a minute because of this situation I have." He really could feel the blood almost bursting out of his face at this point.

Linda chuckled, "Well, I'd feel better if I was here to make sure you didn't fall. I could use a shower as well." She slowly lifted her negligee off her shoulders and let it fall to the tiled floor. She stepped into what looked like a four-person shower with a rain shower head, four wall-mounted sprayers, and two hand-held adjustable heads in the corners. He went into the small room with a water closet next to the shower to relieve his bladder. He dropped his robe and entered the shower with her.

The water was at a perfect temperature which felt great on his body. He thought to himself this feels like a dream. He remembered having a crush on this woman while in school, but he was a year younger and not ready to make a move on this goddess. No more than he was now, he thought. She turned to face him. She noticed his stiffness and was impressed. She squirted some liquid soap onto him and began washing his body. He just stood there mesmerized while feeling the heated water pelt into his sore muscles and at that point could not resist putting his arms around Linda as she pressed her body into his while she soaped him. He said, "Thank you for helping me, this feels spectacular. I can't remember ever being this aroused. I had a major crush on you in school and would never in my wildest fantasies think I would be in this situation." He leaned down and kissed her raised lips. She kissed him back, HARD.

Christie was standing in the middle of her brother's spacious condo downtown. It was Saturday night and she had been trying to find him for a week. She had a key but had never used it until now. As she walked around, she was impressed by the décor. She wondered if some woman he dated had assembled the furnishing or if he himself had designed the home. She had not found his car but took a chance on finding him. No luck. She was really beginning to worry especially after the conversation she had with him last Friday before she left the office. She remembered the things he said about the Galway brothers and Victor Sinclair but shivered when she thought again about what he didn't say. He never said he didn't kill anyone and that had haunted her all weekend. More and more now, that he was not to be found anywhere. She wondered, did he do it, and was he now on the run? Was he innocent and hiding out until things blew over or did something happened to him like had happened to the Galways? She almost jumped a foot in the air as the phone she was holding rang. It was Perry who asked. "Where are you, doll?"

Christie gathered herself a bit and said, "Hi Perry. I am at my brother Matt's place in the city. He's not here." A bell went off in her head. Maybe Matt was at his place in Glenwood skiing, she wondered.

Perry was talking, "You know I never did ask more about Erik and Kris Volsier or Freddy Gilroy when we spoke earlier in the week." Christie answered, "Now is not a great time Perry, I have briefs to prepare; and I am still looking for my brother." Perry said, "Ok I will check with you in the morning. Are you in court all day Monday?" Christie thought wanting to delay the meeting until she found her brother Matt, "Sunday is my prep day for court. I am in court much of the day Monday. I will call you if I get a break of any kind. Then we can follow up on the conversation. She drove back to East Aurora and crashed into bed.

Very early Sunday, Christie jumped back in her Mustang and headed South to Glenwood. It took her no time at all. She was there in 20 minutes. South on Center Road where she lived to Crump Rd. Then west to Dog Run and into Kissing Bridge. Matt's condo was just passed the Kissing Bridge Ski Resort, right on State Rd. Her heart lept for joy as she saw his white Cadillac in his driveway. She parked behind him and went to the door. She knocked several times but got no answer. Then it dawned on her that he was probably skiing. She thought for a moment then realized she may have stuck a key in her bag as she used this place every so often. She found it, opened the door, and went in. She yelled but got only silence back. There on the kitchen table was Matt's phone. It was off. She turned it on. It flashed low battery when she picked it up. Christie quickly looked around in his office/bedroom, finding his phone charger plugged into the wall. She plugged the phone into the charger and returned to the kitchen.

She grabbed a piece of paper and pen from his office and left a note on the kitchen table. *'Hi, Matt- Stopped in to check on you as I was getting no answers from the calls and texts to your phone. You're probably out skiing so I won't wait as I must get back to town so I can prepare for court in the morning. Call me on my cell as soon as you read this. I've been worried sick all week. Love Sis.'*

Christie was really getting worried. Seeing Matt's phone here and no Matt was disconcerting. She really hoped he was alright. She locked up the place and drove home. It had been a busy week and she'd blown off Perry rudely. She would call him when she got back to her house.

Linda and Matt went skiing more than once as he was now fully recovered but most of their time was spent in her villa. She had groceries delivered and he had liquor delivered so he didn't feel like he was being a total mooch.

Their lovemaking just seemed to be getting more intense and comfortable increasing by multiples of ten. He sat in the living room looking out onto the hill at Kissing Bridge which sat 200 yards away. It looked great during the day but was a romantic movie from that vantage point in the evening. It was evening on Saturday night. Linda was freshening their drinks. She made a mean margarita. He was thinking of returning to his place tomorrow then driving back into Buffalo on Sunday afternoon.

He wanted to be back in the office Monday morning. He had really enjoyed the week tremendously and even got in some skiing. Linda walked in with the drink. He reveled at her body. She wore the skimpiest of thongs, bright yellow, and a pale yellow short see-through negligee. She noticed him looking when she handed him his drink, "What?" He paused for a second and said, "I was just taking a picture of what you look like for my memory. I can't believe how beautiful you are, Linda." She blushed as she sat next to him on the couch. It was their favorite place to sit and talk when not eating or making mad passionate love. She thought, I have heard that so often in my life, I have been really blessed. "When I hear it from you, Matthew, (which she loved to call him), it feels very special. It saddens me to think I'll be moving back to Reno in a short time," she said, "Thank you Matthew, it means a lot coming from you." He replied almost hesitantly, "I need to thank you again for pulling me out of the snow and nursing me back to health. Also, I think I am going to go back to my place tomorrow, check my messages and head back into Buffalo so I can be ready to go back to work on Monday." Linda started to say something, but he interrupted, "What are your plans, going forward?" "Well," she said, "if you leave tomorrow, I will probably go into town as well as I can do a couple of meetings before I jet off to Paris for that photo shoot. I should be back in two or three days. Until then, Matthew, I would like very much if you'd take me to bed one last time. You're making me wet just sitting there in that sexy robe." Matt rose and picked her up in his arms and walked into the bedroom. Then they made sweet love.

After the loving, they were both breathless. Matt was feeling his body was at its limit. She had healed his body only to spend the next several days wearing him out both physically and mentally. Linda thought she knew what her plan was in her mind but instead she said, "Well, I may take some vacation time after the new exercise video. It has been a great week and I loved every minute, but our worlds are very far apart. It would be difficult to cultivate a relationship under those circumstances, I am sorry to say."

Matt was both relieved and saddened. He replied, "Linda, you are a very special lady, and it has been a dream come true to spend this kind of intimate time with you. We have a great chemistry but sadly, I agree that a relationship would be impossible given our current paths. It would be great to have one last special night with you. How about we go out to the Embers Restaurant tonight, my treat. It's relatively close and away from the maddening crowd, so to speak." Linda smiled, "That is one of my favorite restaurants, I'll call right now and ask for my special table. It's only 10 minutes up Rte. 240 from here. That would be great. Thank you." Linda called and made reservations for 7:00 p.m. They showered and dressed and left for the Embers.

Dinner was spectacular as they would each always remember it. Simple, yet elegant. They skipped the dessert and after-dinner drink and decided to head back to have dessert back at Linda's place. When they were back in her villa, they went straight to the bedroom to change and get comfortable. They enjoyed just lounging around in the terrycloth robes she had. The sight of her changing in front of him was too much for him and he crawled across the bed and wrapped his arms around her. All she had left on was her tiny thong. He was in his boxers when he began his impulsive quest. They caressed and kissed. The heat from their passion was unparalleled for each of them. Next thing they knew, they were side by side atop the large comforter on her bed. Then they made love. It lasted longer than usual as both sensed it was their last opportunity to enjoy each other for who knew how long. They lay breathless staring into each other's eyes. It felt magical for them both.

Matt looked at her clock alarm on the nightstand. It read 12:20 a.m. It seemed like minutes had passed when they returned from dinner, but it had been hours. They both realized how tired they were. They slept. The sun woke Matt on that Sunday morning. He felt the bed next to him and she was there just waking up. They kissed, showered, and dressed. She offered to make breakfast, but he declined.

He decided to leave. Thanking her profusely again and gave her a final kiss. They each planned to keep in touch with each other knowing they would probably not. He took the KB sled home which Linda said she would have picked up.

Matt walked into his place in Glenwood. He looked at his phone which was plugged into the charger. He remembered not charging it as he was bound and determined not to take calls while he was out here skiing and relaxing. Then he saw Christie's note. He must have just missed her as it looked like she would be back in court tomorrow, Monday and this was Sunday. She was probably just driving, so he decided to wait to call her. He locked up the lodge as he called it, jumped back in his car, and headed back into Buffalo. He was going to call her but thought he'd wait until he got back so he wouldn't disturb her Sunday preparation for court on Monday. He got back to the loft in Buffalo and called his sister.

She answered the phone on the first ring, thinking it might be Perry, "Hello there" she said in as sultry a voice as she could conjure. "Hey, Sis." Is what she heard; she took a beat, let out a sigh of relief that he was OK, then said, "Where the hell are you, Little Brother?" Matt laughed, "I just got home from KB. I must have just missed you earlier. What time were you out there?" Christie looked at the clock on her desk and said, "I think it was eight a.m. or so. Were you out on an early run?" Matt thought quickly, "Well, I was unavoidably detained by a beautiful damsel over the past few days. My phone was off; I just wanted to clear my head and relax." Christie thought a minute, then said, "Matt, I think the police want to talk to you about the murders. They may have a couple of motives. Let's do it on, our terms. Meet me at my office in the morning at 7:30 a.m. We'll strategize then call them to come over to my office. So lay low until morning? Matt replied, "Sounds like a plan, Sis, Thanks." They hung up the phone and she began to prepare for the questioning.

She had no court time on Monday like she had told Perry so her day would probably be filled with this latest challenge. She thought as she wrote questions to prepare for Monday, I wonder if my brother had anything to do with the killings. She shuddered. She was relatively confident he did not but hoped he was innocent.

More importantly, she hoped that he had some strong alibis for the time frame that the police would have put together in their investigation. She called her trusty secretary, Wendy McKeller. She was always offering to work any time Christie needed her. Today, Christie was hoping she was available as they had loads to do before morning. "Hello, Christie," said Wendy, "Yes, I am available today. What do you need?" Christie just laughed out loud, "Hi, Wendy. How did you know?" Wendy replied, "Well you never call on Sunday and I didn't think you were calling in sick for tomorrow." They laughed as that was always their running joke.

The rest of the next eight hours were filled with these ladies putting together a defense strategy. They began with questions, then a timeline of their own. Wendy had some rather interesting insights about the whole case. Christie was impressed but they focused on Matt's questioning on Monday until they broke for dinner at 7 p.m.

Christie thanked her profusely for the help. Wendy was glad to help and was ready to assist as she'd been thinking about this whole affair for weeks.

Monday morning, Matt was sitting on the floor in front of Mahern, Miller, and Associates at 7:15 a.m. Christie got off the elevator at 7:20, walking up to Matt and hugging him warmly said, "Great to see you, Brother. I must say, I was a bit worried about you until I heard your voice yesterday." As they entered the office, they heard the elevator ding on its arrival at the second floor. Out walked Wendy McKeller. They smiled and headed into the office where for the next hour, the ladies bustled around Matt as he sat and watched.

They asked questions. They provided the timeline they had prepared; and insured Matt had a scenario for each possible question on his whereabouts when the murders were assumed to have taken place. At 8:30 a.m., Christie called Perry, "Perry, this is Christie. I have my client, Matthew Fogelburg sitting in my conference room awaiting your arrival for questioning if you have some time this morning." Perry responded with, "Whom did you say was calling?" They both chuckled. Perry said, "We'll be there inside of ten minutes.?" And hung up.

Perry grabbed Paul and Parker and said, "Come with me gentlemen, we are going to question Matt Fogelburg!" Both men scrambled for their jackets and walked out of headquarters following Detective Perry Kline. Perry explained the call from Christie as they drove left on Delaware around Niagara circle to then left at the corner of West Mohawk. They parked in front and rode the elevator to the second floor. Wendy greeted them at the door and escorted them to the conference room. She grabbed a carafe of coffee and poured them each a cup as Christie rose to greet them.

"Good morning officers, please take a seat wherever you are comfortable. Matt is ready for your questions whenever you'd like to begin. Perry began with their rehearsed strategy. "Mr. Fogelburg, did you like Johnny Galway?" Matt quickly replied, "I hated his guts! I felt like killing him after both losing the election to the cheating so and so; and the awful things, he said about me on the news. Then after he and his brother Frank announced, they were planning to what amounted to abusing their power on the waterfront deal, I wanted both him and his brother dead."

Christie's eyes were wide open in shock; she couldn't breathe. It felt like someone slapped her in the face, she was able to lean over and whisper to Matt, "Think about what you're saying, Matt. These gentlemen are the police; they have reason to believe you may have committed these murders."

Matt turned to her and said out loud, "I don't care, Sis, I did not kill anyone but there were days…" his voice trailed off.

"Matthew", Perry began again, "tell us how you felt about the mayor's brother Frank." Matt said quickly, "Oh that horse's ass!" Christie threw up her hands and said, "Matthew, why am I here?" Matt turned to Perry and said, "Mr. Kline, I don't think I want to answer any more questions." Perry responded, "I don't think we are done here, Mr. Fogelburg. We can do them here or down at headquarters. Now, I need to know your whereabouts on December 6th through the 9th and December 16th through the 18th."

Christie interjected, "Detective, I spoke to my brother early this morning and we have prepared a written statement of his whereabouts on all of those indicated dates." Wendy, as if on cue, entered the room and handed three copies of the statement to Perry, Paul, and Parker respectively. Matt added, "Perry, I am sorry

I let my anger get the best of me, but I did not kill either of the Galways. They were NOT worth the effort."

The officers in the room took a moment to read the statement that Christie had prepared. Perry said, "Paul can you run down these alibis for us?" Paul nodded. Perry continued, "Matt, where were you this last week?" Matt looked at Christie before he spoke. Christie answered, "Detective, my client was skiing at Kissing Bridge for the week. He unfortunately had an accident, slamming into a tree and was knocked unconscious. He was rescued by an old friend and was with them for the remainder of the week until yesterday at 10 a.m." Perry said to Matt and Christie, "OK, we have no further questions at this time, however, you are to remain within the city limits until Friday at 5 pm. If your statements turn out to be corroborated, you and your attorney will be notified. If they can't be, we will need to resume further questioning on Friday at Police Headquarters. You are released on your own recognizance. Oh, by the way, who was the old friend who rescued you as I will need to confirm that alibi as well?"

As the three officers got up out of their chairs simultaneously, Matt said, "Linda Carnello. I stayed with her much of the week." No one responded but Perry said to Christie, "Thank you, Ms. Mahern, for calling and setting up this interview."

The police then left the conference room. Christie just looked at Matt, "Are you involved with her?" Matt laughed, "Sis, I am sorry about my outburst and yes, we had a great week. I have got to get to my office. Thanks for this."

Matt left Christie's office and headed to his office in City Hall. Christie took advantage of the spring-like temperatures in Buffalo this Monday morning and changed into her running clothes. She texted Joni Wilsco to see if she was available but got a quick text back which read, 'Sorry can't today and damn you, you lucky dog.

Wanna meet for a bite after work; Say 6 at Chef's?' Christie wrote back, 'Perfect, see you at 6.' She then headed out the door telling her secretary she was off on a jog. She stretched in the elevator as it was empty. She was glad she had not scheduled any court time or other meetings today so she could do some catching up on case preparation and maybe begin an investigation of her own on these murders. She made a mental note to contact Micah Blair after her run. Off she went toward the marina. She took Delaware to Niagara Square. Then Niagara Street to Franklin. Right on to Franklin to Erie Street under the Skyway then past the Marine Drive Apartments to the Marina. It was a forty-minute jog, but she was usually gone an hour as she stopped at the Observation Deck at the end of the Marina to look out over Lake Erie as she took a break.

This Monday was a bit different. As she got past the Marine Drive apartments and turned into the Marina, she spotted a white Cadillac like her brother Matt's. As she passed it coming out of the parking lot, she noticed it began to follow her. As she got close to the Observation Deck, she thought she'd stop and have a chat with him. As she turned, she saw it headed right toward her and it was gaining speed. She was frozen in her tracks.

Christie sensed the danger and had the wherewithal to jump onto the sidewalk. The Cadillac was now on the sidewalk too. She ran and quickly jumped into the doorway of the deck just in time. The car almost scraped the wall as it sped past the doorway and spun off the sidewalk into a snow pile at the curve around the deck where plows had cleared the street over the past few days. She looked in the tinted windows, but couldn't ID the driver.

They had on a hoodie and large dark glasses. Christie's heart was beating fast, and it wasn't from the run. She quickly ran to the other side of the stairwell in the deck and looked out the other door as the white Cadillac sped off, tires squealing past her out of the

Marina. She noticed the last three digits on the plate, it read-745. She took out her phone and dialed Perry. He answered, "Hello, is this, a sales call?" She was obviously not in the mood. She just began yelling, "Perry, they just tried to kill me! They tried to kill me!! There was this white Cadillac following me on my run. I thought it was my brother. As I got into the marina, it jumped onto the sidewalk and sped up trying to run me down." Perry yelled, "Christie, WAIT!" She stopped and took a deep breath. "Where are you now?" he finished. She answered, "The Marina Point, come here, NOW. I'm really scared!"

"On my way" said Perry, 'Don't hang up. Stay on the line until I get there." He was already in his cruiser, and he turned on the siren. He got on the radio and called dispatch. They answered, "Buffalo Police". He said, "Donna, this is Perry Kline, send units to the Erie Basin Marina, Officer needs assistance!" He clicked off. Christie was listening to him request backup. She heard the sirens approaching. She watched very intently for the possible return of the white Cadillac. She saw nothing. It seemed like forever, but she saw Perry's cruiser approached the Observation Deck; she stepped out onto the sidewalk as he pulled to a stop, right at the doorway. He jumped out and she ran into his arms. She shook. "Are you alright?", he said. "Now that you're here I am," she said crying.

She calmed quickly as she noticed the black and white arrive with two officers inside. She wiped her eyes with her sweatshirt sleeves. She looked at Perry and said, "Thank you for coming so quickly. I thought the white Cadillac was my brother, Matt. As I got a quick look, it didn't seem like him, but the driver had a hooded sweatshirt over their head and large dark glasses." Perry let her go, resting her on his cruiser. He approached the officers in the first black and white which had arrived, "Hi, Larry. Ms. Mahern here was almost run over by a white Cadillac about 10-12 minutes ago." Christie yelled, "The last three digits on the plate were 745."

The second officer, Scott Layman, picked up the radio from their cruiser and said, "This is unit 4. On the call to the Marina. Attempted hit and run. Put out an APB for a late model white Cadillac with partial plate's last 3 digits '7-4-5'. Also, run it through DMV to see if you can get any info. Over." Perry gave him a "thumbs up" and as he turned back to Christie, he saw something flash in the sunlight on the ground on the street's curve behind her. He asked her, "So how did this go down?" Christie began, "When I heard the car rev its engine and jump the sidewalk, I was lucky enough to run into the doorway of the Observation deck. I saw the car go off the sidewalk back to the road and fishtail into the snowbank over there." She pointed to where Perry had just seen the flash of a reflection. He walked over to the snowbank and looked down. Christie was right behind him. When Perry crouched down for a closer look, he heard Christie yelp behind him. What they both saw was a hand with one of its fingers exposed in the snowbank. There was a large gold ring on what looked like the left hand's fifth digit. Perry looked back at Christie who said, "I recognize the ring! It belongs to Victor Sinclair." Perry spun around and yelled to Larry Rammunski, "Larry, we've got another body here. Call HQ and get Parker and the crew out here. You guys start a tape barrier."

Parker Clark arrived wthin minutes after notification. He walked up to Perry Kline and said, "Well, what have you got?" Perry replied, "Well Chief, I think that is Victor Sinclair under the snow pile." Parker said, "Looks like the 'Snow Villain' has struck again." Perry continued, "A white Cadillac nearly ran Christie Mahern over as she was out jogging here in the Marina. As she dove into the building, she tried to get a look at the driver, but they had large dark glasses and a sweatshirt hood covering their head. She got a partial plate number "7-4-5". She reports it was a New York plate. We had HQ put out an APB on the tag. I remember that her brother Matt drives a white Cadillac." Parker interjected, "So did Victor Sinclair, Perry!"

Parker remembered that he would be on the lookout for that make and model when he was secretly dating Charmaine Sinclair, however, he kept those thoughts to himself. "What else did you find?" asked Parker.

Perry shrugged his shoulders, "Let's see what we find when they dig him out, Chief." Perry and Parker walked over to where Ted Zak was supervising his team of forensic specialists digging the body out of the snow drift. Parker was on his phone as they walked, "Donna, this is Parker. Do me a favor and get the plate number of Victor Sinclair's Cadillac. I'll wait." The forensic team was just rolling the body over. There was a bullet hole in the back of the head. The more frightening thing they saw was a Red Tag in his shirt's breast pocket. Perry said to Ted, "Zak, please pull that red thing out of his pocket." Ted pulled his tweezers from his coat pocket and grabbed the tag. He held the tag up to show Perry and Parker that it said- 'HYATT HOTEL- ROOM 220. There was an audible gasp from both Perry, Parker and now Christie who was standing behind them watching. Perry said, "Ted, bag it and tag it. I would like to check over at the Hyatt with George the manager. That's way too many keys for that room to be found." Parker said into his phone, "Ok Donna, Thanks. Now do me a favor and walk down to the property room and look in the evidence room with whomever is on duty and tell me how many keys we have bagged and tagged for the Hyatt. Call me back." Turning to Perry, "That was Victor's car. The full plate was VASCO 7-4-5."

"Perry why don't you and I go see George at the Hyatt. "Paul", he yelled to Paul Gorci, "Paul, do me a favor, take your cruiser over to see if you can find Charmaine Sinclair. Get the exact address from VASCO. Perry and I will take my car and visit the Hyatt. Call me if you find her. I want to see if she has the car. If she does, bring her into HQ. I want to personally question her." Paul said to Perry, "I am gonna give Christie a ride back to her office then head to the Sinclairs. I'll call as soon as I know anything." "Great." said Perry, "Seems we are going in circles here. See you, later."

The CNN truck drove into the Marina, parked. Out stepped Bernard Shaw and his cameraman, Donny Jaluska. They got info from the forensics team. Bernard called his station and they prepared to do a live feed from the Marina. They reported to the nation that there was a third murder in Buffalo. The same scenarios were found. All three were prominent leaders in the community and were shot execution style. He also reported that the FBI was being called into the case as well as the New York State Police. He then told his audience that he was staying on the case and would report all subsequent findings.

As Parker and Perry walked into George's office at the Hyatt Hotel, there sat Matt Fogelburg and George Stepanovik watching a CNN report from the location they had just left minutes before. They all sat with their jaws opened listening to the report from Bernard Shaw, this young unfamiliar reporter from Ted Turner's new comprehensive news network, CNN. Perry said to Parker, "One of the reporters must have overheard you calling the FBI and State Police. It looks like we're going to need some help as all our suspects are getting knocked off. Matt, I'd watch my back if I were you." Parker then asked George, "Mr. S., how many keys do you have for Room 220 in the house right now?" George picked up the phone and called the desk, "Jackie, is anyone in Room 220 now; how many keys for 220 do we have up there?"

He shook his head no, no one was in Room 220 to those in the office with him. "How many keys are in the drawer for that room? George waited as Jackie looked and responded. "OK, put those in your pocket and bring them to my office, please." Parker asked George as he hung up the phone, "George, do you have those keys made on sight?" George replied, "Yes, the machine is right here." We usually make three. Two for the guests and one spare." Jackie walked in with one key.

He spun his desk chair around and opened the closet behind him with a key from his master ring. There on the door was a small machine bracketed to the inside of the door. He opened the plastic cover on it with yet a second key. There was a key cutter below which held blanks. There was also a large box below with extra key tags. That too had a separate key. "Wow", said Perry, "You keep that very secure. You need a key for the office, one for the closet, and one for each, the machine, storage, and key blanks." "Yes", said George, "You need five keys to make a duplicate. All five are not on the same ring. Your next question will be, 'How many of these key sets are there, George?'" Perry smiled and shook his head in agreement. "George told the group, "Two, which belong to Matt and me. The sixth key needed to get the key for the tags is the key to my desk. Only I have that spare key locked in my desk. We change them all every 2 years." Parker said, "How often is that key used by others?" He said, "Never!"

As Perry and Parker drove back to HQ, Perry's phone rang. It was Paul Gorci. He said, "Perry, I had DMV do a search of white Cadillacs in Western New York over the past five years. I had them email it to you, Parker, and me. I checked my email after dropping off Christie at her office while waiting for VASCO to get me

Sinclairs' address. There are only eight registered. You'll notice there are five ending in 745.

The list reads:

Year	Make	Model	Color	Owner		Plate No	City	State
1985	Cadillac	Eldorado	White	Frederick	Gilroy	BO-43-7745	Buffalo	NY
1986	Cadillac	Deville	White	Dennis	Shooda	EC-14-745	Lackawanna	NY
1984	Cadillac	Fleetwood	White	John	Galway	45-EE-2199	Buffalo	NY
1988	Cadillac	Fleetwood	White	Mario	Baldelli	BIGM-745	Niagara Falls	NY
1987	Cadillac	Seville	White	Matt	Fogelburg	57-EE-8745	Buffalo	NY
1987	Cadillac	Eldorado	White	Victor	Sinclair	VASCO-745	Buffalo	NY
1987	Cadillac	Seville	White	James	Maltry	CC-1977-05	North Evans	NY
1986	Cadillac	Fleetwood	White	Linda	Carnello	67-LHS-345	Glendale	NY

"I will talk to you later," said Paul then hung up.

Perry looked at Parker and said, "Chief, this case is getting stranger and stranger as the days go by. There are five, white Cadillacs in the vicinity that have a plate with the 7-4-5 as the last three digits." "Mother of Mercy", said Parker, "are we ever going to get a break in this case?" Perry thought for a minute. He said, "Chief, I was thinking about what you said, early on, in the case, about not missing anything because of its high profile. Why don't you and I team up tomorrow and visit all the murder locations and put together a chart of similarities and differences? Maybe we can pick up on a different trend that we're not seeing to this point. If nothing else, maybe we can determine motives that correspond to each incident." Parker replied, "You bring the files, I'll pick you up at Central Perk on Elmwood at 8 am. I'll drive and you can take notes." Perry concurred and they pulled up to Precinct #3, Headquarters. This time as they entered the building, Parker's phone rang. "Hello, Clark!" said the chief into his phone. He listened and swore under his breath. Perry walked away.

Perry got to his cubicle and picked up the phone and called Christie Mahern. Christie answered, "Hello, this is Christie Mahern. How can I help you?" He said, "It's me. How are you?" She said, "May I ask who's calling?" They both laughed.

Christie then asked, "Hey Perry, any chance you and I could have dinner sometime tomorrow? I know you are probably swamped but I need a chance to properly thank you for your Knight in Shining Armor performance this afternoon in the Marina. I was thinking maybe 7 o'clock at my place and bring your toothbrush." Perry was pleased and yes very excited that she called. He responded with, "Oh my, Miss Mahern. Whatever are you suggesting?" Again, they laughed. They each needed a break from their constant work.

The murder cases on Perry's agenda and their investigations were all-consuming. Similarly on Christie's agenda, her court cases were now affected by these murders as well. Perry said in a serious voice, "Christie, I will be with Parker all day tomorrow and we'll hopefully be done by then.

So yes, I would love to see you and it may be closer to 8 o'clock but I'll ring you if I am gonna be any later than that." Christie and Perry exchanged goodbyes before hanging up their phones. Perry refocused on the printout.

Year	Make	Model	Color	Owner		Plate No	City	State
1985	Cadillac	Eldorado	White	Frederick	Gilroy	BO-43-7745	Buffalo	NY
1986	Cadillac	Deville	White	Dennis	Shooda	EC-14-745	Lackawanna	NY
1984	Cadillac	Fleetwood	White	John	Galway	45-EE-2199	Buffalo	NY
1988	Cadillac	Fleetwood	White	Mario	Baldelli	BIGM-745	Niagara Falls	NY
1987	Cadillac	Seville	White	Matt	Fogelburg	57-EE-8745	Buffalo	NY
1987	Cadillac	Eldorado	White	Victor	Sinclair	VASCO-745	Buffalo	NY
1987	Cadillac	Seville	White	James	Maltry	CC-1977-05	North Evans	NY
1986	Cadillac	Fleetwood	White	Linda	Carnello	67-LHS-345	Glendale	NY

He began writing notes in preparation for tomorrow's venture with Parker. Could any of these vehicles be linked to multiple scenes? Was there a link that all these people shared? He had so many questions running around in his head, he was beginning to get one of his killer headaches. The ones that were only eased by laying quietly in a dark room for an hour or so.

He went upstairs to the fifth floor and visited his friend, Donna Smith who he knew would be working in the evidence room. He walked in and she was sitting at her desk in a crisp white shirt. Her face lit up like a Christmas tree when she saw him. "Hey Smitty", he offered. "Hey PK" was her retort. "I need your couch for an hour, headache!", he begged. "No worries, Perry," she said, "I am going downstairs for a sandwich. Want anything?" He replied, "No, I'm good. Thanks." "There's Tylenol in the desk drawer if you need some." Then she was gone.

Joni called Christie first thing in the morning. "Hey, Girl. Wanna meet today for a jog? I can meet at our usual time; 11:45 a.m." Christie thought a second and said, "who is this calling?" They both laughed. She thought of Perry as it was his favorite phone joke. "Yeah!! My partner is back in action. See you at eleven forty-five. Gotta run, Bye"

Delaware at Church is where they met most days during the week then they would head to the Marina. Joni was there when Christie arrived. She was jogging in place to keep warm. As Christie got there, the light changed; and they were off.

"Hey, Lady", Christie began, "I have so much to tell you." Joni interjected, "I have a bunch to tell you as well. Paul…" Christie continued like she was not interrupted, "The one day you miss our run, I almost got run over by what we think was the Snow Villain, but I also discovered the body of another victim at the Marina." Joni stopped in her tracks, "WHAT!!", she yelled, "Christie, WAIT!!" Christie looked over her shoulder and came back the twenty feet she went past Joni. Joni started, "You didn't call me? What the hell happened?" Christie said, "OK let's walk. I was running to the Marina and just parked in the Apartments was a white Cadillac like my brother Matt's.

I couldn't see if it was him but as I got past it about 50 yards, I heard its engine rev and looked over my shoulder to see it was headed straight for me. By that time, I was close to the observation deck and got up on the sidewalk. I looked again and the damn thing was also up on the sidewalk.

Luckily, I was able to dive into the open doorway of the building. I almost broke my neck. I rolled on my shoulder and slammed into the staircase. I heard the car squeal around the curve and head out of the Marina. I only could make out the last three digits on the plate as it was half covered in snow. I then called Perry screaming to get there ASAP. I knew that it wasn't my brother and didn't want them to come back to get another shot at me."

"Oh, my Lord", said Joni, "why the heck are we headed there now?" Christie said, "Perry said not to run alone. Only with a friend. I don't think they would try anything again so soon. I might be running with a police officer for protection." "But I am NOT a police officer, Christie!" screamed Joni, "let's go back please." Christie said, "No, it'll be fine. They have an unmarked car stationed there just in case." Joni asked, "So you found another victim?" Christie replied, "Yep. As the Cadillac side-swiped the snow drift around the circle, it partially uncovered the body it probably dropped there. Its hand was out of the snow and the sun reflected off a ring on the man's finger. I knew that ring. It belonged to Victor Sinclair. He was shot in the back of the head with the same kind of gun as the Galways." "Get out!" said Joni, "that's three murders. You're lucky you weren't number four." As they approached the Marina, they saw the end taped off.

As they turned around and headed back to work, Joni said, "So what about your court cases?" Christie said, "Well, it looks like all three will need to be put on hold for who knows how long."

That's great," said Joni, "A couple of the girls and I are going to Key West for eight days. We are flying on Friday noon and coming back the following Saturday. I took the liberty of getting you a room in one of the four two-bedroom suites. I also got your air reservations scheduled. What do you think?" Christie stopped, grabbed Joni, and kissed her. "You are the best, Lady! Thank you. I would love to go. I will pack tonight. I need a mani-pedi and a haircut. I should go shopping for a new bikini. Busy later? My treat." As they got back to their starting point where they separated to return to their perspective workplaces, Joni said, "I will be ready at six. Just text me where to meet." They hugged and jogged off in opposite directions.

Just as Christie reached the front door of her office building on West Mohawk, she noticed a white Cadillac speed by her to the corner of South Elmwood. She couldn't see the plate because of the sun glare but it gave her a chill. Maybe getting out of town was the best idea yet.

She walked into her office and Wendy McKellar was at the desk. Christie said, "Clear my calendar from Friday through next Friday. I am going to visit family out in Denver." Wendy said, "That's great. You need a break from all this madness. Do I need to help with anything?" "Yes, see if you can get me in to see my hairdresser, Cindy Deeps. I am then going shopping for a new swimsuit."

"My cousin in Denver has an indoor heated pool. Everything else is taken care of. I am going to jump in the shower." "On it!" said Wendy. She was already dialing the phone. Christie walked into her office and shut the door. She thought about whether to tell anyone where she was really headed. Maybe Perry. Just in case I need him. Wendy popped her head into Christie's office, "Cindy is free at 3:00 p.m. today. Do you need a ride? Anything else I can do?

Cleaners, bank, people to let know you are unavailable until after next week, a number to reach you in case of an emergency?"

Christie had just come out of the shower with a towel around her head and she was drying off with the other. Wendy whistled, "Geez. Your body looks fantastic, Lady. I guess that running around Buffalo during your lunch hours has tightened things up very nicely!!"

Christie blushed. She was used to women in the gym locker room making comments about her body, but she was a bit taken back when she heard it from such a close friend.

She said, "Yeah, thanks, Wendy. I guess I have put a lot of work into keeping this figure together." Wendy laughed, "Yeah, it's together alright! If you don't mind me being a little bit specific, not only are all the parts there but the presentation is exquisite! In other words, WOW!"

Parker looked at Perry and said, "Paul just stopped Victor's car. Margie Galway was driving it. He is bringing her in for questioning now." Perry looked shocked, "What is your take on this Chief?" Parker thought a minute and replied, "I really don't have any idea what is going on. I need a cup of coffee and write down some questions." Perry grabbed a legal pad and walked back into the Chief's office. He said, "I'll write down the questions and we'll both try to generate them." "Thanks", said Parker, "First we'll want to know if she has been driving his car the last few days. Then maybe, why she would have his car to begin with." Perry was writing and added, "We may want to ask the last time she saw Victor, time, and place. Then maybe try to figure out whether she had substantial motives to kill Johnny, Frank, and Victor. If she did, then who might have been her accomplice." Perry continued to write on the legal pad but looked at Parker for any reaction.

He saw none but wondered why he was visibly upset after Paul told him on the phone that he found Margie driving Victor's car. Parker gave Perry a funny look and said, "Do you want me to ask her about an accomplice too, so you can observe both of our reactions?" Perry was very careful here, "Well Chief, Margie has been dating you. She has also dated Victor. I don't know if those two things overlapped. Maybe you do? You are lots of things, Chief but one of them is not a good actor. I'll be watching for Margie's reaction." Parker just grinned, "I wonder if she has an alibi for the afternoon at the Marina when Christie Mahern was almost run down."

Perry continued to write notes frantically, "This should be one heck of a conversation Boss!" Parker agreed but was quiet. Truth be told, he was nervous to hear what Ms. Margie Keen Galway had to say to all the questions. Parker then spoke, "I also want to ask her about Room 220 at the Hyatt. Was it her that registered? Was she there on any of the dates we think Johnny's murder occurred?" Perry threw his pen down, "OK, Chief, I am officially not writing any more questions. My hand can't hold the pen anymore and I think it may be out of ink as well." They both laughed.

Perry continued, "We are absolutely going to video this. I will be behind the glass. Here is a copy of the questions. If I think of any more to ask, I'll text them to you. Do you want anyone in the room with the two of you? Maybe Paul or Donna from upstairs?" Parker thought before he spoke, "I don't want her to feel pressured with too many people in the room. Maybe I'll do this alone, she may be more relaxed and speak her mind more freely. When Paul brings her in, I'll send him for coffee. Let him know you're ready and he can give me a positive nod when he brings in the coffee. Then he can leave the room."

Paul Gorci walked into Headquarters with Margie Galway. They took the elevator to the second floor and walk to the conference room where Parker was waiting. Parker stood as they entered. Paul said, "Ms. Galway, can I get you a coffee?" Margie replied, "Hot and black, please Paul." She shook Parker's hand and sat in the adjacent chair at the conference table.

She wore a powder blue parka which she removed and placed in the next chair. She had on a powder blue sweater and navy skirt just above the knee and dark blue patent leather four-inch heels. Parker began, "Thank you for coming in today, Ms. Galway. I have a few questions for you, and I'd like to record your responses; so, I don't have to take so many notes, if that is OK with you?" Margie just grinned and said, "I will gladly answer all your questions Detective Clark and please call me Margie."

"Thank you, Margie," said Parker as he turned on the recorder, "Thank you again for coming in today. We have questions about Mr. Sinclair. When is the last time you saw Victor Sinclair?" Margie said, "Four days ago. We had dinner and he asked me to drive him to the airport. He was visiting a friend in Reno for a few days. He asked me to drive his car while he was gone so it wouldn't sit around idle." That was Friday, correct?" asked Parker. "Yes, today is Tuesday," answered Margie. Parker continued, "Margie, Victor was found shot to death on Monday. His body was found at the Marina buried in the snow." He watched her reactions closely. "No! No!" she screamed, Oh my heavens, Parker. That's three murders now. What the hell is going on in this town?" Parker replied calmly, "That is precisely what we are trying to find out, Margie.

So let me ask, why were you registered at the Hyatt Hotel for seven nights from December 10th through December 16th?"

"Was I registered at the Hyatt? HERE?" asked Margie, "No! I was certainly not registered at the Hyatt! Why on earth would I do that?" Parker continued, "Margie, did you have anything to do with Victor Sinclair's death?" "Parker, I know you're just doing your job but how could you even ask me that. You know how fond I am of Victor. We had a nice friendship. It was nothing like what you and I had. By the way, isn't this when I should ask for a lawyer? Am I a suspect in this murder?" Parker was sure by Margie's reactions that she was innocent. He still had to be professional as the tape was running. "Margie, you may be the last person to see Victor alive. You're driving his car and he was an enemy of your late husband Johnny's. So, I suppose there are those who might think you were a potential suspect. Where were you yesterday between noon and 2 pm?"

Perry, Donna Smith, and Paul were all watching and listening to the interrogation of Margie Galway. They were all very quiet until Perry broke the silence when he whispered to Paul, "See if you can get Matt Fogelberg to come in for a few "follow-up questions" maybe without his lawyer. Maybe we should see if Linda Carnello is also available." They then heard Parker ask her about where she was the prior afternoon. Margie responded, "I was sitting in a salon chair having my hair and nails done. Cindy Deeps's place. 'Deeps C Do's" at 57 S Elmwood. She can verify this and the times I was there. Why do you ask; if I might be so bold?" Parker didn't want to play all his cards, but he said, "Victor's car was seen somewhere and did something ticket worthy, however, the car got away before one of our units was on the scene." Parker breathed a sigh of relief as Margie just provided a solid alibi. He followed up, "Did you drive Victor's car there? Is there anyone else who could have had the car while you were at the hair salon?" Margie thought for a moment. She knew exactly who was driving the car but all she said was. "I had my own car. His car was at my house." Parker saw something in Margie's eyes that told him this was a fib. He had interviewed so many others before but none as close to him as was Margie.

He thought it best to follow up later. He said, "Well thank you so much for coming in. Can I drop you somewhere?" She replied, "I see it is after one o'clock and I haven't had lunch. Would you care to join me? Chef's. My treat." Parker smiled. This would give him a chance to clear up the car thing and he always enjoyed her company. "That would be great. We'll just stop in my office on the way out so you can sign the copy of the interview we just did." Margie asked, "Can I get a copy?" She knew she would be presented a copy of this as she used to transcribe them for Johnny years ago when she worked for him. Parker rose and said, "Off we go then. Why don't you head to my office? I am going to make a quick pit stop, first." Margie just waved and continued to his office. Parker stopped into the viewing room to see what his coworkers thought of the interview.

He opened the door to the room as they were just getting up to leave. He asked, "So guys, what did you think?" Perry seemed to speak for the group, "We thought it went well Chief. I did see her give you a look when you asked about driving his car to the hair salon. Maybe you could follow up off the record?" Parker was about to get defensive but changed his mind and said, "You have good instincts Kline. I was just reflecting on that as we left the room. I think I will follow up with that and see where it goes. Margie and I have known each other…", he stuttered for a second, "for a long time and I think I'll be able to tell if she is hiding something. I'll ask her at lunch."

Perry and Paul walked into the bullpen area of the office. Paul spoke first, "Brother, I thought you didn't like heights? You were walking the high wire just then with Parker. You know he is gonna talk to her about that exact thing on the way to or at lunch at Chef's. Why would you stick your neck out?" Perry laughed, "You know me, partner, I just wanted the old man to know I saw what he saw.

Remember when I told him earlier that he wasn't such a good actor? Well, he's not. I was watching him as soon as I saw the look, she gave him. He visibly grimaced for a second. Then he quickly recovered. I don't even know if Margie saw it in his eyes.

Any luck with Fogelberg or Carnello?" Paul said, "Matt said he would be here at three. Linda wants us to meet her at Jacobi's Restaurant in Lackawanna any time after five o'clock.

She has a meeting there until then and would probably buy us dinner if we get there soon enough." "Nice work partner," said Perry, "I love their linguini with clam sauce. It's Dennis the chef's best meal. I can't believe he was just a pizza maker for years then became such a great chef. Who knew?" "Okay," said Paul, "I won't have anything heavy until then. Do you want to review the transcript of the Hyatt staff interviews?" Perry said, "I was just about to suggest that.

Great minds, Paul. George from the Hyatt sent over the video as well so that will help a lot. We'll set up in the conference room until Matt gets here."

Micah Blair walked into Headquarters and searched for Perry. He was told to look in the conference room and he indeed found him there with Paul Gorci. They were just about to roll the film. Micah said, "Hey Fellas. I have some news." He handed Paul a zip drive and said, "Plug that in. I want to show you guys something." Paul unplugged the drive from the Hyatt interviews and replaced it with Micah's drive. Micah said, "May I?" pointing to Paul's chair. Paul relinquished his seat. Micah began the clips. "Here is the guy getting the Room 220 key from Reggie at the Hyatt. I blew this up and was able to see a neck tattoo."

The clip zoomed into below the left ear. It was a small gold halfmoon crescent with a floating diamond in the center. A very shiny diamond. "Now here is Johnny's funeral. If you want to know how many people, have visible tattoos in this town, let me know. I have a blown-up photo of a lot of headshots on here." The clip then showed Matt Fogelberg. Then a close-up of his ear that showed a very large diamond stud in the left ear but no tattoo. Now Victor Sinclair appeared with a similar but larger diamond stud earring next on the screen but no tattoo. Then Linda Carnello appears. Left ear close-up zoomed in…. a small gold halfmoon crescent with a floating diamond in the center tattooed on her neck.

"What in the name of all that's holy!!", screamed Perry, "How long did it take you to find that little nugget, Micah?" Micah smiled as both the officers in the room had their mouths wide open in shock, "it was a lot of hours but after I found no men with a tattoo like that, I thought, could it have been a woman? The first one I looked at, was Linda." Paul said, "We better copy this for evidence, Perry. Now Micah, we'll need you to go to Jacobi's Restaurant on Abbott Rd. in Lackawanna around four o'clock to see who Linda is meeting with.

We'll be around the corner waiting. Can you fit that into your schedule?" Micah laughed. "I am her 4 o'clock appointment!" Perry spoke first, "What in God's name are you meeting with her about?" Micah just laughed."

"Linda says she has got some information she wants you guys to have but doesn't want it coming from her. If it gets back to her contacts in Reno or Vegas, it will upset the fellas if they didn't get it from her firsthand.

She was mysterious about it all and said she'd explain today at Jacobi's." Perry asked him, "Do you think she did the murders and is trying to lead us off her trail?" Micah responded, "Well, that certainly could be the case. I think rather than that, she might have information on the real murderer or at least how it went down. It should be an interesting conversation."

Paul said, "Do you think she'd check you for a wire? We could set you up, very quickly." Micah laughed, "You guys have been watching too many episodes of 'Hill Street Blues'. If I told you I have a wire on now, would you think I was a bad person?"

"Yes, I would, Mr. Blair!" Parker Clark said in his most booming voice as he entered the room. The room otherwise was quiet. Micah laughed, "Well, look who came to the party. Mr. Clark, just to ease your mind, I was having a little fun with your boys here, or is that not allowed?" Parker looked at the other officers in the conference room. They both stood and began roughhousing Micah like they were patting him down. "It's not even on guys, it's not even on!" pleaded Micah. At that point, they were all laughing except Parker. Micah said when they stopped, "Here, I'll show you!"

Micah reached to the lapel of his sportscoat and pulled off a diamond stick pin in the shape of an 'M' and held it up at arm's length away from himself. "See this is the microphone and it transmits to my cellphone when I push the button on the back of it. "Testing for the Police. Testing for the Police." Micah then took out his cell phone and played it back. They heard, "Testing for the Police. Testing for the Police." "Wow!" said Paul, "nice technology. Micah said, "and pretty, doggone expensive too, I might add. I have it ready for my meeting with Linda. I'd better get going so I am not late."

Perry said, "We'll be in our unmarked cruiser around the corner. Just let us know when you need us." Micah handed him a small box, "Listen yourself, it's a receiver." He headed out to Lackawanna.

"Well," said Perry, "Looks like the Hyatt staff interviews are on the back burner for now. Paul, could you stay and talk to Matt Fogelberg when he comes in?

I have written down some questions for that. Parker, if you want, you and I can drive to Lackawanna together. Maybe I'll give Capt. Budzinski at LAPD a heads up that we're in the area working the case." Parker added, "OK, good call on both ideas. Let me get my coat."

Paul looked over the questions for Matt and added a few. He then began to view the Hyatt Staff meeting video that George Stepanovik sent over. It began with George sitting in his office and Jackie Cuffaletto in the seat in front of his desk. He knew the camera was rolling and video on so he was as professional as he could be and not let on that they were being recorded. "Jackie" he began, "I looked at the schedule and you were on the desk the 8th, 9th, and 10th of December, that Monday, Tuesday, and Wednesday of that week. Do you remember checking in anyone for Room 220?" Jackie shook her head. George coached her, "Just say yes or no so I can jot down notes while you answer please." Jackie said, "Like I told you that week George, the computer says I checked someone in, but I distinctly remember not checking anyone in either Tuesday or Wednesday of that week because of all the snow we got. So no, to answer your question."

Their conversation got a bit off-topic as they talked about business. George had one last question, "Did you ever see the gentleman who asked Reggie for the 220's room key, pictured here?" George slid the 8 by 10 photo of the well-dressed man from the video that day. Jackie said, "He looks very well dressed and I would certainly remember seeing him, had I. So, no I did not." George excused her asking if she'd call in Lillie Mae Mason. Lillie

Mae entered and boomed her Hello to George. He asked, "Lillie Mae, you have access to the computer on your weekend shifts."

George added, "Do you remember taking the registration for an M. Keen? It was for seven days in December." Lillie Mae said, "I did not Boks", using his childhood nickname. She looked at the picture still on his desk of the well-dressed man and said, "Is this the guy who asked Reggie for the key to 220?" George answered, "Yes, as a matter of fact, it is." "Well, I saw him a couple of times after all the commotion, late at night" replied Lillie, "I even followed him once to see if I could see where he was going but I lost him on the third floor. I asked Cindy Deeps about him. She said she checked him in on that Thursday."

"He checked in as Lance Carter from Reno in Room 320." George thanked her and as she left the office buzzed the desk and asked Jackie to send in Cindy Deeps.

Paul's interest rose as Cindy walked in the door and sat down in front of George's desk. She looked down at the picture. She picked up the picture off the desk saying, "This is the guy or maybe the gal that I checked in on the Thursday of the week of the murder. His clothes were impeccable. I remember thinking, what man dresses this sharp around here. For some reason, I thought he looked rather feminine, but his voice was rather low and gruff." Paul shut off the video as he had all he needed. He called Perry and told him what he'd found. Perry was elated and thought Paul should follow up with a picture of the lady they were waiting to talk to this late afternoon.

Micah got to Jacobi's Restaurant at 3:55 p.m. The hostess, Nancy asked if she could help. When he said he had a meeting with Linda, she cut him off and knew who he was looking for. She took him back into the side foyer and told him to go down into the banquet hall and she would be in the office to the left. As Micah got to the bottom of the stairs, Linda walked out of the office to greet him. Micah said, "Sharp outfit." He notices her large diamond earrings but NO NECK TATTOO!!! He is stunned and didn't hear her at first. Linda repeated, "Micah, why don't we sit at the table here as no one will disturb us until after 6:30 p.m." Micah apologized offering a weak excuse, "Sorry, Linda, I was just a bit overcome by how much more beautiful you are in person than in pictures."

Linda queried, "You've seen me in pictures?" Micah had to think fast, "Yes, I am a photographer and took some pictures of the funeral as we were looking for someone." Linda responded, "Was I the person you were looking for?" Micah got a bit nervous then began, "Well, to be perfectly honest, yes, you were on the list of potential suspects. I was able to contact Lacey Curnic, a photographer from New York City. I asked her about you as you both were very close in high school." Linda said, "Oh, you know Lacey? Yes, of course, we were thick as thieves in school. She was always more beautiful than I, but she liked being behind the camera more. I am just an old ham. I love being the center of attention.

So, Micah, tell me what makes folks think I am a potential suspect in all the things that have been happening?" Micah parried, "Let me start by asking you a few questions, and then that will give me a better handle on whether you should be considered as a suspect. First, you were seen at the Hyatt Hotel on Thursday, December 11 checking into Room 320. Is that correct?" "Yes." Her only response. Micah asked, "You were seen at Johnny Galway's funeral at the Basilica with a very tasteful yet distinctive tattoo on your neck. The tattoo of a crescent half-moon with a diamond in the center. Is that correct?" Linda laughed, "Do you see any tattoos on my neck, Micah?" Micah flipped open a file folder and grabbed a photo and slid it across the desk to Linda. She picked it up and laughed.

"Mr. Blair," Linda said with a sarcastic tone, "pictures can be doctored these days! I think it may be time to contact my lawyer, Mr. Alfred Mireno."

Micah thought about showing the picture of the man at the Hyatt with the tattoo that curiously resembled Miss Carnello if she was dressed as a man, however, he decided that he needed to wait for the police to go down that road with her. He then said, "Well, Linda, I supposed it's in your rights to call your lawyer but if you can clear this up now, it will be so much easier to clarify that to the police. Whatever makes you feel more comfortable."

"Mr. Blair, you still haven't told me whether I am being considered a suspect for anything," said Linda, (in an attempt, to throw him off that line of questioning). Micah knew exactly where she was going, so he continued, "Linda, I am certainly not the police. I should remind you that YOU were the one that called this meeting. I have some more questions but why don't you tell me why you wanted to see me."

A moment of silence caused Micah's ears to ring a bit as he felt a bit of tension. Linda laughed that elegant laugh of hers that seemed to be so melodic to Micah. He wondered in how many other situations Linda used that laugh. She began, "Okay, Micah, I will be brutally honest with you. I came back to Western New York because I am doing a story for the 'Atlantic' magazine out of Boston, Massachusetts. I have always enjoyed doing research and writing and I like politics, so it was a natural marriage for me.

I am doing an article about small-town politics and where better to find a juicy story than Western New York. Wasn't I surprised when I came here to find the Mayor of Buffalo had just won re-election then was murdered? I began doing some research and while in the middle of going around asking questions, I heard that Frank was murdered as well. This murder stuff is certainly not my area of expertise, so I thought I had better find a free-lance guy to work with. Your name came up. So, I called this meeting."

Micah was shocked, "So, you are just here to do a political article and the biggest political suspense thriller begins as you return to your roots in Western New York?" Not waiting for her to answer, Micah continued, "So you didn't kill Johnny Galway to get a good story?" Linda almost fell off her chair laughing.

"Micah, I don't need to create this madness for a story. I just was in the right place at the right time, and this all exploded. I spoke to Christie who is an old friend from high school and a great lawyer. She is the person who gave me your name. My best friend Lacey Curnic is a model and great photographer in New York City. She and I have discussed you several times when your name came up during one of my visits with her. She just knew you as a photographer, but we were surprised to learn you were a Private Investigator. Christie and I spoke several times but that was more to get the history of the political scene than to investigate these murders. That said, would you be interested in helping me?"

Micah was a bit taken back by this turn of events. He said, "Well, now I have a different set of questions. What's in it for me? What kind of source confidentiality can I be assured of? If in fact, you are not the murderer, I may consider it. If you were the murderer, wouldn't I just be helping you avoid a possible police trail of investigation by being a partner in the investigation with you? Do you even remember having dated me in high school?" There was that melodic laugh again. Micah thought to himself, 'How can someone sound so sexy just laughing. I am physically moved by the sound of her laughter.'

Linda collected herself and said, "Wow, Micah. You really are an intense guy. Ok, let me think. The 'What's in it for you?' question; I would pay for your time working together with me and a substantial minimum bonus which may increase if the article sells. The issue of confidentiality is simple. You decide who if anyone would know you and I were partners, and you were a source. That would range from no one to everyone. The question of me being the murderer though funny to me is probably a consideration for you and I can give you several alibis and reasons I would never do ANY murder, but I would rather tell you when you're not wearing a wire." Micah was starting to sweat and flinched but tried not to show it. Linda continued, "If you want me to give you my editor's contact info, I will. You can verify with her that I began this process on a phone call prior to the murder of Johnny Galway. My focus for the article centers around the one-party monopoly in this town. Really the area of Western New York. I have been intrigued for years about how utterly despicable politicians are in the pursuit of their success rather than the people they serve.

Last but certainly not least, yes Micah, I remember dating you. I had a mad crush on you when we sat in homeroom. You sat in front of me there and in study hall and always tried to look up my dresses and I always flirted with you. I remember the movie we saw at the drive-in and how wonderful your kisses were. I hadn't had that much fun on a date in, well never. Now if you want to think about the partnership, that's okay. We can discuss it further over dinner if you trust I won't make you the fourth victim in my rampage as the Snow Villain."

There was that laughter again. Micah was now so totally mesmerized. So many things ran through his head he caught himself not breathing for a minute. "Micah. Are you alright?" said Linda shaking him on the arm. Micah's mind returned to the room at Jacobi's and saw Linda's beautiful eyes smiling at him.

He began, "That was a lot to digest Miss Carnello. Thank you for answering my questions and as usual knocking me off my game. You used to do the same thing in high school. That date was one of my fondest memories of my years in school. Now to begin, I really would like to work with you, and I don't REALLY think you are the murderer."

"I would love to go to dinner with you whenever you are free. Most importantly, I am not wearing a wire." Linda just smiled as he watched her look right at his lapel which housed the stick pin with the gold 'M'. "Are you free tomorrow night? she asked. "What time and where can I pick you up?" he answered. Linda looked in her small calendar and said, "As you know, I am staying at the Hyatt on the waterfront. Why don't you pick me up at seven tomorrow and we'll go to Chef's Restaurant? Sound like a plan?" Micah said, "Great. It's a date." Linda said, "Do you have any more questions for me, Micah?" "Maybe tomorrow but now I will let you go. I have a lot to think about before then," he said standing to leave. Linda rose and shook his hand. She thought about kissing him but thought better of it. Micah walked up the stairs and was going to walk into the bar for a drink but decided to leave instead.

Parker said, "Here we sit in the street listening to their conversation and it looks like our prime suspect just gave us the slip." Perry replied, "Well Chief, don't forget that Miss Carnello is a renowned actress or at least a seasoned veteran of theatrics!" Parker looked at Perry across the car, "What is your take on all this then?" Perry knew Parker wanted answers and reassurance that Perry was, indeed, on the case. He said, "I have thought of nothing else since we found Johnny that night. When you think about them one at a time, Johnny was probably killed at the Hyatt. Even if he wasn't, he was not killed along the 400 in West Seneca and left until spring only to be unearthed by Christie Mahern sliding off the icy highway. So, who could have done the murder and moved the bodies alone? It had to have been one strong person, I'm guessing a male or two people. In Frank's murder, it seems that he too was killed somewhere other than the parking lot of the VFW. In both cases, there was no blood at the scene. Frank Galway was an enormous guy so one person was likely unable to move him. Here again, I am thinking our perp is a man. Now, we have Victor Sinclair found at the marina. No signs of blood at the scene. His body was dumped in a snow drift. No easy task for even the strongest woman. We can't forget the keys to the Hyatt found at all three sites. I think it is time to talk seriously with Matt Fogelberg.

Let's go back to HQ and talk to Paul and see how that interview went." Perry started the car and they drove left on Abbott Rd. then made a right onto Ridge Rd. He took the Thruway 90 East to the 190 and headed downtown. Parker asked, "Why did you go this way?" Perry replied, "Just quicker to get out of Lackawanna and out of potential slow traffic.

Now that I am thinking about everything Chief, what have we missed?" Parker thought a minute and said, "Perry, we have three very prominent men murdered within two weeks. We have the same M.O. and it looks to have been a man. The man most likely has been heard to say he would like to see all three of them out of the picture for political, personal, and financial reasons. How did we not spend more time going in that direction rather than looking at a love-based motive? I agree, it is time to indict, Mr. Fogelberg." Perry picked up the radio receiver, "Car 15 to base, Car 15 to base. Come in." Static came from the radio.

"Yes, Detective Kline, this is HQ." said the operator. "Patch me into Paul Gorci if he is still in the building, please." "Just a minute" was her reply. "Hello, this is Gorci." Perry said, "Hey Paul, Perry here with Parker. How did your chat with Fogelberg go?" "Well Perry, it was a bust. He never showed. I have been on the phone calling him everywhere I know about and have gotten no response." Parker added, "Isn't that interesting. I guess he was uncomfortable talking without his lawyer." "Thanks, Paul. We're on our way in."

Perry then picked up his cell and dialed Christie at her office. "Mahern, Miller and Associates," said Wendy McKeller. "Perry answered, "Hello, this is Detective Kline with the Buffalo Police, Is Christie available? "Hi Perry, it's Wendy. I am sorry she is in conference presently." "I'm guessing she is talking to her "Brother", said Perry without giving any acknowledgment of Wendy's comment. Wendy quickly replied, "I am sorry, Detective Kline, I am not at liberty to say who she is in the office with right now. Did you want me to have her call you as soon as she is free?" Perry said, "Yes, Thanks, Wendy. See you soon." Perry looked over at Parker and said, "Chief, I have a hunch that Fogelberg is with Christie right now. I think we should take a quick ride there. I'll send a car over to watch the door in case I tipped them off. We have enough evidence to charge him, don't we?" Parker said, "Absolutely, and then some.

He has said to several people, even us, that he would rather see all of them out of his way, he drives a white Cadillac, he had the opportunity, he has access to the Hyatt where he could make keys. Let's go bring him into HQ."

Minutes later, Perry and Parker stood in front of Wendy McKeller's desk. Parker said, "Miss McKeller, can you have Ms. Mahern join us immediately please?" Wendy replied, "I am sorry, Detectives, Ms. Mahern is in conference with a client." Parker said, "I am sorry as well. She either comes out here immediately or we will interrupt her meeting. Your choice." Wendy held up one finger, punched in some numbers into her phone, and said into her headset, "Christie, sorry but Detectives Clark and Kline are here at the desk and insist on seeing you immediately."

She listened. Perry said into his portable radio, "Watch the back exit, we have the front." Wendy paled perceptibly and said, "Okay, I will send them back. Gentlemen, I assume you know your way?" Parker said," I'll go." He walked toward the hall heading to Christie's corner office. He knocked and walked in. Christie was sitting at her desk, alone. She said, "Hello Parker, how can I help you?" Parker was a bit taken back but regained his composure and said, "Christie, we are looking for your brother Matthew. Was he just in here?" Christie began asking, "Why is it so urgent to see my brother, Parker?"

As she said that, they both heard a scuffle in the outer hall. They could hear a man say, "You have no warrant to arrest me! I have done nothing wrong." They both recognized Matt Fogelberg's voice. Parker looked at Christie and said, "Shame on you, Counselor. We would have gotten him soon enough. This just makes him, and you look guilty. I am surprised." Parker walked behind the desk to through the sliding door into her private office and out the exit door into the hall. Perry was already there putting handcuffs on the wrists of Mr. Fogelberg while he Mirandized him, "You have the right to remain silent. Anything you say may and will be used against you in a court of law. If you have no attorney, one will be appointed to you."

Christie was really upset. She would have to go to an arraignment in the morning, talk with her brother and then begin her briefs for defense. She would contact her partner, Wilson Miller to act as the primary defense attorney in the case. She had already told her brother that this would happen. They agreed she would go on vacation and take up his defense upon her return. They would ask that he be released into Wilson's custody if necessary.

As Perry and Parker returned to HQ, Parker immediately got on the phone with the District Attorney Dr. Patrick Hartley. "Dr. Hartley", said Parker, "how are things going over in justice? Parker Clark here." Dr. Hartley replied, "Just fine, Detective Clark. What can I do for you this fine afternoon?" Parker said, "I need a Judge's order for Matthew Fogelberg, we have evidence that he is the killer we've been looking for all this time." Dr. Hartley said, "I will have one of my clerks run it over within the hour." "Thanks so much!" said Parker. The call ended.

Perry called Christie on her cellphone. It went immediately to voicemail, "Hello, Ms. Mahern. This is Detective Kline calling. I tried to call earlier to give you a heads up about coming to see you, but your secretary would not forward my call. Please call me anytime today so I can speak with you about your case before you leave for vacation. Thanks."

Christie was on her office phone talking to Joni when she saw Perry's call come through to her cell phone. Joni and she were making plans for getting to the airport later in the week. Joni suggested that Christie come into her place Friday morning. Then she would have her friend, Dennis Shooda, drive them to the airport and pick them up next week. That would save any parking costs. Christie ended the call by saying, "That sounds great Joni. Thanks. See you soon."

Christie then listened to the voicemail Perry left. She would call him later and give him a hard time but not too hard as she expected the move as her sources told her they would be coming for her brother. That is why she had Matt come to her office today. She thought to herself, I'll cook his favorite meal for dinner tonight as she wouldn't see him for a week as she would leave the next day.

Meanwhile, Christie buzzed Wilson's office across the hall. He picked up the receiver as his secretary, Allie Hartley, was taking shorthand for a statement he needed for a court case the next day, "Yes, Christie?" "Wilson, my brother Matt has been arrested and will likely be charged with the recent murders. If you have time today, we should strategize our plan. I'm thinking you could be the lead and I'll assist you by doing much of the work." "Be right over." said Wilson grabbing his legal pad and excusing his secretary thinking 'this will be interesting.'

Perry and Parker asked Matt Fogelburg questions and Paul Gorci jotted down notes. A Police stenographer was taking the official transcript of the proceeding. Perry began, "Mr. Fogelburg, did you murder Johnny Galway?" As Wilson Miller, his attorney was seated next to him, Matt replied, "No, Sir. I killed no one." Perry noted his whole demeanor had changed from the last time they spoke, "You have stated often in front of groups of people that you would like to see Johnny and Victor Sinclair out of your way. What did you mean by that?"

Matt paused then replied, "Detective Kline, I said those things because it generates support for my candidacy and as I have explained many times, both those men are doing so many injustices and illegal undertakings toward the members of the community and should not be as powerful as they are."

The questioning lasted about an hour and a half. Nothing of significance was uncovered and Matt would be arraigned in the morning.

The arraignment went well. Dr. Hartley, the District Attorney read all the charges that were being filed against Matt Fogelberg. The prosecution seemed to have done their homework and had only charged him with one murder. That murder was of Johnny Galway. They had plenty of evidence examples of Matt telling people in public on multiple occasions that he not only disliked the mayor but also would like to have seen him removed from the political scene in Buffalo. The D.A. also indicated there was some supporting physical evidence as well as motive and opportunity. To the untrained eye, the confidence of Dr. Hartley would have indicated the case was open and shut.

Christie on the other hand knew that they really didn't have as much evidence as they stated, or she would have known about it. The defense, in the person of Wilson Miller, really had to fight for bail on Matt's own recognizance due to Matthew being gone for a week. When it was explained he was hurt during a ski vacation, it was granted by the Honorable Fredrick Sedita, who presided. Christie breathed a sigh of relief.

Christie spoke softly to her brother, Matt, "Do you think you can keep your nose clean for the next week or so while I am on vacation? I need to get away and don't want to have to be worrying about you." Matt smiled and said, "Sis, you know I am a 'live by the rules guy'. I will not give you any reason to worry. By the way, where are you going?"

Christie said, "I am going to see a friend in Denver. I'll talk to you soon."

Christie left and approached Dr. Hartley as the courtroom began to clear and the judge had retired to his chambers. She said, "Excuse me, Dr. Hartley, can we speak privately for a few minutes about this case?" Pat Hartley turned to Ms. Mahern and replied, "Ms. Mahern, I was surprised not to have seen you representing your brother here this morning. I always have a few minutes to chat with you. Why don't we use my office down the hall?" Christie was glad he was in a good mood as she was about to burst his bubble.

They walked out of the courtroom and down to the end of the hall where they entered the corner office of the District Attorney. Often, she mused whether she had taken the wrong side of the bench and gone with defense rather than prosecution. She would have aspired to this office. They entered his private chambers. He offered her a chair. She remained standing saying, "Patrick, our defense case is solid. I will be the lead attorney in this case. We have all the required rebuttal evidence to refute the charges. Have a great week. See you when I return from vacation. Thanks for your time, Sir."

As Christie walked back down the hall, she thought that telling Hartley she was going to blow his case out of the water would make him press the police for more evidence to strengthen his case against Fogelberg. She knew that all the evidence they talked about was circumstantial and there was no physical evidence to link Matthew to any of the murders. She felt good about having done her preparation so well. She had questioned Matthew rather vigorously in her office with Wendy taking video. As they replayed the video, she was able to coach Matthew on how to keep calm during questioning so either the judge or a jury would not be swayed into a decision about the truth because of his temper and impulsive desire to blurt out what he thought was the absolute truth. He had learned well. She wondered if it would be enough during the trial if it came to having one.

Now she could relax when she got to Florida. She'd tell Perry where she really was going at their dinner tonight.

PART THREE

Friday morning, Joni and Christie left for the airport with an escort from Dennis Shooda. He dropped them off at Buffalo International near the American Airlines check-in. They walked into the terminal and met Linda and Charmaine in line. Linda said, "Margie and Catie had already checked in and would meet them at the gate." The rest of the check-in process went quickly and the ladies were boarded and seated in rows 9, 10, and 11. Each aisle seat was occupied by a member of the group. The chatter was non-stop, but the flight had a stop in Washington. They would arrive at 3:30 pm. Just in time for an hour or so of sun and tropical drinks before dinner.

Christie was thinking of skipping dinner. She had strategized with her partner Wilson Miller. They came up with what she considered an airtight defense plan. Her phone was off, and she would only check voice mails each morning for her messages or have Wendy take care of it. She owed herself this respite and planned to thoroughly enjoy the time off. She joined the group for dinner.

They had planned on going to Disney originally but after some chatting, the ladies thought Key West would be a bit less crowded and more adult. So, they landed safely almost 40 minutes early and got a jitney service to the hotel. The driver was a very tall, dark Caribbean fellow with a great accent and enormous muscles all the ladies noticed. He loaded all their bags and them into the bus in minutes.

It was a 50-minute ride to the hotel, but he made it in 40 minutes. After getting a $100 tip, he thanked them as he loaded the three luggage carts. They checked in at 4 pm and were at the pool bar by 4:15. They were all clad in bikinis and Linda was the only one with a tan. Typically, they each compared their body to the others when Linda spoke, "I was thinking I would be the one with the best body here, but I can't hold a candle to you ladies." Laughter filled the bar area. The two bartenders were scurrying around like crazy getting the ladies their second drinks already.

They all tried to charge their drinks to their suites, however, Linda had already instructed them to charge it to her card. What a great start to a relaxing week, Christie thought. She made a mental note to talk to Linda about her week with Matthew out at Kissing Bridge. After the third cocktail, Catie Fuda said, "Ladies, I don't know about any of you but if I don't eat something, it will be a long night hugging the toilet." They giggled as most agreed. Catie Fuda asked the bartender, "Can we get a table at Milagro's in an hour and a half?" Juan the dark-skinned blonde picked up the phone and spoke in Creole she later found out. After two minutes he said, "Your table will be ready at 7:30 pm. It will be under the name of Catie Fuda." She said, "Thanks for the table and knowing my name."

The room arrangements by consensus were Linda and Charmaine, Christie with Joni, and Catie Fuda and Margie. They all were delighted with Joni's choice of hotels. The rooms all had facing balconies to the pool area and from the second-floor rooms, they could even see the ocean. The kitchen was large and fully stocked. All they needed was food. Catie Fuda, Margie, and Joni volunteered to do food shopping the next day early. They had agreed on a schedule of making dinner every other day.

The bedrooms had two king-sized beds and large TVs. The dining and living rooms were large. Dining room could seat eight comfortably. The living room was spacious as well. Everything from the walls to the furniture was white. They would be able to watch the sailboats and large yachts from their balconies. As they were all in adjacent rooms, they could all sit out and have conversations if they wanted and they took advantage of this feature all week. The ladies adjourned to their respective rooms to get ready for dinner. They decided on Key West "Chic" for their attire. Lots of chatter in each of the rooms and they each showered and picked out an outfit while unpacking.

At 7:25, Christie and Joni were the first to come down to the bar where they were to meet. Christie started the tab by ordering a cabernet wine from California. She found a nice wine by the glass from Robert Craig. Joni ordered her usual Jack Daniels and coke. Just as the drinks arrived, Margie and Catie came in. They seemed to be in a deep conversation which they abruptly stopped when they got to the bar. Margie ordered a local beer. Juan who was now working at the inside bar recommended the Rams Head for her. Catie ordered a Sauvignon Blanc. Next to arrive was Charmaine. She hugged everyone and said to the group how happy she was to be with them all, away from the cold weather. Christie asked, "Where is Linda?" Charmaine replied, "Oh she was fussing with her hair then got a phone call. She said to not wait to be seated and she'd be down shortly." Then to Juan, "Mr. Juan, can I pay for all the ladies' drinks and include two margaritas for me and my late arriving roomie? Juan looked at Christie and Christie said, "I started a tab Char, so put it on that, Juan. We'll do dinner separate." "Okay, Thanks Christie", said Charmaine.

Just as Juan set the two margaritas in front of Charmaine, Linda came in and reached over her asking, "Is one of those mine, I hope?" Christie answered, "Ladies, let us raise our glasses in a toast. To a great week of relaxation and fun. Also, I would like to express condolences to both Margie and Charmaine who both lost loved ones." The ladies raised their drinks and glasses clinked. Christie was thinking to herself, any of these ladies could in fact be the murderer.

They were all on her list as well as the list the police were considering. Yet, her brother was being charged for them and going to court. The hostess entered the bar with menus in hand and announced that their table was ready. Everyone picked up their drinks and followed the attractive blonde. As they were seated, the hostess with Rhonda on her name tag introduced them to their waiter who was holding a chair for each of them as they sat, "Ladies, this is Armando. He will be at your beck and call this evening. Please enjoy."

Armando got them comfortable and checked to see if anyone needed drinks. They all ordered a second round. He took their drink orders and never wrote anything down.

He returned as some looked at the menus and others began to chat about what they would do after dinner and the next day. As Juan returned with the drinks, he sat down a Rams Head in front of Margie, a Sauvignon Blanc in front of Catie, a Robert Craig cabernet in front of Christie, a Jack and coke in front of Joni, and margaritas for both Linda and Charmaine. The ladies were impressed. He asked, "Are you ready to order?"

Matt Fogelberg hung up the phone and was saddened by the fact that he could not leave the state. He heard from Christie's secretary that Linda was one of the ladies in the group going to Key West but not which hotel they were staying. He now planned to rendezvous with Linda there for a day or two. Oh well, he thought. I better prepare for the upcoming hearing in two weeks with Wilson Miller so they would have a solid defense prepared. He also wondered why she said she was going to Denver.

Perry Kline was back in the film room reviewing the videos that Micah Blair had taken at the funeral. He was specifically looking for Matt Fogelberg and his interaction if any with the rest of the possible suspects or either Frank Galway or Victor Sinclair.

He thought it odd that the ladies who they dated, were married to or were in business with all three of the men murdered, just happened to be in a group together vacationing in Key West.

Parker Clark was sitting in his office going over the transcripts of the staff interviews from the Hyatt. He was also researching when Matt Fogelberg had purchased a major ownership of the hotel. He had many questions about how he could afford to own a hotel on the salary of a Councilman.

In the squad room, Donna Smith and Paul Gorci were at her desk researching all the females that had been on the suspect list. Their strategy was to eliminate these women based on lack of motive, lack of opportunity, lack of capability, or lack of plausibility based upon their relationships with these men and the others in their lives.

Micah Blair was just getting off a plane in Key West. It was 8:00 pm and he had brought his surveillance equipment to see what he could learn from the group of ladies from Buffalo who were vacationing at Santa Maria Suites. He jumped into a large panel van with all his equipment and rode to his friend's home.

The driver of the van was Kirt Leoz. Kirt was the golf pro working 4-5 days a week at the Key West Golf Club. He was also a former private investigator and old golfing buddy of Micah's when they had been younger. Micah asked if he would assist him as all the ladies were very familiar with Micah, but none knew Kirt. Kirt did have an office that he leased from Open Ocean Watersports on Simonton Street in the strip mall adjacent to the Santa Maria Suites location. How fortuitous Micah said to Kirt when he called two days ago making these plans. Micah had rented a room in an Air BNB right across the street from the Suites where the ladies were staying. His window overlooked the pool and bar area at their hotel. He found out he could also see their balconies.

Saturday morning, they awoke in Key West to dark clouds and chilly 65-degree weather. Christie and Joni had a room service breakfast and decided to go shopping on Duval Street. They sat on the patio and drank coffee. Joni looked to the balcony on either side of them before asking, "Christie, I just got a text from my neighbor, Linda Weeks, saying she heard that your brother was arrested and charged with the murders. If that is true, why didn't you say anything to me?" Christie waited to set down her coffee cup and answered, "Well, it just happened Thursday. You and I haven't been alone long enough for us to chat about personal stuff. Now that you ask, I'll tell you, he is innocent. My brother Matt has a big mouth. He says things without thinking which is really a dumb habit; especially for a politician looking to win an election. He assured me that he had no clue about those murders. I, myself, am worried that he could be the next target." Joni listened intently and was quiet for a minute.

A half block away, Micah sat inside his room at the hotel across the street with the balcony doors open while listening to their conversation with a long-range surveillance microphone set up on his desk to listen to their audio from across the street. Then Joni asked Christie, "Who do you think has been murdering these people back home?"

Christie looked to both the adjacent balconies as well and said, "I have a hunch that no one that has been named as a suspect is likely the killer. I have been thinking about this since my car unearthed Johnny Galway a few weeks ago off the Route 400 highway. I am talking low just in case someone can hear but I see the doors are closed on the rooms next door. Johnny was loved by so many but hated by some very important and powerful people.

If we look at those he has hurt, my brother is on that list but if we look at women there is a longer list." Christie began naming the ladies with her fingers raising to keep count. "Margie Galway could have. Linda dated him twice. Charmaine Sinclair was secretly dating him. I even dated him." Joni had a look of shock on her face, "Girl, was I out of the country when that happened?" Christie laughed, "It was only two dinners. We never got past the fact that I was eye candy for him after he formally left Margie. When he began to spread his wings, I cut him loose on the second date at the Policeman's Ball. I found him fascinating to talk to and his knowledge of the political scene in this town was a treasure trove for a young lawyer who had been lucky enough to be tossed into that arena years ago by Ed Rotski when he ran for County Executive. I learn from him that knowing what the other party is focusing on really is the best way to beat them in an election. 'Gotta know the players, or you can't know the program' is what Johnny used to say."

It was silent for a minute then Joni asked, "Christie, don't hate me for asking this question but shouldn't you be on the list, too? You dated them all and certainly have had some...I don't want to say bad, but less than cordial dealings with these guys. Did you commit these murders?

Christie made no response. After a pregnant paused, she laughed out loud.

Next door to them in room 219, the balcony doors opened. Out stepped Catie Fuda. She stretched her arms over her head. She was in a silky negligee that flattered her figure gracefully. She looked over toward them and waved, "Morning ladies. I just checked the weather. The weather service says the rain will turn into bright sunshine for the rest of the day around noon. Have you planned anything yet?" Christie looked at Joni who nodded, then said, "Joni and I were gonna go over to Duval Street and do some shopping before lunch then hit the pool. Wanna join us?"

"Oh, cool" said Catie, "I am just finishing a cup of coffee. When are you leaving? Do I have time for a shower?" Christie replied, "Sure, we were just headed in to shower ourselves. How about in 30 minutes we meet in the lobby?" "Thanks ladies, see you downstairs in 30", said Catie closing the doors again.

Almost on cue, the door for room 215 on the other side of Christie and Joni opened. Out stepped Linda. She was dressed which shocked everyone, even Micah. He was still listening having called Kirt and asked him to follow the ladies to Duval Street.

Kirt knew Juan from the Santa Maria and let him know if the ladies from up north wanted a vehicle, he was just around the corner. He was headed to see Micah this morning so he could be there in seconds.

Linda asked Christie what the plans were if any. Christie said, "We are meeting down in the lobby in thirty minutes if anyone wants to shop on Duval. Do you and Charmaine want to go? I am calling Juan downstairs to set up transportation. She responded, "Just a second." Linda leaned into the room and apparently asked Charmaine if she was interested. "We're both in," said Linda, "see you in the lobby." Christie walked into their room saying to Joni, "Why don't you shower while I make a couple of calls." Joni was naked and walked into the bathroom shower and turned on the jets. Christie called the desk. Juan answered, "Santa Maria Concierge, this is Juan. How may I help you?" "Hey, Juan, this is Christie from 2-1-7. We need a car for six in 30 minutes to go shopping on Duval and Whitehead. Can you set it up?" Juan said, "Yes Miss Christie, I'll have a jitney waiting for you when you get down here. Anything else?" Christie said, "No thanks. We'll be down in a half hour."

30 minutes later, Kirt had left Micah's apartment having gotten a call from Juan and pulled up to the front entrance of the Santa Maria and waited. He tooted the horn twice to let Juan know he

was there. The six ladies exited the hotel escorted by Juan to the jitney.

Kirt loaded the ladies into the vehicle. Kirt would drive them and offer his services all day. He said to Christie who acted like the leader of the excursion, "Where to Miss?" Christie answered, "The Shops at Mallory Square, please." Off they went. As they drove up Simonton, Kirt said to all the ladies, "My name is Kirt. I can drive you back down to the Suites when you are ready." Linda spoke up and said, "That would be great as we would like to come back down for lunch to Louie's Backyard. Can we call for you?" Kirt answered, "Yep. I have a meeting near the shops, so I will wait to hear from you. Here is my number." handing his card to whomever wanted to grab it. Charmaine was closest so she grabbed it.

They arrived at the Shops at Mallory Square just after 10 am. Kirt bid them a good morning of shopping and said he would be where he dropped them off, "If you are ready sooner, just call and I'll come as soon as you call." He drove off to his appointment. Kirt was, in fact, meeting Micah to discuss more surveillance of the ladies. Micah was now in his second office on Duval Street.

The ladies decided to split up into different pairs. They went with someone other than their roommate. This would be a trend throughout their trip they decided. There was just starting to be more foot traffic in the shops as it got closer to noon. This was the agreed-upon meeting time to regroup and go to lunch. Margie and Christie found Kirt in the jitney at 11:55 am. They really enjoyed their time. Margie asked Christie all about the murders as they walked through the stores. Christie was keeping things a bit close to the vest as she really didn't know Margie all that well and she had dated her late husband after their marriage ended. Christie said, "Margie, I hope things do not get uncomfortable between us. I know I dated Johnny after you two broke up. I found it interesting talking with Johnny. I especially liked listening about all his political knowledge and experience."

Christie ended the statement by saying, "We never really got beyond the dinner and a kiss goodnight stage because...he... well he decided to move on." Margie laughed, "I guess, he moved on from all of us. He and I had a good run, but we just grew apart. It was interesting to see the variety of different women he dated after we parted. I hold no grudges and I especially wanted to thank you for finding him in the snow that night. When you think about it, he may have been there a long time until the snow melted, and even then, we might not have found him so thank you." Christie said, "Gee Margie, I never thought about it like that. Thanks, I feel better about it now."

Micah was on the roof of the Cuban Coffee Queen in the shopping plaza. He had listened to most of the conversations between Margie and Christie. He listened to Linda and Joni as well as Charmaine and Catie. He noted all the pairs got along quite well during their two hours of shopping. He was particularly intrigued with the conversation he had recorded between Catie and Charmaine. Catie had a similar conversation to one Margie and Christie had.

Catie said to Charmaine, "You know I went out with your late husband once. He was really, quite handsome and a very, smooth talker, but I guess you of all people would know that. He was nice to talk with, but I realized at our dinner that he was a bit too...I don't want to say old, but he was mature beyond his years. It made him seem like he was not anything I was looking for in a partner or even someone I'd date again. When he was found murdered, you must have been devastated."

Charmaine had remained silent through Catie's speech then said, "Victor was a complex man who liked having beautiful women around him but sadly it was never enough to satisfy him. You are right, he was aloof and almost distant. That is what attracted me to him and made him seem so sexy to me. After being with him for a while, however, he made me feel so inadequate that I went into a shell for a while then realized that I was missing living my life. So, we had an agreement to have an open marriage but one of discretion. We have built so much in business together and worked so well together that it was difficult to break away from the relationship even after he hurt me so often by flaunting his women in my face in public way too many times. I really despised him for that."

Catie was silent for a minute. She was dumb-founded when Charmaine finished. She could think of nothing to respond with; she changed the subject and started talking about the dress that Charmaine had purchased and how beautiful it looked on her. Catie commented how her breasts looked so elegant in it. She herself always had difficulty finding a dress or any clothes for that matter that made her own large breasts look classy. This dress she felt seemed way too sexy to wear for dinner with the girls, but she was maybe learning what made Charmaine tick.

Micah noted that Linda and Joni were very animated in their discussions but were whispering the entire morning. Micah was unable to hear them.

Micah watched all six of the Buffalo ladies as they scampered into Kirt's jitney. They were on their way to Louie's Backyard he had heard them say as they got into the vehicle. Kirt mentioned to them that a new restaurant opened across the street from Louie's Backyard, "It's called 'The Buffalo Café'. I think, Neal Seagle just opened it a month ago. If not today, make sure you stop in before you head back north."

On the drive down Duval Street, Kirt cut over to Simonton as it was a less traveled route during the day, especially on a Saturday. The ladies decided to take his advice and try the Buffalo Café. A few of the ladies knew Neal from his being on the Council. They hoped that he was there so they could say hello. Linda said to Kirt, "We've decided to go to the Buffalo Café on your advisement Kirt." "Great," said Kirt, "we're almost there. It is one of the best new places down here. I hope you like it."

The Buffalo Café turned out to be an excellent choice. Neal was there tending bar when they walked in. He was excited to see his friends. Greeting them, he said, "How in God's name did you ladies show up here?" Joni replied, "There is no hiding from us, Seagle! We wanted to track you down and keep you on your toes." Everyone laughed even Neal who replied, "Hey Joni, is that a short comment? 'Keep on my toes?' The ladies were giggling again as he took their order."

They chose a table in the bar area rather than the dining room so they could continue to chit-chat with Neal. As he brought their drinks, Christie began a toast, "Here's to Neal and the Buffalo Café. May it prosper and grow as you wish and for as long as you wish." "Here, Here." They all shouted.

Neal thanked them and took their lunch orders. Half chose the chicken sandwich but half of them ordered the wings and fries. They all ordered lite beer on tap. Joni went to the bar and spoke to Neal for a few minutes. When she returned, she said," Neal said he wants us to meet him tomorrow night for drinks at Sloppy Joe's at 8:30 P.M. It is Buffalo night there. He said he has a surprise that we can't miss. It won't be longer than an hour and a half because he will have to be back here to close the restaurant. We can stay if you'd like."

Charmaine said, "Cool. We should call Kirt again and invite him in for a drink and he can bring us back down to the hotel and we can either continue the party there or come back here with Neal." Neal then brought them over another round of drinks saying, "Ladies it was a supreme pleasure to see all of you here. These are on the house. Tomorrow will be fun if you can make it. I will be gone after that as I'm taking the red eye back to Buffalo for some meetings."

The ladies decided to go back to the hotel. Kirt walked in the door as if he had been listening to their conversation. Christie got the eerie feeling again about the coincidences and she thought of the guy looking and listening from across the street. "Kirt" yelled Margie, "how about a lift back to the hotel?" Kirt walked by the table to the bar and said, "Sure, give me two minutes to wet my whistle and square up my tab with Neal for my meal today. Cola please Mr. Seagle!"

Christie and Linda both got up to go to the ladies' room. Neal pointed them toward the dining room. In the hallway, there in its magnificent splendor was a 6-foot by 6- foot portrait of Johnny Galway. The ladies both gasped audibly, upon seeing it. "Oh, my gracious." said Christie, "should we show this to Margie?" Linda said, "I think she'd love it." There were many other photos to be viewed in that long hallway, however, Johnny's portrait was the most majestic. "I wonder who painted that?" said Christie. Linda responded, "I will bet you dinner tonight it was Neal." "Really?" said Christie.

She knew Neal from school and the political arena in Buffalo but never knew he was an artist. Nor did she think him the entrepreneur he seemed to be. She thought to herself 'maybe I should be planning on a business operation for when I quit lawyering.' The hustle in the courts was really starting to take its toll on Christie. I will talk to Joni tonight in the room and see what we can put together. Then she thought about Perry Kline. She wondered if they would be together long-term or not. Would he be interested in creating a retirement business after he retired from the police force?

Margie and Catie were walking toward the ladies' bathroom as Linda and Christie exited it. Margie gasped as she saw Johnny's portrait. Catie was in awe as well. Linda said, "we are going to ask Neal if he painted this before we leave." Margie said, "I'll have to grab my phone and take a picture before we leave."

Margie continued, "That is a great capture of his most adorable expression of being mischievous. Can't wait to hear if Neal did it and how long ago it was that Johnny sat for it."

Charmaine and Joni entered the hallway looking for the others. As Joni saw it, she was shocked to see Johnny's portrait. She wondered how Margie would feel as she let out an involuntary gasp. Margie had just exited the ladies' bathroom as Joni gasped. Margie said to her, "Doesn't it capture his impish personality perfectly, Joni? At one point, I would have loved to have this for my home. Now it might be better, placed in City Hall somewhere, don't you think?" Joni said, "Do we know who painted this?"

"I did!" said Neal walking up behind them, "I am sorry to have shocked you with this, but I totally forgot it was here. Johnny sat for some photos after a Council meeting about a year ago. All of them hugged Neal and each other as they shed tears remembering Johnny as Neal had captured him. He said, "I finished it four months ago and when he came down to visit the last time; we had an unveiling ceremony for him. He loved it. Margie, I have some pictures I was going to send him of the ceremony if you'd like them." Margie said, "That would be great Neal, thank you."

The ladies said the goodbyes and paid their tab having to fight Neal to accept their money. Linda said finally, "If you don't take our money, you'll get in the habit and close this down before you know it." Neal thanked them all and graciously took their money.

Kirt was waiting outside as the ladies exited the Buffalo Café. "Back to the Santa Maria?" he bellowed. They all yelled back, "Yes and fast before we lose the sunshine!" They laughed and thanked Kirt for bringing them here. They might never have thought to try the restaurant if he had not suggested it. Christie thought to herself on the ride back to the hotel that something about this trip was amiss. She couldn't put her finger on it but there was something strange about all the coincidences that have happened already. She needed to talk to Perry.

Maybe if she got some alone time, she'd try to call Perry later tonight to run things by him. He could always seem to see through the clouds of situations like this.

Perry and Paul had just left the Mulligan's Brick Bar on Allen Street in Buffalo. They each decided to call it an early day as they had been working today on a Saturday which was rare but not unheard of for them. Perry was close to home turning the corner onto Richmond Avenue and into his driveway as his phone rang. "Hello, this is Perry Kline, Can I help you?" "Hello, Mr. Kline. I am taking a survey of Buffalo Police officers. I wondered if you could spare a few moments to talk?"

"Could you tell me how much you miss the cute brunette, you've been seeing lately?" Perry laughed as always, "Hey Darling, how are you? Great to hear from you. Enjoying the R and R?" Christie asked, "Are you alone?" Perry said, "Yes, Ms. Mahern, I just pulled into my drive. Paul and I just had a couple of beers after work at the Brick Bar. I am now in my kitchen. What's up?"

Christie was walking around the pool looking to see if any of the girls were out on the balcony so she could talk freely. She saw no one. "Perry, I would like to get your take on things here. They are getting more weird by the hour.

Christie noticed in a 2nd floor office across the street, there seemed to be a pair of large binoculars set up on a tripod with what looked like a large circular speaker pointed right at her. She saw no one there but decided to move. As she walked toward the front entrance of the property, she noticed someone stand and look through the binoculars. As she reached the street and saw the free Duval loop bus approaching on Simonton, she flagged it down and jumped on.

She rode for a few blocks talking to Perry when she exited the bus. There in front of her was an ice cream store. She ordered a vanilla cone, no sprinkles. She said to Perry, "Thank you for waiting. I was at the pool so I could talk to you alone and saw a man across the street from the hotel in an office with the balcony door open and a pair of large telescopic binoculars pointed down at the pool area and next to it was a large speaker thing like an audio surveillance microphone. Maybe I am just paranoid but better to be safe than sorry." Perry interjected, "So, tell me what's wrong Christie?"

Christie took a deep breath. She did not want to cry and upset him 1500 miles away. She took another breath and said, "Well, it has been a little bit crazy down here and I needed your calmness right now." "Anytime doll. Go ahead," said Perry. Christie began her saga. She described the ladies and their pairings but got quickly to the fact that their driver, Kirt, was from Buffalo working down here semi-retired. He brought us to a place a couple of blocks away called the Buffalo Café. The owner is Neal Seagle." Perry said, "I just heard about him opening the Café about two hours ago when

I ran into Tina Oliver at the Brick Bar. She and Neal were school-mates since first grade or something.

When I heard Key West as she was talking to the group, my ears perked up. I guess he had been planning that for years." Christie went on, "He seems like a nice enough guy but when I went to the ladies' bathroom at his place, I saw this monster large painted picture of Johnny Galway in the hallway. There were other Buffalo famous dignitaries on the wall. There is even a picture of your police graduating class. I did not say anything, I kept any comments to myself, but the picture freaked me out. Then when I noticed the room across the street with the zoom-in binoculars and listening device, that sealed it for me."

Perry asked, "So how have all the ladies been getting on with each other? You do have two widows with the group and as I thought about it, you were all mentioned as suspects at some point in the investigation." Christie had to take another deep breath as she walked across the street to catch the on-coming bus to return to the hotel.

Christie saw a trash can at the stop and tossed out her melting, almost untouched ice cream cone. She continued, "We all, seem to be getting along. Everyone is on their best behavior and there has not been a cross word heard. So, what do you make of this? Anything?" Perry thought to himself to be sensitive and supportive even though he thought Christie was off the rail a bit, "Well kiddo, I see where you might start to put all the coincidences together. The driver from home, taking you to a restaurant run by a guy from home. My suggestion is to keep an eye out over your shoulder. It may be nothing more than you, using your detective skills which certainly have served you well over the years to create a possible uncomfortable scenario. I will call Micah. He or his team may be down to Key West to see what you ladies are up to. I will keep you apprised of anything I hear if anything. Does that help at all?"

Christie was getting on the bus which had just pulled up, "Perry, thank you so much for just listening. I think you're right. It may be nothing but you never know. I'll call you again if I see anything untoward. You're the best Kline, Thanks!" Perry replied, "Take care and have fun. Talk to you soon." They ended the call. She thought, they never said 'I love you' to each other. She felt she loved him, but I guess, she thought, 'I'm waiting for him'. She laughed to herself.

The Santa Maria Suites appeared. She rang the bell to get off. It took her time to cross the busy street. As she got to the entrance, she turned and looked back at that room across the street. The balcony doors were shut now. She noticed the lights were now on inside and the telescopic binoculars were pointed skyward. Hmm, she thought, I wonder where I can get a set of binoculars for sightseeing. She walked into the pool area and saw the ladies sitting around in the afternoon sun. Charmaine yelled to Christie, "Hey Lady. We have been looking all over for you. Your phone went to voicemail when I tried to call. Welcome back!"

Linda was just climbing out of the pool. Her red bikini was smaller even than what she wore yesterday. Catie turned around to greet Christie with a glass and a pitcher of margaritas judging by the green color in the pitcher. She said, "Can I wet, your whistle, Miss Christie?" Christie yelled, "Heck yeah! Thanks. I was just out for a walk to get the lay of the land and digest lunch. Now I can have a drink and go to the room and get my suit on. I will wear my black one instead of my red one, so you guys won't mistake me for Linda!" The ladies laughed, especially Linda. Christie downed half her drink then headed to the room for her suit.

It was humid in Key West after the morning rain. Micah had the balcony doors open so the breeze would cool him down. He was listening to the recordings from this morning. He had gone into the bathroom which also had a small window facing the Santa Maria Suites across the street. He noticed Christie on her phone walking off the property alone. He washed his hands and then saw her get on the bus. Micah wondered whether Christie had seen him or his equipment. He shut the doors and turned on the AC which took some time to affect any change to the room. He sat at his desk and the phone rang.

He recognized the caller as Perry Kline showing on his screen. "Hello Perry, how are you?" Perry said, "Hey Micah, I am well. I was looking to find out where you were. I may have an assignment for you." Micah thought he had a hunch now who Christie may have been on the phone with. He decided not to play his hand, so he was vague saying, "I am on the road. What can I help with?" Perry said, "I may want you to travel out of town for a few days. You know there are six ladies from Buffalo down in Key West vacationing together. All of them were on our suspect list so maybe we should keep a close eye on them while they are there. You up for a paid vacation?"

Micah answered carefully, "I can pack a bag and be on a plane in an hour if you want. Whereabouts are they staying? I will bring a couple of folks with me so I can stay in the shadows as they all will recognize me on sight. Just text me the place they are staying." Perry said, "That would be great. You can keep an eye on all their travels, so they remain safe. Especially the Mahern woman who I have developed a fondness for of late. Check-in with me when you get there. We can then speak daily. OK Micah, Thanks." Perry hung up.

He checked his contacts on his cell and found Kenny Thomason. He was an old friend from school who had been a cop in Hamburg and was now working in Key West Florida. He dialed Kenny's number, "Capt. Thomason, please." He waited not even thirty seconds. "Hello, can I help you?" Perry said, "Kenny, it's Perry from Buffalo. How are you?" Kenny Thomason replied, "Hey Detective Kline, how are you doing brother? Coming to our fair city anytime soon?" Perry replied, "No Kenny but I need a favor. I do not know if you heard but we have had our mayor murdered recently along with two other prominent citizens. There are six women who are or were on our suspects' list, staying at the Santa Maria Suites down there. First, I wanted to let you know they were there. Then I was wondering if you could put a local P.I. on their tail for us. One of the ladies is a friend of mine, a lawyer, Christie Mahern, who suspects the group is under surveillance.

Kenny said, "Thanks for the heads up, Perry. I know just the guy to keep an eye on these ladies. He is very, smooth. He has been working for me for years. I am on it, Brother. Next vacation, make a trip down here so we can catch up. Ten four."

Christie returned to the pool and immediately dove into the water. She swam four laps then crawled out and retrieved her drink. She made quick work of that one and asked if she could order another round.

Everyone raised a hand. Juan was just walking toward her as she looked to the Cabana Bar. "Juan, we are in desperate need of additional libations!" said Christie. She pulled a towel off the lounger and dried off. Charmaine exited the water behind her in the skimpiest bikini the ladies had seen yet. Linda said, "Damn Girl, I see I need to work a little more on my gym routines. Your body is smoking hot!" Charmaine said, "Thanks, Linda. As I look around the group, I would say all of us are smoking hot and I am wondering why there are no young men hovering around the pool leering at us!" Laughter ensued. Christie thought that she was in complete agreement with the assessment of the ladies but also wondered if they were all giving off a vibe of untouchability.

Joni perked up from her nap and said, "Ladies, are we giving off a negative vibe to the males around us? I was wondering why we haven't gotten any play as well."

Margie stood up and said, "Well, for one, I am in a relationship as I would guess many of us are. We are, thick-as-thieves, as we have been traveling around town since we arrived so maybe it is the 'GET AWAY' vibe we're offering. I don't know about the rest of you, but I came down here to get away from all the madness in Buffalo. I just wanna have fun." She laughed, "Do I sound like Cindy Lauper?" Then everyone began chattering at once. The talking was on. Then raucous laughter.

Across the street as the afternoon sun began to fade, Micah was beginning to get frustrated with trying to listen to all the banter after the "Cindy Lauper" comment. Kirt walked into Micah's office. "Hey Micah, still monitoring those gorgeous ladies?" Micah sighed, "You have no idea what a challenge it is! I was just listening to them at the pool, and they began to talk about why no guys are hitting on them. That started a bee's nest buzz that has been undiscernible. I have a major headache. I got a phone call a while ago from Detective Kline in Buffalo asking me to come down here and spy on the group to keep them safe. I must call him in an hour and let him know I am here.

I will tell him that I am using you and Neal to assist with the surveillance." Kirt replied, "Wow that is interesting. Lucky for you, he didn't want a conference before you left." Micah laughed, "Boy are you right on that one. I was sweating bullets that he would."

Kirt continued, "Okay, now that you are sitting back down, I can tell you this one. I just got a call myself a half hour ago. It was from Kenny Thomason from the Key West Police Department." Micah spun his chair around and now listened more intently. Kirt continued, "Kenny said a Detective from Buffalo asked him for a favor. He said there was a group of ladies visiting that are or were on his suspect list for the recent murders back there. He wanted KWPD to put some surveillance on them to see if anyone else was watching them or stalking them. He said they didn't want these suspects vulnerable, so they want to make sure they don't miss anything. Isn't that a hoot?" Micah didn't laugh but grabbed the phone. He made a call to another contact in Buffalo, Markus Edwards, his son. Mark was a drummer in a rock group "the Cruisin' Fusion". Mark had worked with his dad many times and was quite good at doing surveillance, being a bodyguard, and attracting the ladies.

Micah didn't think any of them knew they were related or even knew of him so he might be the perfect person for this assignment. He needed him to sniff out if anyone else was watching our ladies and if he could infiltrate them to be closer, that would be an added benefit. "Mark, Dad here. How are you, Smooth? I have an assignment. Are you in Key West or Buffalo?" Markus replied, "I just got off a flight to Key West this morning, Pop. We have two gigs this week. We're playing at Neal's Wednesday and Friday. We're also on the Party Cat Cruise a few nights. What is it you need, Pop?" Micah explained the situation. Markus told him he would gladly have this as a distraction because of all the downtime he would have during the day. "We are even staying at the same place, Santa Maria Suites. You know the owner gives us great rates, so it is a no-brainer. I think I may have seen the ladies at the pool. I will get right on it." Micah said, "My office is across the street remember. Keep, in touch. If I hear they are on the move, I'll buzz you."

Markus added, "Pop, don't forget, we gig on the Party Cat cruise boat from 5-7 p.m. each night to fill in the week so stop by. We do the old standards from when I played with my mom and Uncle Tom. You know he is still doing studio work in New York. He still has a great lip." Micah said, "No worries, I have two other guys helping on this. You just might be the player they are looking for to wine and dine with them. I just heard them say they were surprised no one was hitting on them. Just try not to hit on Catie, her and I have been dating lately." Mark said, "OK, Pops, gotta go. It is time I get ready for the cruise. Talk soon, Love you." The call ended. Micah gazed into the binoculars at his station, now in the bathroom.

Joni got the ladies' attention, "We have some options for the week. We are free tonight, so I thought another nice dinner then some dancing at Mangoes. It is at the corner of Duval and Angela Street. Tomorrow, we are supposed to go to Sloppy Joe's to meet Neal. I also found a sunset cruise for Wednesday night. It is called the Party Cat. It is two hours around the keys with dinner and music on the boat. Thursday night we have tickets and a table reserved for Comedy Key West. Tom Papa and Dave Chappelle are there headlining. Friday is open at this point but that's our last night as we fly out Saturday. Any thoughts?"

Linda said, "I am up for some dancing tonight for sure. After our chat about no men around, I am looking to prowl tonight." Margie said, "I am in. I would like some fun. Joni, you have done a great job putting an itinerary together for us. It all sounds fantastic." Joni said, "It is five o'clock now. Dinner is at 7:30. I thought we would dress up sexy casual, so we will be ready for dancing." Catie laughed and said, "Some of us or maybe all of us only know how to dress sexy casual." Christie said, "Hey is that really a thing? Sexy casual." Joni ended the topic, "It is, because I said it is!" They all laughed and jumped into the pool. Swam and frolicked for another 15 minutes then they got out to finish their drinks. All of them meandered to their rooms to prepare for dinner.

The weather had cooled to a balmy 74 degrees. Linda and Charmaine left their balcony doors open as they were getting a heavenly breeze. They each were lying on Linda's bed as they had their outfits laid out on Charmaine's. They were topless. Micah focused his lenses appropriately and watched with mouth agape as Linda rolled over and began kissing one of Charmaine's breasts and caressing the other. Her caressing hand then slid down Charmaine's stomach into her bikini bottoms and Charmaine could be heard, moaning. Micah visually looked at the other two rooms and only saw one lady and presumed the other was in the shower. As his eyes went back to room 215 with Linda and Charmaine, he was sad to see the wind blow the balcony doors closed and their privacy restored. He called Kirt and let him know they were going to dinner at Mangoes at 7:30 p.m. Kirt said he would hang around their lobby and ask if they needed a ride. When they began to straggle into the lobby, Kirt was standing at the desk talking to Juan, who seemed to be everywhere, at the Santa Maria Suites. Christie saw him first and said, "Kirt, are you following us?"

Mark Edwards went to the lobby in time to see the ladies assembling to head out for dinner. He walked by the group and accidentally bumped into Linda. "Wow, pardon me Miss. I am really embarrassed. I was so taken by how beautiful each of you is dressed this evening, that I was not really watching where I was going. My humble apologies. Are you ok Miss?" Linda looked at his strong body seeing how strong and handsome he was. She hardly heard a word he said. All the ladies were a bit giggly at that moment. Christie said, "I think, you stunned all of us.

I'm Christie. The girls and I are just going out for dinner. I think, Linda is okay, but she is a bit shy." All the ladies laughed. Linda regained her poise and said, "I am okay. I am Linda. Are you staying here?" Mark said humbly, "Yes, I am Mark Edwards. As, a matter of fact, I am staying here with my band from up north for a week of gigs in town. I apologize again for the intrusion. As an apology, would you ladies be interested in being our guests on Wednesday night at the Buffalo Café? Our treat."

He was really taken with all of them even though they were somewhat older. They were all beautiful. He especially was attracted to Charmaine and Linda. If his dad had not given him the heads up on Catie, she may have been his first choice. Joni then entered the conversation, "Mark, thank you so much for the invitation, we'll consider that after looking at our itinerary. You must excuse us; we don't want to be late for dinner. Nice to have met you. See you around the pool. Mark walked back toward the elevator saying, "Okay Ladies, have a great night. Here is my card if you decide to join us."

As they got into the jitney with Kirt, they all started whispering about the nice young man they had met in the lobby. Linda said loudly, "Ladies, we certainly need to maybe relook at our itinerary." They all laughed. Christie thought that when they got to Mangoes, she would again ask Kirt about following them as he seemed a bit tense when she asked the first time. They arrived at Mangoes. Christie was the last one out so she stopped and asked Kirt as he helped her out of the vehicle, "Well are you going to answer my question?" Kirt feigning ignorance, "What question was that again?" Christie knew she had him and pressed on, "Okay Mr. Leoz, why are you following us? Why aren't you charging us for driving us all over Key West?" She waited. A glance at the door saw the ladies waiting so she waved at them to go in.

Perry Kline was researching the whole investigation, looking for something to jump out at him. He felt he was missing something and was reviewing and reviewing until his head could take no more. He went home and jumped into the shower. The steam cleared his head a bit. As he rinsed off, he thought, 'Why am I not thinking like a criminal? It has always worked in the past.'

He stepped out of the shower and missed his favorite lawyer at that moment. He wondered how she and the ladies were doing in sunny Florida. He threw on light sweats and a tank top and retired to the den. It was his favorite place to think.

He began with Margie Galway. He did a series of 'what ifs' in his head. Why would she kill Johnny who had already left her? He had run around on her with other women and was still, considered a skirt chaser after he left. The political arena was obviously, Johnny's domain so that did not seem probable. Money? Perry thought, 'I wonder how much money or political influence Margie had extended to Johnny for him to win the last election. If she invested loads of cash or major favors to push him across the finish line and Johnny reneged on his promises to her, that might be the straw that broke her patience with him. The problem then was, how was she able to kill him then move the body and dump him in a shallow ditch off the 400?'

He entertained the man/woman idea that Paul had raised. Perry thought if she was working in partnership with a man; 'who might that man be?' Could it have been Parker Clark her current beau or Matt Fogelberg the election loser or Frank Galway the brother who was always in his shadow. Wait a minute he thought, didn't Christie tell me that she heard from maybe Ronnie Olsen that Frank also dated Margie. If that was true, then who killed Frank.

Did Margie kill him and get another man to assist with the cleanup, and help her move the body? If that was true, then she would have another accomplice that she would need to eliminate. Hmmm. She may have gone to Victor to help her. He may have helped her, but Frank would have been a challenge even for just those two. She did however have Victor's car after he was, killed. I might be on to something. I just have a few pieces wrong. If this all was the case, then possibly a third accomplice was there to remove Frank and help her kill Victor. Margie would still have an accomplice that needed removal. Now let me look at the same scenario using a different person as the Snow Villain.

Kirt Leoz looked at Christie and laughed, "You must be a lawyer or private detective, Miss Christie. You are letting your drinking in the sun affect your rational thought. Just so you know, Juan from here at Santa Maria Suites called me the first day you all got here and asked if I could be on call. You guys were a special group and he wanted to extend a special courtesy to you for transportation around town. I am a freelancer. My schedule was open and here we are."

Christie thought a second and asked, "How come you never accept any money?" Kirt knew he had convinced her, "Juan and I have a good working agreement that is beneficial for us both. Do not worry about me I do okay but thanks for your concern."

Christie knew she would need more information from Juan but that would come later. She did not want them to get spooked, so she said, "Thanks Kirt. That really eases my mind. Have a good night." Kirt said, "Just call later if you need a ride back to the hotel."

The ladies were seated by a large, open window looking out onto Duval Street. The waiter came to take their drink order. Linda and Charmaine ordered Margaritas, Christie and Catie ordered wine; Joni and Margie ordered local Goose Island beer. Their waiter

Chaz was very handsome and seemed to be flirting with Catie who was blushing the whole time. As he left to get their drinks, Catie said, "what was it we were complaining about not getting any, attention?" They laughed which was what all of them expressed earlier to be exactly what each of them needed for a variety of reasons.

When Chaz returned with the drinks, he asked, "Ready to order?" They had been chatting the whole time, not all had even opened the menu. Joni took charge as usual and said, "I think, we are ready and by then the others should have decided. I am starving. Chaz, I will start. Bring me the Tropical Caesar salad and the Braised Short Ribs." Linda was ready and ordered, "I'll just have the house salad and the Togarashi Tuna Steak." Charmaine said, "I'll have just the Yellowtail Snapper."

Margie was just putting her menu down and said, "I'd like the Caesar salad and the Blackened Cobia shrimp." Catie looked like she needed help deciding so Chaz walked behind her; she was blushing the whole time as she noticed him gazing down her blouse. She quickly ordered, "Chaz, I will have a house salad with Italian dressing and the tuna steak." Chaz smiled, "Thank you miss. And you, miss?" turning to Christie. Christie said, "I'll do a Taco salad and another wine." Chaz left to place the order and grab another round of drinks as the ladies each held their empty glasses up.

Micah was sitting in his friend Neal's apartment on Duval and Angela Street. It was upstairs from the Island Memories store on the adjacent corner, overlooking Mangoes Restaurant. He listened to the conversation between Kirt and Christie.

He thought Kirt fielded the question well. He also knew that when Christie followed up with Juan, in the future, Juan would assure her that the hotel owner wanted to make sure that the special guests were, taken care of as much as they could. Transportation was an easy perk, they could offer.

Micah again had some difficulty hearing the conversations so he decided that his crew would cover the ladies, so he went down the street to get dinner himself. He walked into Fogarty's on Duval and got a Shrimp Po Boy which came with fries. He sat at the Monkey Bar and check his email. Then he called Perry Kline.

"Hello, Detective Kline. It's Micah. I am here in Key West. My team down here has the ladies under surveillance as they are dining at Mangoes on Duval Street. My office is set up across the street and I can keep an eye on the pool and outside bar. Luckily, I can observe them on their balconies as they all face the pool. How are things back in Buffalo?" Perry was glad to hear so quickly from Micah, "That is great news, Micah. I was reviewing all the investigation materials and have come up, with a potential scenario for the murders. If you have a minute, I'd like to run the idea by you. I was thinking that if it was a woman, she may have had a male accomplice. That would explain her being able to move the bodies.

She may even have had the accomplice after Victor's murder. Or Victor might have been the accomplice and she took care of that one herself. If all of that makes sense, then it could have been any of the ladies vacationing in Key West. Any thoughts?" Micah had just finished his Po Boy and was wiping his mouth, so he answered with, "That makes sense from a criminal point of view. What if it was all the women here or a combination of those vacationing together here in Key West?" Perry's head was spinning, and he had trouble speaking. These were all possibilities, "Wow", he said after Micah called his name again, "that makes it imperative they're kept safe."

After Perry hung up the phone having spoken to Micah, he began to think about the scenario he first thought about and substituted Linda. He noted she was a much larger woman than Margie but thin. He thought she may have been able to muscle Johnny and Victor around but certainly not Frank Galway. She could have used an accomplice as well. She also drove a white Cadillac. She had motives for all the murders too.

He asked himself if it could have been two women or all the women together. He knew Christie well but the reason she was a suspect was due to her unearthing Johnny Galway's body when she slid off the highway. Perry had been with her a while now. They had a close intimacy. He could not remember her ever mentioning any of the murder victims other than Johnny who she found. She also was in a court case against him while representing Victor and his company. Her relationship with Frank was fleeting at best and she did not seem to harbor any ill feeling toward him. Joni was an outlier. There was really no record of dating any of them but could have secretly been involved with them. She could have been an accomplice to any of them if that scenario held water.

Catie was also not a central character in all the relationships with these men but had dated them. She was a close friend to most of the other ladies on the Key West Trip. Finally, he looked at Charmaine. She certainly was in the mix.

Being married to Victor, who flaunted his relationships with other women in public may have caused some major embarrassment to Charmaine. She was close to all the women and not really shaken by the murder of her estranged husband, Victor Sinclair.

Perry was distracted from these thoughts as his home phone rang, startling him. He said, "Hello, this is Perry." He looked and saw no caller I.D. on his phone. A woman's voice said, "Detective, you should be following the suspects in this case more closely because they are actively planning another prominent Buffalo resident's demise. I certainly hope you solve the case soon because we can't afford to lose any more important citizens in our city. Just a warning though, we are watching you and all the people you have assigned to this investigation. The people that have committed these crimes are watching you also. Please be very, careful, Mr. Kline." The line went dead.

What, the hell was that, thought Perry. He called Parker Clark, "Chief, I just got a call from some woman. I tried to record it but missed the first part. She started by saying I should be following the suspects closely because... Here's what I recorded:

...they are actively planning another prominent Buffalo resident's demise. I certainly hope you solve the case soon because we can't afford to lose any more important citizens in our town. Just a warning though, we are watching you and all the people you have assigned to this investigation. The people that have committed these crimes are watching you as well. Please, be very careful, Mr. Kline.

Parker was jotting down notes, "Perry, the woman said, 'They are actively planning another murder', which could mean there is more than one Snow Villain. She said, 'They are watching you and the people you have assigned.' What does that mean? I thought we were being covert. Can you explain this?"

Perry replied, "Parker, I was hoping you could make sense of this. I sent Micah down to Key West to keep an eye on the ladies for us.

"He is not making contact as they would obviously know him. He has a team working down there already but I wanted his expertise there. Christie, I think made someone across the street with high-powered binoculars and a listening microphone, but I told her, I would check it out. Now that I think about it, that was more than likely, Micah's team. I will double-check that and make sure they stay covert. I just got a couple of scenarios worked out and was about to call you to run them by you." Perry then ran down the female with accomplice theory and let him know he was just finishing Linda, Margie, and Christie. Linda was a maybe and the other two were not. He had yet to put the other three into the possible scenario when he got on this call with Parker. He then told Parker, "I just got a call from Micah tonight confirming he was there in Key West. I ran the scenarios by him. He gave me the possibility of it being more than one. Maybe it was all the ladies that were on vacation. As I said, I discounted a couple but what are your thoughts on multiple ladies from that group?"

Parker said, "This case has more twists and turns than a Grisham novel. Let's chat again in the morning. I need to sleep on this and see if I can figure it out. Good night, Perry." "See you in the morning, Chief", said Perry as he hung up the phone. Perry called Paul Gorci. Paul answered, "Hey Perry. Don't you ever sleep?" "Sorry partner. There are developments you need to hear." Perry spent 20 minutes filling Paul in on Micah being now in Key West, his call to Key West Police for back up on surveillance for the ladies, his scenarios, and his conversations with Parker and Micah.

Paul said, "Okay, I am awake now partner! Now I have one for you. I got a call earlier from Melanie Barstow from the Ace of Clubs. She told me the guy she has been seeing got wasted drunk one-night, last week and spilled to her that he was in on the disposal of a couple of bodies for this 'out of town chick'. He would not name any names for her. She surmised that he was talking about the Galways and Victor. She was going to keep it to herself so her guy, Freddy Gilroy, would not have to go back to the slammer as he is out on parole as it is. The reason she called is that she has not heard from him since that week. She confirmed after I asked that it was last Thursday."

"Given your scenario possibilities," Paul continued, "he could have been working as an accomplice to our Snow Villain. When he or she was, done with him, he was killed. I was trying to put it all together to see if it made sense but now that I've heard your scenarios, it makes perfect sense."

Perry's response was, "So, we still need to identify our main suspect. We should do a couple of things. First, we will call Parker and keep him in the loop. Then we need to find Mr. Gilroy. Could you start on that one? Check with his parole officer. See if he has any hangouts that Melanie did not check. Who does he run with, etc. Then maybe I will call Micah back and see if he has any thoughts about this guy. It could be that we have a fourth murder, partner. Call me if you make any headway. If not, I'll see you in the morning."

Micah had just gotten back from dinner and was just looking in on the ladies. They were just getting into Kirt's jitney, so he was glad he didn't have that second drink. His phone rang. It was Perry. "Hello Perry, what's up? said Micah. Perry took a deep breath which Micah listened to him exhale slowly. Micah said, "That silent moan sounds serious Brother."

Perry began calmly, "Micah, Freddy Gilroy admitted to Mel he moved some bodies for some lady. He is now missing back in Buffalo. Melanie called Paul very upset. Paul related to me that she had told him, "Freddy has been missing from work, his apartment and his cell phone seems to be dead. I hope, he isn't.' Then she asked Paul, 'Can you help?' Paul said to her that he could. He then told me, 'I told her I would look for him.' Then he called me. We have an APB out on him and are looking for his car. Guess what kind he drives? Would you believe he drives a late-model white

Cadillac? Don't these people ever drive Chevrolets? Do you have any thoughts on his whereabouts?" Micah said, "Perry, that's a lot of information to digest. Let me think about it and maybe call some contacts back in town and I'll get back to you." They ended the call.

Dinner at Mangoes was divine. This was the consensus of the ladies at the table. Linda noticed as Chaz, their waiter, brought the bill, she saw Catie slip him a note which she assumed was her phone number. The ladies paid the bill, deciding to go for a nightcap to the Green Parrot. It was a block and a half, so they decided to walk, even in their heels. They went west on Angela then turned right and headed North almost to the end of the block. "As their website noted," said Joni, "the Green Parrot is a fun corner bar that's a must-stop on the walk to or from a visit to the Hemingway home. Lots of locals, as well as wandering tourists, drop in here. This eclectic bar has gone through several changes throughout its time but has remained a staple for great music and comradery in Key West. The walls are decorated with signs, memorabilia, and assorted junk, and most everything has an interesting story or history."

The ladies all laughed as they enter the Parrot because Joni read them something about every place they had been to since arriving. They referred to her as the Tour Guide. Christie told her when they stood at the bar, "Joni, we're kidding, of course, but we all really appreciate all the research you have done since you began planning this trip. Thank you." Joni hugged her, "Love you girl. Thanks. I needed that. I was starting to get a complex."

The ladies all ordered the Green Parrot which seemed to be a concoction of a lime juice mix and tequila with pineapple. It was a hit with all of them. They realized the place was loaded with a somewhat younger crowd but that didn't seem to matter. There were two groups of men around where they stood. The ladies were chatting to both. After about an hour, they decided to move back down to the Buffalo Café for a couple of drinks and see if the crowd was any more appealing. Christie called Kirt as it was quite a way away from the Parrot. He arrived in three minutes. Charmaine said to him, "Gee Kirt, you were fast. Are you following us?" Christie's ear perked up to listen to his response.

He simply said, "Well you guys were in luck. I was just leaving the Coco Plum Inn bar which is right next door." The ladies were loaded into the jitney and chatted about Catie's new beau.

They teased Catie all the way to Neal's place. At the Buffalo Café, Kirt came in for a nightcap. Neal was gone but the crowd was more mature and suited to their taste. The barmaid made room at the bar as she recognized them from their previous visit. They all had margaritas and the night continued until way after midnight. They had a grand time and met yet another couple from Buffalo. The Volsiers, Erik who was from Long Island, and Kris who was originally from Syracuse.

Paul Gorci walked into the Ace of Clubs. Melanie was surprisingly tending bar tonight. He sat down near the server section where she would largely be filling waitresses' drink orders. He ordered a Molson's Canadian. Melanie said, "Perfect timing Paul. I get off in five minutes and we can sit at a table and chat if you have time. Paul finished his beer and Melanie cashed him out but handed him another beer, "This one is on me. Thanks for coming so quickly", said Melanie. They sat at a small table up against the back wall.

Paul began, "I have some questions if I can start." Mel nodded her head while lighting a cigarette. Paul continued, "When was the last time you saw Freddy Gilroy?" Mel exhaled and said, "Like I mentioned on the phone, he was at my house on Wednesday night last week.

He was drinking when he got home. He had two shots of Jack Daniels and laid down in bed. When I woke up at 6:00 a.m. Thursday morning, he was already gone. I am usually not a heavy sleeper and if he stirred in the night or got out of bed, it would wake me. Then I would go back to sleep. I never heard him leave. I didn't hear from him on Thursday. On Friday, before I left for work at noon, I called him. There was no answer on his cell and his voice mail was full was what I heard. I called him at his apartment, no answer again. I called him at the bar he works part-time and they said he had not been in missing his shift on Thursday. I even called his mother; she has not seen him either since Wednesday."

Paul asked, "Melanie, I hate to ask but are you and he dating exclusively? Could he be laid up at another woman's place?" Melanie said, "Well, I never considered that, but it doesn't sound like him. I have not known him to stray before. He is too predictable. He especially doesn't miss work at Smitty's Tavern.

I am really upset and worried." Paul said, "Does he have a close friend that he hangs out with? Are there any places he frequently when he's not working? Mel said, "Paul I know this is official business, but I'd prefer if you called me Mel. He usually hangs out at the Ace of Clubs, Smitty's, or Jacobi's in Lackawanna. I called them all this morning; no one has seen him since early last week. He has friends but he is a loner by nature. He and I hang out when neither of us is working." Paul closed with, "Mel, is there anything else you can tell me? Maybe his car? We could have the patrols begin to look for it as well." Mel replied, "He drives a late model white Cadillac. It's a Fleetwood and it is a great-looking car but too big for me to drive. I just registered his plates two weeks ago. It is 15-BUH-745.

Paul returned to Headquarters after cordially ending his chat with Melanie. He parked out front as the plows had been through after he left so the two feet of snow they had since the weekend was cleared. He thought about Freddy Gilroy missing and the large deposit of snow, 'Could they find another victim of the Snow Villain or would it take until the next thaw. He went to Donna Smith's office and asked her to run the plate to see if it was stolen and who owned it. It came back belonging to Freddy Gilroy, but the plates were registered to Melanie Barstow. He was not surprised. Paul asked her if she'd sent an APB out for Freddy and the car to see what they'd get.

Paul and Perry had put a tail on Matt Fogelberg to see if they could catch him doing something and secondarily to keep him from being another victim. They had called Micah and asked if his son was available only to find out he was down in Key West with Micah. Micah gave him his old partner, Danny Hitchcock to call. Danny was available so Paul put him on the case of finding Freddy Gilroy.

Perry was sitting in his cubicle rewatching the videos that Micah had left with them from Johnny Galway's funeral. He was specifically looking at finding Freddy Gilroy to see if he was there and who he might have spoken with. It was well after noon and Perry had finished half of the double order of his Chicken wings from The Pearl Street Grill. He left the unfinished half on Paul's desk. Paul was out and about looking for Freddy Gilroy and would return soon.

Perry went back to viewing the videos. He noticed Christie was with Mel Barstow at the church. He noticed two other ladies in their party but didn't recognize them. He snapped a screenshot and saved it to ask Paul when he got back. He then saw Charmaine and Victor Sinclair walk in. Victor leading the way and stopping to talk to some very attractive woman. She had her back to the camera but looked like a model. Big wide brimmed hat and pencil skirt with red high heels.

A light bulb went off in his head. He had seen that hat before. He was sure it was Linda Carnello. She turned and gave Victor a quick hug and then he saw Charmaine behind Victor talking to some younger guy. He was tall, thin, and very well dressed. His purple shirt and tie ensemble stood out in the video. He wondered if that was Gilroy. Perry zoomed in on the video and noticed the two of them were holding hands.

Perry had to rewind it a bit then he took a screenshot and saved it to his computer. Paul walked in and thanked him for the lunch on his desk knowing it was from Perry. Perry showed Paul a picture. "Yep, that's Gilroy," said Paul, "oh and they seem very friendly, don't you think?" Perry agreed.

The barmaid at the Buffalo Café, Jodi Petrissi was an old friend of Catie Fuda's, both originally from Syracuse, New York. They screamed at each other when the ladies walked into the Buffalo Café. Christie thought, 'this Buffalo and Key West connection was getting too much for her to handle. Why were so many people here from Western New York? Christie asked Jodi when things settled down a bit, "Hey Jodi, how long have you been down here?" Jodi replied, "I started coming down here about five years ago.

I work mostly baseball season up north for the Bisons in their accounting office. I decided to come to the warmth. Someone said that there were a bunch of folks from home down here in Key West. It has been great. Working for Neal is great because he is up and down because of his political job but he lets me run the place because of all my experience.

Word of mouth travels fast so for me, when people ask where I've been from October to April, I tell them the Key West story. I imagine everyone else does the same."

It was getting late. All the ladies looked like it was time to hit the road. Linda said, "I wonder if Kirt is still here? We could use a ride back to the hotel." As if he was listening on a headset, in he walked from the restroom. They looked at him like he was a ghost. "What?" he said, "did I do something?" Charmaine said, "Linda just asked if you were still here and as if you were listening to our conversations, you magically appear." Kirt laughed, "I was in the dining room talking to Erik Volsier about some work he might have for me when we get back to Buffalo. Did you guys need a ride?" Margie perked up and said, "you even know what we were talking about?" Kirt laughed again, "No Ladies, you are getting a bit paranoid. You are all holding your purses and your drinks have been cleared. Just deductive reasoning."

Kirt dropped them off and said goodnight. Catie asked if anyone wanted to stop at the bar for a nightcap. No one seemed interested. She heard a lot of, 'Gee, I'm tired' & 'I need a shower' comments. She acquiesced and went to her room as well. Joni jumped into the shower, so Christie went out on the balcony. Next door, Charmaine was sitting on her balcony with her back to Christie and she was on the phone.

She was angry at the caller. She whispered then her voice now escalated to yelling. She screamed into the phone, Matthew, I know you spent time with Linda. I think you should stay away from her because she's got a new love. Go back to Buffalo."

Christie quietly went inside and closed the door. Joni was standing naked toweling off as she began to put on her sleepwear. She asked, "Was that Charmaine yelling at you?" Christie said, "No she was on the phone. I came in to give her some privacy."

Linda came out of her shower and saw Charmaine come in from the balcony and slammed the doors. "What's wrong, Babe? You look upset." Charmaine sighed, "Oh, it's nothing. I was just talking business with one of Victor's old partners who doesn't want to listen to my requests. I'm fine now, sexy." They kissed quickly as Charmaine left to go shower saying, "Don't go far, I'll be right back!"

While Margie was also showering, Catie got a call from Chaz Valdez. He asked her out, but she declined telling him she had a steady fella back home and they were faithful to each other. He apologized and hung up. Margie came out of the shower with her pajamas full of ducks. Catie said, "I love those, they look so comfortable."

Micah was listening to all the chatters as best he could. Charmaine's was the easiest because he could almost hear her without the listening device. She was screaming at Matt somebody, maybe Fogelberg. Was he here in Key West? Perry said Matt was remanded to stay in Buffalo.

Next morning, the ladies were having breakfast at the pool. It was more of a brunch as it was 11 am. Christie and Linda ran in the morning. Charmaine and Catie went to a fitness gym and did Pilates. Margie and Joni swam laps in the pool at 9 am. They regrouped at their favorite table and Juan took their order for a combination of breakfast and lunch. The food ranged from omelets to quesadillas. At noon, the ladies began with cocktails. Margaritas were made in pitchers and Juan brought three large pitchers to the table. Some swam, some were sunning, and some even did the hot tub.

Christie and Charmaine were in the hot tub. It was on the opposite side of the pool away from the table. Christie wondered if she should ask Charmaine about the phone call then said, "I was out on the balcony last night and overheard your telephone call. I went in as soon as you began yelling but not before I heard you tell some guy named Matt to go home. I was wondering if you were talking to Matt Fogelberg?" Charmaine kept a straight face to hide her emotions and embarrassment, "Yeah, your brother is the only Matt in the world, I guess."

Christie was now convinced it was her brother, "Let me ask, was he down here in Key West trying to see Linda? Charmaine said, "Why don't you ask your brother?" Christie got angry and her lawyer came out, "Listen Mrs. Sinclair, I am not trying to be difficult, however, if in fact it was my brother, as he did, in fact, spend time with Linda out in Kissing Bridge, I'd like to know why you were so angry at him for wanting to see her, number one. Number two, why are you avoiding the truth here?"

Charmaine thought a minute before she answered, "Christie, I am sorry. I guess I let my anger affect our relationship. It was your brother I was speaking to. Yes, he did say he was in Key West but didn't know where we were staying because he wasn't supposed to leave Buffalo according to the court. Frankly, I was jealous of him trying to rekindle the relationship with Linda because I, in fact, have developed a very strong feeling for her myself. Now if I could ask that you not broadcast this to the rest of the ladies as a personal favor to me, I would really appreciate it." Christie was, to say the least, flabbergasted. She was at a loss for how to respond. Finally, she said, "Charmaine, I will chastise my brother for leaving town after he was ordered not to by the court. Maybe I should just teach him a lesson and have the authorities pick him up at the airport. Do you happen to know if he went back to Buffalo or is he still here in Key West?" Charmaine said, "I don't know. I hung up before he could say any more to me."

Catie was talking to Linda as they walked back to the Hotel after their run. She said, "Linda, you weren't easy to keep up with, you with those long ass legs!" Linda just laughed, "Thank goodness I have them because your quickness gave you quite the advantage. Your body shows that you run and keep fit. I bet you look fabulous naked!" Catie blushed, "Thanks. I guess I've gotten no complaints from my male suitors." They were back at the hotel. Then both took off their sneakers and jumped into the pool.

Margie and Joni got splashed. Joni jumped out of the pool and returned to the table as Margie began a splashing war with Linda and Catie.

Christie said to Charmaine, "Maybe I won't say anything to Matt. He's a big boy. No worries, Charmaine. I need a drink." Christie left the hot tub and dove into the pool. She wanted to cool off and think. Catie seeing Joni alone at the table, climbed out and sat down guzzling her drink. She turned to Juan and said, "Por favor, Senor!" Then she turned to Joni and said in a low tone, "Can I talk to you?" Joni was surprised at her approach but curious said, "Sure, what's up?" Catie began, "How well do you know Kirt Leoz?" Joni said, "I've known him a long time. We used to date years ago and have remained friends. Why?" Catie asked, "How much do you know about his involvement in drug trafficking?"

She paused for effect and continued, "I was in line waiting for the ladies' room availability at the Buffalo Café last night and I overheard Kirt talking to Erik, Kim's husband. I don't even know their last name. Anyway, they were discussing the drugs coming into Key West from Cuba. Erik seemed to be in-charge of getting the drugs out of Cuba through a rendezvous with Cuban traffickers on boats halfway between the two countries. He would then bring them back here to Key West and Kirt would then store them with Jodi, the barmaid at Neal's place. I didn't clearly hear the person's name who brings them up north, but it sounded like Sonny Swordman and some other guys. Freddy whose last name I missed and Matt something, I didn't hear because two women came out of the restroom laughing so loud, Erik and Kirt stopped talking. I know I am dropping a whole lot on you, but I had to tell somebody.

I knew you were close to Kirt and a friend of Christie's. I came to you first to bounce it off someone." Joni looked shocked. This gave Catie a good feeling that she was not involved. She only said, "WOW!"

Tuesday night the ladies went to Louis' Backyard. It was nice and casual. The drinking was kept to a minimum. Kirt again arrived on cue and drove them to Sloppy Joe's to meet Neal. Neal and Jodi were there with several friends and folks who used to live in Buffalo. No one knew those in the group but all of them had an enjoyable evening. They called it an early night to go back for a night swim.

Tuesday late afternoon, Buffalo Police patrol found the automobile of Freddy Gilroy sitting in the parking lot of the Delaware Golf course. As they approach the vehicle, the officers notice a blood splattering pattern on the inside of the driver's window. There is nobody inside the vehicle but a distinguishable set of snowmobile tracks from the right of the vehicle circling around to the driver's side. A light snow hides any further traces of evidence, however, the snowmobile heads out toward middle of the golf course. The officers call for backup and instruct HQ to notify Detectives Kline and Clark of their findings. The lead officer, John Pacetti, stays with the Gilroy vehicle and his partner begins to track the snowmobile as the tracks are deep in the snow. Larry Rammunski is tracking the snowmobile through the ninth green around to the Buffalo Zoo parking lot.

After he walked a few minutes, Larry came to the parking lot at the end of the Park's property. He noticed the snowplow ends its route and pushed the snow into a pile. He sees some footprints off the snowmobile, five feet from the snow pile. He can't quite tell why the snowmobile stopped there. It seems someone may have unloaded something. Maybe something dragged through the snow to the snow pile. There are footprints returning to the vehicle. The snowmobile tracks head over the pile into the lot then tracks disappear.

Almost as if there were a carrier of some sort parked there. The carrier could then have exited Parkside Street and been gone from the park with no further trace. Larry radioed John as he walks back to the snow pile and at the foot of it, he sees something black at the bottom. "John, Larry here. It looks like the snowmobile drove to Zoo parking lot and unloaded something or someone at the snow pile the plow leaves after clearing the lot. It may have headed out of the park on a carrier or trailer because the tracks end there. Do you want me to walk back or wait until you can meet me at the back end of the Zoo lot or the Clubhouse for the course near Parkside?" "Larry, the Detectives, and a backup unit are here. They heard your message. We're all headed over to you at the Zoo. See you in a minute. Over."

As Larry waited at the snow pile in the Zoo parking lot, he again noticed something black at the edge of the pile. He walked over to it. He took out his nightstick and poked around at it. It was a boot heel. He went no further not wanting to disturb any possible evidence. He suspected it was the body of Freddy Gilroy beneath the snow. Perry and Paul pulled up on the exit road from the course with his partner John Pacetti right behind them. "Perry, I think there is a body under here", said Larry. It was Freddy. They had done this before. Call Forensics, Parker Clark, et al.

After the body was transported to the morgue, Ted Zak worked on the body of Mr. Gilroy and made his report to the department. Freddy Gilroy was shot in the back of the head with the same caliber gun as were Johnny & Frank Galway and Victor Sinclair. The bullets removed from the four gentlemen all matched. He had only been dead a few hours when the car was found.

As the police report indicated, he was shot while in the vehicle then placed onto a snowmobile and transported to the other side of the golf course. Ted said in his report that they missed seeing the shooting within the hour or two as the body was nowhere near Regi mortise. With all the snow this morning, the car quickly was covered and the patrol that noticed it saw a reflection from the side mirror when they turned around across the street. Whoever did this must have shoveled the snow as best they could to hide the body but missed the right boot heel.

Paul dropped Parker off at HQ and said he was going to tell Melanie of Freddy's demise. Parker said he would fill Perry in as well. Paul walked into the Ace of Clubs. Melanie was tending bar again. There was no one at the bar drinking. She was at the service bar making drinks for Marie the other waitress. He sat at the bar and waited. Mel came down and asked, "What'll it be Detective?" Melanie looked at his face and knew, "You found him. Is he dead?" Paul was trapped.

He wanted to tell her in private, but she seemed to already know. He started softly, "I'm sorry, Mel. Yes, we found him and yes, he's been killed."

Mel put her face in her hands and cried softly. She grabbed a tissue off the back of the bar and asked, "Where did you find him?" Paul sighed, "I am not at liberty to tell you because of the ongoing investigation. We called his sister to positively identify him. I thought it was better than you having to go down to the morgue. Mel regained her composure and said, "Thanks, Paul. This doesn't surprise me, but it makes me sad."

In Key West, Margie was done swimming and jumped into the hot tub. Linda was there and was about to go for more drinks, but Margie had brought a pitcher of margaritas when she walked over from the pool. Margie said, "Mind if I join you?" Linda responded,

"Not if you share your pitcher of that life-saving elixir!" They laughed, filled their glasses, and settled into the bubbling water. Margie began, "I know you and my late husband were an item for a while. I was curious to know what you found attractive in him." Linda was very open and said, "Johnny was a brilliant political mind but more than that I was fascinated by how he could connect with people. People from every walk of life. He was just a likeable guy. Underneath all that charm, however, was a man who was so insecure that he often became rude, discourteous, and sometimes violent. I am guessing this is no surprise to you and if it ended my relationship with him, it may have been the Achilles heel in all his ventures whether it was politics, business, or love. I'd be interested to know what split you guys apart."

Margie smiled, "My life with Johnny was interesting. I too saw that boyish charm and fell for it. He was magnetic in his appeal. That appeal was universal. He couldn't get enough attention, especially from the ladies. He seemed to have a thirst to satisfy as many as he could proving that he was not only attractive but a Don Juan with women. What tore us apart was that and his taking all the credit for his success. He was a public embodiment of Johnny Galway, but I was really the brains behind the political juggernaut that was Johnny Galway's power and influence. He never would give me any credit or appreciation. He also began trying to squeeze me out of my own wealth by making deals behind my back. Deals both in business, politics and unfortunately in love."

Perry walked into the Ace of Clubs to give his personal condolences to Melanie Barstow. She and Freddy Gilroy were together off and on for many years and he knew how she stood by him and wanted to offer any help he could to her. Melanie hugged him when he came to the end of the bar. Paul was still sitting on the last barstool near the service bar. Perry said, "Mel, I am so sorry it ended this way. I've heard from a dozen people already that he was a great guy and always treated you well. If there is anything I can do, please let me know." "Thank you, Perry. You and Paul coming in personally to share the news means a lot. I just wish I knew who he was working for because I think we'd know who the murderer was." As Perry sat down next to Paul, Mel handed him a Grey Goose and soda. She leaned over and said in a soft whisper, "You know he helped the killer remove the bodies because he needed the money. We were going to get married and what he earned would have helped but I really did think he wanted to get out of the racket."

The week was flying by. On Wednesday, Joni talked to Christie as they got ready for dinner. They were going out on a dinner cruise called the Party Cat. Joni said, "Christie, what do you think of all the Buffalo citizens down here in Key West? I wanted to get away from Buffalo and it feels like either folks are following us, or we coincidently landed in the Buffalo retirement village." Christie laughed, "You know, Joni, I wondered if you knew all of this going in, as you planned the trip for us."

I have talked to Perry because I saw someone with large binoculars and a listening microphone across the street when we got here. I thought I was being paranoid, then I found out, Neal Seagle has a bar here, your friend, Kirt Leoz has retired here, even Kenny Thomason is a cop in town here. Then we find out Catie's friend, Jodi is a barmaid/manager, at Neal's place. The night we were there, I saw Kirt talking to Erik Volsier who is rumored to be involved in some drug trafficking. Do you find this at all strange? Joni looked at Christie and said, "It all makes me nervous. You are so high profile that since you uncovered Galway's body, your cases have almost all blown up and you were even almost run over at the marina. I am looking over my shoulder all the time. I spoke to Kirt.

He said he was asked by the owner of the Santa Maria Suites to look after us. That's why he has been chauffeuring us around." "Who owns the Hotel.?

Why are they so concerned about us?" said Christie. Joni replied, "I asked but he said the person wants to remain anonymous." Christie said, "Let me check into that. I may be able to call my friend in real estate, Jon Hartley to see if he can find out."

The Party Cat Cruise was a real hit with the ladies. It was a fun group of about eighty people. They arrived at 5:55 pm and were whisked on the vessel by two cute sailors who the ladies flirted with shamelessly. Having had a drink, or two, at the Santa Maria Bar before Kirt drove them here might have caused their late arrival. The night was perfect for a cruise as the winds were calm and the temperature was 78 degrees. They settled in at their assigned table ordering drinks from one of the sailors who escorted them onto the yacht. Soon, they heard music coming from the upstairs level and Linda and Joni decided to check it out.

Linda noticed immediately that the drummer was the guy that almost knocked her over at the hotel. He nodded to her as he noticed they were watching. The band was playing some old standards by Frank Sinatra, but they looked nothing like the old crooner from Hoboken. The drummer, Mark, was dressed in a black, short sleeve tee-shirt that showed his full sleeves of tattoos on each arm. Linda was very attracted to this young man.

Joni texted Christie and told her the band was really rocking. The girls all appeared in three minutes. Jody Vandal was the lead singer and he and Mark Edwards did most of the vocals and as Margie said, "They sang like angels!" Sinatra was one of her favorite singers, so she was swooning during each old standard they played. After 45 minutes, they took a short fifteen-minute break. Mark went to the bar and was approached by Linda, "Hi Stranger, bump into anyone lately? Mark laughed as she hugged him around the waist, "Miss Linda, if I could bump into you every day, it would certainly be a real pleasure." Linda finished her drink and said, "I would like to show you some real pleasure later if you're available." Mark said, "I have to load up my stuff and get paid then I am yours to play with as you see fit." Linda said, "Do you have your own room at the hotel because I have a roommate.?" Mark replied, "I will meet you at the hotel."

Linda was pleased. He continued, "then we can have a drink and discuss where to take it from there." Linda said, "That will be great. I will see you later then."

As the ladies left the ship, they talked about where to go after as it was only 8:30 pm. They decided to go to Neal's for a drink then decide where else to go from there. Linda had already talked to Charmaine about bringing the drummer back to the hotel, "Would you like to join us for a threesome? It might be fun, and I am sure Mark will enjoy us." Charmaine declined the invite but said she wasn't into that. Christie was on the phone with Jon Hartley after the ride. She asked if he knew who owned this hotel. He said, "Parker Clark. A cop from up north. Do you know him?" Christie couldn't catch her breath.

Melanie Barstow was at Freddy Gilroy's apartment. He had told her long ago that if anything happened to him, there would be money hidden. He said a notebook of all his relationships in business dealings would be in his safe so that someone would know who the last person was he had done business with, and that person would be the first to look at as a potential suspect in his demise. Mel sat and cried for the first half hour she was in the apartment. She took out her wallet. In the change section was the combination to the large safe in his bedroom. It had been built into the wall and was 5 feet high by 2.5 feet deep and 30.5 inches wide. As she opened the door, she got very nervous.

She saw the guns. There were two long rifles he had used for hunting. There were also two Glocks that were in shoulder holsters. He must have had one with him because she was sure he had three pistols. She found an envelope with Mel on it. She opened it and found $32,000 in large bills. She almost fainted. Beside the envelope was a notebook wrapped in a large elastic band. She had a tough time taking off the strap but once completed, she was able to open the book. She looked at the last page. The heading said…She was startled by keys jiggling as someone began opening the outside door. She closed the book and threw it and the money in her purse. She walked back into the kitchen with a suit and shirt she had laid out to take to the funeral home. Into the house walked his sister Rosa. She screamed and so did Mel. They looked at each other, then they hugged. They both cried for a minute or two and once calmed, Mel said, "You scared the living daylights out of me, but I am glad it's just you."

Rosa said, "You were scared? I almost wet my pants! I was coming to grab some of his clothes. I see you beat me to it." Mel said, "I will just get his shoes and leave to take them to the funeral home." Rosa said, "Whatever you want, you can have if there is anything that is sentimental. You know, he bought the apartment building here and gets rent from the other three apartments. I was managing it, but it is a full-time job so if you want to move in here, it would be rent-free. You could help with managing because you'd be right here. I'll understand if you can't." Mel was initially sad but realized she needed a change like this. It would keep her close to Freddy's memory and the free rent would be a lifesaver. She told Rosa, "I would love to move here and help you manage things. It will really help. Thank you."

The ladies were ready for their last night in Key West. They decided to have a nice dinner at one of the best restaurants in town. They had reservations at Bagatelle's on Duval Street. Steak and seafood filled the orders and plenty of margaritas. The ladies all got very comfortable with the Tequila drink. They ordered Don Julio Blanco and two of the ladies, Charmaine and Linda would always drink it straight with limes and salt.

Dinner was delicious and it seemed like there were five or six waiters attending to the table. The ladies were impressed. The Maitre d' hotel checked on them at least five times himself. He was a tall thin older gentleman looking very similar to Victor Sinclair. As you might imagine, Charmaine was quite taken with him and flirted unabashedly throughout the meal. Margie seemed to have her eye on the lead waiter Cisco who was late thirties with blonde hair and a handlebar mustache. Christie tried to enjoy herself but kept thinking about all the murders and her brother Matt's hearings. She felt very strongly that he was innocent but his uncontrolled mouth and flippant utterances to the wrong people could lead to his demise.

PART FOUR

The ladies from Buffalo hit several bars on Duval for some drinking and dancing. After Sloppy Joe's, the last stop was Margaritaville. They met several groups of guys that varied in age but none of them clicked with the ladies. Christie called Kirt at 11 p.m. for a ride back to the hotel and he arrived in two minutes. He had been across the street below Micah's new location in his car waiting for this call. They were very tipsy and need help getting into the jitney. Kirt, ever the gentleman, assisted valiantly. Their plan was to sleep in, get some morning sun and a swim then head for their 2 pm flight back to Buffalo, New York. The temperature in Buffalo was 34 degrees and had been snowing all week. At 2:05 pm, their Southwest flight began the return. So long, Buffalo-South.

The ladies had a great time relaxing and being away from the weather and madness that currently existed in Buffalo. They were back. It was Monday morning. Back to the grind for most. Linda flew off to Paris for a few days of photo shoots. Catie was busy running her company WIFI (World Insurance Fraud Investigation) as well as getting ready to open her new restaurant "Magdalene's" which was located on the newly renovated West Chippewa Street near Delaware. Margie Galway began the process of selling her home and moving into the new high-rise condos at Canalside on Prime Street and Hanover on the water. Joni Wilsco returned to her new bank position as Chief Loan Officer. Charmaine Sinclair went back to her house on Depew Street and began the installation of Solarium with an outdoor inground heated pool behind her back patio. It also had plans for a walkway from the main house which doubled as a greenhouse so she could garden all year long. Christie was the busiest of the group as she opened two new cases and the first thing on her agenda Monday morning was to visit Parker Clark at his office in Police HQ. She arrived unannounced at 9:30 a.m. She walked up the stairs to the second floor and went to the desk of his admin assistant, Kat Allura and said, "My name is Christie

Mahern and I'd like to speak to Chief of Detectives, Parker Clark, please." Kat said, "He's on the phone right now. Have a seat and I'll just slip into his office and let him know you're here."

Christie waited all of three minutes after Kat returned to her seat at the desk. Parker opened his office door and boomed, "Well Ms. Mahern, to what do I owe the honor of this early morning visit and this your first day back from vacation?" Christie rose and walked past him in silence avoiding his outstretched handshake offer. She sat in the large leather chair in front of his desk. She noticed he left the door opened as he returned to his chair. Christie said, "Close your door Parker, you don't want anyone to overhear what I have to say to you, and it might get loud in here!" Parker quickly rose and walked back over to the door saying, "I generally leave the door open when I have a woman alone in here so there is no question of any impropriety. It has always been a good rule to follow."

Paul Gorci walked into the cubicle saying to Perry, "Did you see Christie just walk into Parker's office?" Perry looked up from his computer and said, "What?" Paul said, "I just saw Christie Mahern walk into Parker's office and he closed the door. He never closes the door when there is a woman in alone with him!"

Christie watched Parker take his seat again. He was about to say something to her, but she began first, "Parker, I am here today to get several things off my chest. First, while in Florida, I stayed at the Santa Maria Suites in Key West. I and the group I was with were provided daily transportation everywhere we wanted to go free of charge. This was provided by the owner of the hotel. After a little searching, I find that you, Parker Clark, are that owner. I would like to know, why the free jitney? Second, and you can answer when I am finished so take notes, after further investigation, I was interested in finding out what other business interests you had that may or may not be in conflict of interest to your current employment in the city's police department.

I learned that you also are the principal owner of the Hyatt Hotel down on the waterfront. That would surely afford you the opportunity to have knowledge of all that happens in those accommodations. Third, I was able to speak to several employees of yours in these private businesses that confirmed your leadership in some illegal drug trafficking out of Cuba." She watched Parker's face begin to perspire as she continued. "And finally, Mr. Clark, when I put my list of potential suspects together in my head the night you drove me home, I kept them all to myself because you were on the list. You had dated all of us ladies who were on that list. You always seem to know everything about people.

It also would not surprise me if you had people listening to all of our conversations while the group of us vacationed at your hotel. I say this because I observed on two different occasions at two different locations people were watching us with high-powered binoculars and listening to us with long range audio listening devices. Now, Mr. Clark, as you are the Chief of Detectives here in Buffalo, I would not presume to have any jurisdiction over your dealings on or off the force, but just so you know that I have made a copy of this speech in case anything happens to me.

Parker began to speak but Christie interrupted him, "Parker I have three minutes, what do you have to say?" Parker sighed, "Christie, you gave quite a speech. Some of it true …some of it not. I will just say, I have no illegal dealings and I am appalled that you have made these allegations, but you are certainly entitled to your opinions. Now if you'll excuse me, I have an important meeting to attend." With that, they both rose, she turned on her heel and walked out saying, "Have a wonderful day, Mr. Clark." "Take care." was his retort.

She was on her way downstairs. As she got to Perry's cubicle, he looked up and she said, "Take me for coffee some place I'm not being bugged." She turned and walked to the stairs. Perry grabbed his coat and followed close behind. They got outside and he offered his cruiser as he opened the door. She declined and said, "Let's walk." He followed her and waited to hear what she had to say. They walked east on Church across Franklin to Pearl Street and into the Main Place Mall. There was a coffee shop on the first floor. Christie said, "Make mine black please." Perry ordered two black coffees. He returned to the table, where Christie sat. He said nothing. She took a sip of the coffee, sighed deeply, and sighed again. Then she spoke, "I just spent ten minutes with Parker Clark." She sighed again. "Perry, I think he could be the murderer!" Perry was speechless. He was silent as he felt there was more coming. Christie continued, "There were people watching us down in Key West. I think, I saw Micah for sure at one location across the street from our hotel and then a different person uptown on Duval Street. We had free transportation the whole time provided by the hotel's owner. That owner my friend is Parker Clark.

The last thing I told him was that on the night I unearthed Johnny Galway, he drove me home and knew when to turn into my driveway. How many times did you come to my house before you could remember where the driveway was?" Perry thought to himself, thirty. "When he drove me home that night" she continued, "he asked if I had a list of suspects because I said I have some obvious ideas of who could have wanted him dead. I declined to answer that night but today I told him that he was on that list.

Linda was getting off the plane in Paris and a car was picking her up. The driver had a sign held up that said 'Linda C.' on it. The driver was none other than Matt Fogelberg. Linda screeched when she noticed him, "What in God's name are you doing out of the country?" Matt smiled as he grabbed her bag, "If your girlfriend won't let me see you in America, I thought what better idea than to come to France to see you. I paid the guy five hundred dollars to borrow his sign, hat and I almost talked him into the limousine, but he said it was $50 K for that. Hi, Linda, how are you beautiful?"

Catie Fuda got a phone call at 10 a.m. while sitting in the kitchen of her new restaurant planning menus and making a shopping list. She said, "Hello." It was Micah who said, "Welcome back to the 'big B' doll. How was your trip?" Catie said, "It was very relaxing. If anyone would know you would." Micah knew immediately that he'd been made in Key West but continued with, "How about a late dinner tonight?" Catie said, "I am very busy with the restaurant. I could do it tomorrow around six. Does that work for you?" Micah was relieved that she would see him. She may even be open to listening to his reasons for being there, "That's great. I will pick you up at your condo at 6:00 p.m. sharp. I've gotta go. I'll leave you to it. Bye Lover." He hung up.

Joni liked her new office on the 37th floor. She had a double office which had windows on three sides. Her desk was on the south wall so she could look straight up Main Street on the opposite windowed wall facing north. The wall to the right, faced east and overlooked Erie County as far as you could see but also had a bird's eye view of the Bison's ballpark below. She had three secretaries in her office. She had a grouping of eight stuffed leather chairs facing her desk. Her credenza behind her as she spun her chair overlooked Lake Erie to the South. On the north wall, she had a bank of small file cabinets for her personal files and also a grouping of five couches. On the west wall was a large screen TV that she could turn remotely and see from her desk. On the wall facing east was a conference table that sat 22 people or her entire staff. As she began her Monday morning meeting, she got a text from Christie 'Call me ASAP'.

Perry's jaw felt like someone punched him and seemed to be lying on the table next to his coffee after Christie told him about her conversation with Parker Clark. He finally said, "You planned all this and didn't call to tell me last night? I didn't call you because you were flying yesterday and would be preparing briefs so if you had time, you would have called me. Jeepers Lady, a guy needs a little warning when you drop a bomb off in his lap like this." Christie looked at him for his reaction and was satisfied he was as surprised as he was.

Perry continued, "Well, I have some news for you as well. Micah was down in Key West keeping an eye on you and we think there were two other groups keeping surveillance on the group. Micah overheard some conversations that lead us to believe that either Linda or Charmaine is the murderer or maybe both are involved." Now it was Christie's turn to be shocked. She said, "I thought they looked very chummy down there and Linda told me while we were alone one day that she and Charmaine had a thing. What are we gonna do?"

Perry laughed, "You, young lady, are NOT going to do anything but keep your sweet behind safe and in the future, if you are going to berate my boss and make any allegations about his being a murderer, PLEASE give me a heads up."

Christie said, "Well, I will watch my back but what do you think YOU are going to do Detective? And by the way, can I get a ride back to my office?"

Perry said, "I am going to think about this some more then put a plan in place. I have some ideas but, in the meantime, keeping you safe is a priority as well. Let's walk back to HQ and I'll drive you."

Christie stopped him. Do me a favor. "Can you run back and get the car?" I'll wait here.

I don't want Parker to see us together. Keep in mind, he'll probably put together that we've talked, I just don't want him to see us together today." Perry said, "I'll be right back. Stay by this door. Inside."

Off he ran. Christie thought I don't know if I've ever seen him run. He was back in the car in two minutes. They drove to her office. They kissed then she ran in.

Wednesday morning, Parker sat at his desk and began opening his mail. He noticed one that was addressed to him that said, 'Personal & Confidential' He carefully opened this one as it looked very official. It read:

> *Hello, this is the Buffalo Police Department. You have been our lead suspect since we found Johnny. We have watched you since then but obviously not close enough as you have three additional victims. We now have you on 24-hour watch and audio surveillance as we have placed listening devices in your residence, car, and office. We will be in touch with you by Friday at noon. If you come into the Police Headquarters prior to that with your attorney and confess, you will be in a much better place for plea bargaining. You will, however, be charged with these crimes as the evidence makes the case a lock. Check-in at the front desk.*

Parker read it again. He wondered who sent this. Was it Perry or Paul or was this a hoax? He thought they had taken him off the suspect list when they met at Chef's Restaurant weeks ago. He thought, I better show this to Perry.

Christie got to the office early on Wednesday. She had not heard from Parker Clark at all which was a relief, but she wondered. Wendy came in a half hour early and brought the mail up from downstairs. Wendy yelled into Christie, "Morning. I picked up the mail. Did you make coffee yet? Christie replied, "Hi Wendy, No I did not make any yet, I was just finishing my Starbucks. I'll make a pot now." Wendy replied, "OK if you want to, I'll sort through the mail." Minutes later, Christie came to Wendy's desk.

She gave her a steaming cup of coffee for her. "Thanks, Boss, here is your mail." Christie said, "Not a problem, I wanted another cup as well." She grabbed her mail and went into her office. She looked through it and saw bills, letters from three potential clients with standard information that she had requested. Then she saw a letter marked 'Personal & Confidential'. She began by opening that one.

It read:

> Hello, this is the Buffalo Police Department. You have been our lead suspect since we found Johnny. We have watched you since then but obviously not close enough as you have three additional victims. We now have you on 24-hour watch and audio surveillance as we have placed listening devices in your residence, car, and office. We will be in touch with you by Friday at noon. If you come into the Police Headquarters prior to that with your attorney and confess, you will be in a much better place for plea bargaining. You will, however, be charged with these crimes as the evidence makes the case a lock. Check-in at the front desk.

Christie was floored. She thought and could still hear Perry not answering her when she asked him if she was being considered a suspect. Was this on the level? Was she, their suspect? Is that why she saw people watching and listening to her in Key West? She had to think about how to respond.

Charmaine had just gotten back from the gym on Wednesday. As she pulled into the circle drive, the mailman was just walking away from her front door. She waved to him. She thought I think his name is Charlie but wasn't sure enough to call out to him. She parked the car, grabbed her gym bag, and went into the house after picking up the mail. She set down her bag in the kitchen, got a cup of coffee that she had on a timer. She sat at the kitchen table and blew on her coffee as it was steaming hot. She looked at the pile of mail. Right on top was a letter that was addressed 'Personal and Confidential'. She sliced it open with her fancy letter opener.

It read:

> *Hello, this is the Buffalo Police Department. You have been our lead suspect since we found Johnny. We have watched you since then but obviously not close enough as you have three additional victims…. It continued the same as the others.*

Charmaine was angry. Was Parker trying to be funny? Was this a real letter? Was this someone else's idea of a joke? She wondered who she should call first.

Joni loved going into her new 37th floor office early each morning to watch the sun come up. She would work out in her home gym rather early, shower, have coffee then head to the office. She arrived in time to make coffee, pour herself a cup, and watched the sun rise in the eastern sky above Buffalo, New York. It was exhilarating every time. It was almost a religious experience. Then minutes later as she poured herself another cup of coffee, three being her limit, her lead secretary, Sassy Lincoln, knocked on her door and brought in the mail. She had sorted it already into business and personal. Joni opened the letter she saw marked, 'Personal & Confidential. It read:

Hello, this is the Buffalo Police Department. You have been our lead suspect since we found Johnny. We have watched you since then but obviously not close enough as you have three additional victims...

It ended just like the others. What was this, she thought, a prank? Then she wondered if it was a real letter. Who could possibly think I would...NO, she thought? I better call someone...but whom? Do I call the police? Maybe I should call Christie.

Catie Fuda was working at home today. She was sending off an email to her customers and potential customers about a NEW YEAR's sale opportunity. It was a one-day preliminary look at a potential fraud situation in their company(s). It would give them a solid footing for a possible investigation. Catie's current companies received emails. She had a bag full of hard copies for new companies. Her mailman, Andrew, started his route on her block as it was furthest from the post office. As a result, she got her mail early.

She left the bag for outgoing mail for him. She heard him out front so, she went to get her mail if any, there were three. Two bills and a letter marked 'Personal & Confidential, she opened it first.

It read:

Hello, this is the Buffalo Police Department. You have been our lead suspect since we found Johnny.... another of these letters.

Catie was furious. After all, she had seen and heard down in Key West, she was getting this from the police. It was an outrage. She then thought, are they serious? Who do I call? Should I just show up? It doesn't even say who to see about this. Maybe I should call a lawyer. Maybe I should call Christie. No, I will just pop into the Police Headquarters and look up Christie's boyfriend Perry.

Linda had landed Thursday morning in Buffalo back from her trip to Paris. She planned to close her condo in town and then fly out to Las Vegas. She picked up her car from long term parking at the airport and drove home. She went to the mail office down on the first floor of the building to pick up her mail. There was a stack all tied together neatly. She got into her condo at 10:30 in the morning. She thought it is too early for a drink, so she made a cup of tea in the microwave. She went and changed into sweats then returned to the kitchen, made the tea, and sat at the table to go through all the stack of mail. There was a lot of junk mail with advertisements, post card from Charmaine reminding Linda of the dinner party at her place on Saturday night, some bills, two checks from her agent, which she opened and got ready to take to the bank then there was this letter marked 'Personal and Confidential'.

It read:

> *Hello, this is the Buffalo Police Department. You have been our lead suspect since we found Johnny. We have watched you since then but obviously not close enough as you have three additional victims* …. The letter ended just like all the others.

Linda couldn't believe her eyes. This was great! She would use this in her article for the magazine. It was a joke of course. Or was it real? She thought, maybe I should call ... Christie? Parker? Charmaine? Micah? Who?

Margie had been busy since returning from Florida. Doing her volunteer work and getting back into her gym routine. Her mornings were the busiest. When she got home every day around one p.m., she would make herself a salad or something else light and open the mail, pay bills, etc. This day was unusual. There was one letter in the box. It was marked, Personal & Confidential. It read:

Hello, this is the Buffalo Police Department. You have been our lead suspect since we found Johnny. We have watched you since then but obviously not close enough as you have three additional victims. We now have you on 24-hour watch and audio surveillance ... ending just like the others. Margie just couldn't believe what she was reading. She went through five or six emotions. The last being anger. She'd see about this.

No one called or visited the Police Department by Wednesday. He was beginning to wonder if he made an error in judgment of the killer.

Christie hadn't done anything about the letter yet. She wondered if Perry had sent it. Maybe Parker sent it. Is this just a joke? When I get home, I will see if Perry can come over and I'll talk to him about it then.

She grabbed her briefcase and coat, locked up the office, and headed down the elevator to her car on the garage level one. She walked across the garage toward her car with her keys in hand. As she got to her car, she switched her briefcase into her other hand and as she dropped her keys, she heard two loud bangs as she bent over. It was right behind her. She crouched and turned toward the noise. She saw a person dressed in all black with a full black ski hat running toward the garage's outside door.

She was about to give chase but realized her head hurt and she looked down as she felt something trickling down her neck. It was blood. She called 911. "My name is Christie Mahern, I've just been shot. I am in the parking garage west first level of the new Chase bank building at West Mohawk and Delaware. The operator was saying something she couldn't follow them as she sat down being a bit dizzy. The next thing she felt was being shaken and a person calling her name. She opened her eyes and there in front of her was Perry Kline crouched on one knee. Behind him were several Paramedics and she looked down and saw more blood that she'd ever seen before. She passed out again. Christie was placed on a stretcher, placed in the ambulance a rushed to Buffalo General Hospital on High Street.

Matt Fogelberg returned to Buffalo Airport on Wednesday from Paris. He wondered if he could sneak into town unnoticed. He had a large winter hat on and dark glasses. He grabbed his carry-on and went swiftly down the corridor to the parking garage. He hailed a cab and gave the address. He said, "443 Delaware Avenue in downtown Buffalo." As they drove, he checked his email on his phone. Upon arriving, he paid the Fare and took his suitcase to the adjacent parking lot and placed it into the trunk of his car he had left there. He then went upstairs to his office.

Perry was at the hospital almost faster than the ambulance. He was sick to his stomach and wondered why he hadn't put her in protective custody when she returned from Florida. He was really kicking himself even knowing she would have refused it. He knew Dr. Christopher Grace in the ER Department and just happened to see him as Christie was being wheeled in. She was awake and laughing albeit nervously with the two Paramedics rolling her in. Perry said, "Hey Dr. Grace, my friend is just rolling in with a gunshot wound, take your usual good care of her will ya?" Dr. Grace turned and headed to the ER treatment room yelling, "We'll see what we can do Perry. Sit tight."

Perry went over to the waiting room. He took out his cell and called Paul Gorci, "Hey, Partner. I am at the hospital. Christie's been shot. We're waiting to hear how she is." Paul grimaced and said, "Hope she's ok, buddy. Where was she hit?" It was Perry who now grimaced, "In the head. I am hoping it wasn't serious because she was able to call 911 before she passed out. There was a lot of blood when I got there." Paul said, "How did you get there so fast? Perry said, "I didn't shoot her if that's what you're thinking. I was walking past the 911 room and heard the call come in, White female, in the Chase Bank building parking garage', I didn't even miss a beat, I was in my car and to her and beat the ambulance buy two minutes. She was lucid for a minute when I shook her and called her name. Then when she was talking to the Paramedics and saw the blood, she passed out. I am at Buffalo General."

Paul said, "Ok Calm down a minute. Take a deep breath and don't anticipate the worst. Hopefully, she'll be okay. When she's done in ER and you can talk with her, you'll be able to learn more about what happened. Is there anything you want me to do? Perry thought a minute. He did take a deep breath as he realized his hands were clenched, "Paul, thanks, we don't really know anything yet. That's why I sent Micah to Florida to keep an eye on her. I should have continued the coverage and trusted my instincts. I feel like crap now." Paul said, "I'm on my way to keep you company. Sit tight."

Perry wondered if this was a planned attack or was it planned after the letters were sent to all the suspects. He tried to remember who was running with Christie all the time. He thought it was Joni. Naw, they're best friends. Could it have been Linda? Maybe. Then he thought about Parker. Where the hell was Parker this morning? Maybe I will just give the Chief of Detectives a call.

Micah Blair was back in Buffalo and busier than ever. He was helping the police with the case of the century, but he had bookings scheduled that he needed to satisfy. He was waiting for the arrival of the wedding party at the Statler Hotel on Delaware Avenue. It has a large overhang entrance, so he was standing atop the small roof balcony closer to West Mohawk and Delaware and was using this large zoom lens Nikon -S Nikkor 70-200mm atop a Nikon V1.

He was just telling the security guy that let him out on the roof that he used this long-range lens because it only weighed three pounds but had great quality and the reach was perfect for most of what he did. He stood alone waiting for the bridal party. He had a perfect angle to capture them getting out of the limousine.

Suddenly, he heard what sounded like two loud, gunshots. He jumped and almost lost his balance. It seemed to come from across the street at the bank. He turned and looked through his camera and saw a person running out of the garage dressed in all black. Black pants and nylon jacket and a large black ski mask over their head as they ran up W. Mohawk toward Delaware. He took several pictures. They made a right turn onto Delaware and headed straight for the Statler Hotel. Micah stood atop that balcony and clicked picture after picture hoping to get a good look at them. Just as this person got close to the overhand at the entrance to the Statler below him, they took off the ski mask and he got three quick pictures of their blonde hair. Then the assailant was inside the hotel.

He was stunned. He got out his phone and called the Statler. The operator at the main desk answered and Micah said, "Listen very carefully. Grab your phone if you have one on you and take pictures of the blonde who just walked in from Delaware dressed in all black.

They may have just robbed the bank." He hung up as the wedding party just pulled up to the Hotel. He quickly made sure he had enough film and began to take his scheduled wedding pictures. He realized he was shaking not knowing whether it was from the cool wind blowing in his face up on the second floor or his excitement.

Micah had all the shots he needed for the wedding entrance. He was on his way down to the desk to talk to the clerk. When he got to the desk, he saw a man working. Micah asked him, "Excuse me. Was there someone else working the desk 20-25 minutes ago?" The young man behind the counter with a name tag that said Eric said, "Yes sir, that young lady has gone home for the evening. Can I help you with something?"

Micah was frantic but calmed his voice, "Yes, can you tell me her name?" Eric Slay, the clerk said, "I can only give you her first name, it's Sara." Micah asked, "When does she work again? I asked her for a favor. I need to ask her if she did it." The clerk said, "She works again on Monday at 9 a.m. but if you tell me what it was, maybe I can help." Micah said, "No that's okay. I will check with her Monday, thanks." He went up to the second-floor ballroom and continued taking pictures at the wedding.

Perry was pacing in the waiting room when Paul walked into Buffalo General Hospital. Paul handed him a cup of coffee. Perry said, Thanks, Pal. I appreciate you coming and the cup of Joe." Paul asked, Any word yet?" Perry shook his head no. As he went to sit down, he heard his name. "Kline?" It was Dr. Grace who began walking to a side room. He opened the door and motioned for Perry to join him. Perry came over and Dr. Grace shut the door. He turned to Perry and said, "She'll be fine in a couple of days. She lost some blood and she's anemic anyway, so she passed out a couple of times before she got here. The bullet only grazed her thank goodness, but it was deep enough to cause some major bleeding.

She took about fifteen stitches. She lost a little hair, but the nurses hooked her up and made sure she could cover the scar with her hair. She asked to see you if you were here. Don't stay more than five minutes. We gave her a pint of blood and something to calm her. Let her get some rest. We'll admit her.

You might want to have a female officer sit with here 'til morning. Come on, I take you to her." "Thank you so much, Chris. I appreciate all you do." As they walked out of the room, he said to Paul, "Call HQ and get a female officer for her. I want round-the-clock protection for her as the person that shot her may find out where she is, and I don't want to give them another opportunity to complete their assignment. She'll recover and be okay but is staying tonight. Be right back."

Christie was sitting up in bed and was as Dr. Chris said, a little whoozy. Perry was just glad she was alive. She said, "Well Mr. Kline, where were you when I needed you?" He laughed. It was a relief to hear her joking around. He replied, "Well, Miss Mahern, had you been working in your office instead of trying to sneak out before 8 p.m., we wouldn't be in this predicament." Christie smiled. The nurse gave Christie another pill and motioned for Perry to leave. Perry said to Christie, "Did you see who it was?" Christie closed her eyes and said, "Nothing. I got nothing. They had a full black ski mask and all black clothing. Even their sneakers were black. The Dr. said I would be able to go home tomorrow. Would it be too much of an inconvenience if I stayed at your place?" "Not at all, Doll. Just text me when they are kicking you out of here tomorrow and I will come and get you. I am gonna leave and let you get some rest. See you tomorrow. Love you." He leaned over and kissed her sweetly on the lips. The first 'L' word!!

Micah was back in his studio looking at the pictures of the person running. He had taken 40 photos. None of them would be useful for identifying the suspect. He was going to call Perry and tell him what he saw but he thought he would just get his hopes up. The girl at the Statler desk may not have gotten any pictures of the bank robber at all.

As Matt Fogelburg exited the cab at his office, he walked to his car. He took his suitcase and placed it in the trunk of his car that he left in his parking place adjacent to the building. He walked into the office at 12:35 p.m. His secretary, Dana Collage, got a very surprised look on her face, "Matt, the police were here twice looking for you last week. I didn't know what to tell them and they were giving me a third degree. They thought I was hiding something.

I am glad you're back, I just made coffee. I'll bring you a cup. There is a ton of mail on your desk. When you are ready, we can go over your meeting schedule for the week."

Matt sat at his desk and said to Dana, "Sorry I left you out on a limb last week. I really needed to get away and still be close and alone and I stayed at my friend, Sarah Krawley's place over on Jewett Parkway near Delaware Park. She is in New York City shooting for Playboy, so I had the place to myself. Let me go through my mail and we'll sit and catch up."

Matt drank the coffee that Dana brought to him and sorted through his mail. He came upon one marked, 'Personal & Confidential'. He was not surprised by the letter he found. It read:

'Hello, this is the Buffalo Police Department. You have been our lead suspect since we found Johnny'.... it was the same letter the others received but each of them thought it was only them receiving it.

He thought to himself, I better call Christie and let her know about this. He dialed her office. The answering machine picked up in the office saying, "You've reached Mahern, Miller, and

Associates, we are temporarily closed but should open again on Monday. Thank you for your understanding." He immediately called her cell. He knew something was wrong. Christie never closed the office. Wendy was always there. She answered on the first ring, "Hello Mr. Traveler, how are you?" Matt only partially heard her, "Why is your office closed? I got a funny message that you'd be back on Monday. Are you ok?"

Christie was angry and said, "Well, Mr. Fogelberg, if you hadn't been out of town or should I say the country, you would have heard that your sister was shot last night!" Matt screamed, "What? Are you kidding me? What happened? Are you okay? Where are you? Why didn't your secretary call me?" She stopped him, "Matthew! Stop. I am gonna be fine. I was in the parking garage and dropped my keys. When I bent down to get them, I heard 2 loud bangs. Thank goodness, I am clumsy. I saw blood as they ran away. I called 911 and then I think I passed out.

Perry woke me and the ambulance took me to Buffalo General. I got hit in the head, so it didn't hurt this thick skull of mine too bad. I should be home in a day or so. Now let's talk about you!!"

Matt said, "What room are you in? I am on my way to Buffalo General!" He told his secretary, Dana, what happened, and he'd be back later maybe. He promised to keep in touch with her as he'd need her for an alibi down the road. He jumped into his car and headed for the hospital. It was four and a half blocks over up Delaware to Virginia. Virginia to Main and left on Main to High Street. He was in her room in less than ten minutes.

"Geez, Matthew. Did you take a rocket here?" said Christie. Matt looked at the bandage on her head and grimaced, "That must have hurt. Did you get a look at the guy that shot you?" Christie said, "Matt, sit a minute. Let me get used to seeing you back in the States!" "Sis, come on. Do we have to discuss this now?" said Matt.

Christie was grinning, "So you obviously don't take advice from your attorney; nor do you adhere to anything the judge hands down in decision! I was so upset with you. If I had you here when I heard, I would have tried to slap some sense into you. You're a grown man Matthew. You're a role model in the community and you still act like that 12-year-old that used to steal bikes. You make me crazy sometimes." "OK Christie, look. I wanted to see Linda as we had something special down in Kissing Bridge when she rescued me on the hill. I was unsuccessful in Key West, but I knew where she would be in Paris, so I took a shot. I guess my calculations on how great a lover I am were greatly over-estimated. She dropped me like a large boulder. No one is the wiser as you and she are the only ones who officially know I left town. My secretary will attest that I was at Sara's resting so I wouldn't be disturbed. Now how are you really?" Christie knew she couldn't stay mad at her brother for long and just resigned herself to the fact that he will do what he will do, "I am fine. I lost some blood, but the doc said I was anemic and needed some blood anyway. The rest has done me a world of good. To answer your questions, no, I don't know who shot me.

There doesn't seem to be any ill effects other than a sore head where they stitched me up." Matt said, "I got a letter from the police saying I was the lead suspect in the murders. They want me to confess by noon on Friday." Christie looked puzzled, "I got the same, 'Personal & Confidential'" letter.

Micah was still looking at the pictures of the bank robber. He had them on his computer now. He was unlucky as no matter how he blew up the pictures; the fugitive was unrecognizable. He was going to call the Manager of the Statler and get Sara's number. The clerk he had asked to take photos of what looked like a blonde person dressed in all black may be his only chance of identifying the person. He dialed the Statler.

It sounded like Erik Slay was working. Micah asked to speak to Dean Coretti, the Manager. "Just a second, I'll see if he is available. Can I tell him who's calling, please?" Micah said, "tell him Micah is calling. I worked the Seles/Murphy wedding last night in the Ballroom." Micah waited five minutes and heard, "Micah? Dean here. What's up?" Micah told him what happened on the balcony …. He was interrupted, "Micah, Sara called me last night after her shift and let me know what happened. She said she got four pictures of the blonde woman in black, but she was very spooked. The woman saw her with a phone pointed at her and yelled for her to stop then ran out the circle exit. I have the pictures. Now that I know it's you, why are these important? Micah said, "I think someone robbed the new bank up the street. I was on the balcony getting ready to take photos of the wedding party arriving and I heard two gunshots. I saw this person leave the bank garage and run right toward the hotel. They had a ski mask on so I couldn't see them. When can I get the pictures? Can you email them to me? Dean said, is 'Blair Photos.com' still running? Micah confirmed that it was. "I will send them right over and let me know if you catch her." Thanks so much!" said Micah and hung up the phone.

Now he'd wait to see if he could recognize the woman. It took only a few minutes for the emails to arrive. He anxiously opened the emails from Dean. There were the four pictures sent from the Statler Hotel. He opened the first. You could tell it was a blonde but not much else. In the next one, she had her head turned away. The third was her yelling at the clerk but she had her hand up to her face. The final picture was a side shot of the woman with her hand shielding her face. He enlarged the photo. Her left hand had a ring on it. He'd seen it before. He thought it looked familiar. He called Perry Kline.

Perry picked up his phone at his desk, "Detective Kline." Micah said, "Perry, this is Micah. I am back from Florida and catching up on lots of wedding jobs. By any chance was there a bank robbery at the Chase Bank at Delaware and West Mohawk yesterday?" Perry replied, "I don't think so but there was a shooting in the bank garage that day. Why do you ask?" Micah said, "Well I may have pictures of the suspect. I was up on the second-floor balcony of the Statler Hotel waiting to take pictures of a wedding party set to arrive when I heard two shots.

It scared the devil out of me and almost fell. I turned and saw a person in all black running from Mohawk down Delaware to the Statler and they ran inside. I called the desk and was able to have a clerk snap a couple of shots of the fugitive as they ran through the Statler lobby. It was a blonde woman. Are you at your computer?" Perry said he was. Micah continued, "I will email this one picture and you tell me if you recognize anything in the photo. Here it comes." Perry waited and his email popped up. He opened the photo from Micah. It was a blonde woman with the face obscured by their hand, but the hand had a distinctive ring on it. Perry thought out loud, "Hey, isn't that the same ring we saw on Victor Sinclair when he was found at the Marina?" Micah said, "Yeah, you're right. I knew I had seen it before but yes that is the ring.

Could that be Charmaine in the picture? "By the way, what happened at the bank?" Perry said, "I guess you didn't hear. It was Christie Mahern that got shot. Luckily, she had dropped her keys and the bullet hit her in the head but hit nothing vital. There were two shots. That is what you heard, right? All Christie reported is the person was all in black. Micah, send me the rest of the photos. I gotta go and Thanks."

Perry yelled for Paul. He was just around the corner coming from getting them coffee. "What's up, Partner?" Perry showed him the picture. Paul said, "Isn't that Victor Sinclair's ring? Is that Charmaine? Isn't that the Statler Lobby? Perry answered, "Yes to all your questions."

Perry continued, "I printed off several other photos to see if we can confirm that it is her. We will have to track her down and question her and see if she has the ring on." Paul waited with him for the pictures to print.

Joni was sitting in the room with Christie at Buffalo General Hospital. She said, "It sure is taking the doctor long enough to show up. Didn't he say it would be early?" Christie was sitting on the bed, dressed and ready for discharge, "Yes, he did but he is also the ER MD on duty. Things happen and he probably got tied up." Joni said, "I'd like to tie him up, I'll tell you." Christie laughed, and in walked Dr. Grace. Both Christie and Joni began to blush. Dr. Christopher Grace was a very astute young man.

He saw their faces and said, "Were you just talking about me? Sorry I am a little behind as I had two emergencies come in early today." The ladies' faces both got redder. Dr. Grace let them off the hook saying, "Well Ms. Mahern, how are you feeling today? Any dizziness or headaches? How did you sleep last night? Christie was glad to have a distraction from the questions to answer, "Feeling great. No dizziness or headaches and I slept like a log last night." Dr. Grace said, "OK, Counselor, let's break you out of this place. Remember, Nurse, Traci Lynn, she will give you discharge orders that gives you care instructions for the wound which is healing nicely. Most important is no heavy physical activity for a week or so. If you have any headaches, call us immediately. OK?"

Christie knew she would, "Yes Dr. Grace, Traci Lynn has already gone over that very thoroughly, and thank you and your staff for everything." "Ok then, take care," said the doctor as he left the room. The nurse handed her the paperwork and asked if she wanted a wheelchair to the front door. Christie stood and hugged Traci and said, "No, I'll walk. Thanks for everything." Joni walked with her as they took the elevator down to her car at the front door.

Joni said, "OK, we can go to your house unless you'd like to stay with me for a while?" Christie said, "If it wouldn't be inconvenient, I would like that a lot. I would have someone to talk to at night especially. Could we swing out to my place and grab some clothes? I also need my briefcase and computer from my car."

Joni said, "Tell, you what, I'll drop you at my place, run downtown to your car and get your briefcase and computer. I have your keys, so I'll swing by your house and grab some comfortable clothes and some nightwear. Anything else?" Christie said, "Perfect."

Charmaine was sitting in her kitchen looking over the letter from the police again. She decided she'd drive to Parker's office and confront him about the letter. It really angered her that she was sent this accusation.

Joni walked back into her house around 3 p.m. Christie was sitting in her recliner watching Oprah on TV. Joni said, "I am exhausted. I got your computer and briefcase. Got some clothes and picked up your mail. I also stopped and got us a bunch of food from Bar Bill's. Now, I need a drink!"

Christie thanked her about five times before Joni sat on the loveseat next to her. Joni said, "I meant to tell you. I got this letter from the police. It said I was the lead suspect…"; Christie stopped her, laughing, "You got one too? That is hilarious. Well, I got one and Matt got one and you got one. I wonder who else receive one? Let me call Perry. I need to tell him about all this and where I am, so he doesn't worry." Then added, "Or have a conniption!!!" They both laughed.

"Detective Bureau, Kline speaking," said Perry. "Well, Detective. How are you doing? I just wanted to let you know that I have been released from the hospital. I am staying with Joni Wilsco for a few days. You are the only one who knows. I thought it best to lay low, in as much as you have not apprehended the assailant who perpetrated the attack on your favorite counselor."

Perry breathed a sigh of relief, "You really are on your game Mahern. Good thinking. We have some strong leads on the shooter, but I will fill you in when I see you. How are you feeling?" Christie said, "I am doing okay. What have you found out, Perry?"

Perry said, "I should have never said anything. Micah was on the balcony at the Statler Hotel and saw the assailant running from the West Mohawk into the Statler. We have pictures of her. I am going to interview her as we speak. I'll talk to you soon."

Christie's mouth hung open and she closed her phone. "What?" said Joni? Christie said, "They have some picture of the woman in black that ran out of the parking garage into the Statler Hotel lobby." "Really", said Joni.

Charmaine walked into Parker's office. He left the door open as was his usual protocol. "Parker", she began, "I received this letter from…" He held up his letter. "This one?" he asked. "Oh my, YOU got one of these letters? Who sent them?" Parker got up and closed the door. They spoke quietly about who he thought had sent the letters and what they were going to do about it. She was glad he had a plan.

Christie watched Joni, unpack her computer, phone, clothes, and the meal she picked up. She ordered beef on wick, chicken quesadillas, and a bucket of wings and fries from Bar Bill's in East Aurora. Joni said, "I ordered stuff we could share. I didn't know what you'd be in the mood to eat. If this doesn't work, I can cook you something." Christie was so appreciative, "Joni, you did great. I am famished and this all looks superb. If I could have a little of everything, that'd be great. Then I'll probably fall asleep." They laughed. Joni set everything up and asked her if she wanted a glass of wine.

Christie said, "Just water, please. I want to keep my wits about me." Joni said, "Who sent them? Do you know?" Christie was about to say something, but her phone rang. "Hello."

"Hello, Christie, how are you feeling? I just heard what happened to you. This is Catie Fuda." Christie figured Micah had let her know, "I am well. Just a slight inconvenience. Thank you so much for calling. I will probably take a day or two off then return to work." Catie said, "The other reason I called if you have a minute. I received this letter from the police marked…"

Christie interrupted, "Personal & Confidential?" Catie said, "Yes, how did you know?" Christie continued, "I have several folks who received one. My plan is for all of us to gather at the police department and confront them about it. We will meet in the lobby on Friday at 10:30 am. Can you make it?" Catie agreed to be there. "OK Catie, we'll see you on Friday. Thanks again for calling."

Christie thought for a minute. She wondered who else received this letter. She called Linda Carnello. "Hi Linda, this is Christie Mahern. Are you back in town? Linda replied, "Oh Hey Girl, how are you? I just heard someone shot at you. It is so good to hear your voice." Christie said, "Thanks, I am fine. Just taking a couple of days to recoup." Linda said, "I am so glad you called. I wanted to talk to you about this letter I received from the police." Christie chuckled to herself, "Was it addressed Personal & Confidential? Did it say you were the lead suspect?" "Yes!!" Linda almost screamed, "What the heck is going on? Do you know anything about this?" Christie said, "Yes, I am meeting with those that received the letter as I will represent them if necessary. We are meeting at Police Headquarters on Franklin this Friday at 10:30 am. Can you be there?" Linda sighed relief, Oh my goodness, yes. I will see you there. Thanks so much and take care of yourself."

Christie turned to Joni and repeated what Linda had said. She asked Joni for Margie's number. Christie said, "Give me your phone to use." Joni handed her the phone she had in her hand. Christie dialed, "Hey Margie. This is Christie Mahern. How are you, lady? Are you unpacked and back to the normal grind?" Margie looked again at the caller I.D., "Hey Christie, I am back to working hard. I heard you had a nasty incident the other day. Are you okay?" Christie said, "I am fine. I am just taking a few days to recharge then I will be back at it."

Margie asked, "I am rather glad you called because I may have a situation that may need your representation." Christie knew, "You got a letter from the police, didn't you?" Margie was a bit shocked, "Why, yes, I did. How did you know?"

Christie said, "There were a couple sent out. We are meeting at Police Headquarters Friday can you be there?" After giving her the specifics, Margie said she would be there with bells on.

Parker said to Charmaine as she was leaving his office, "Let's meet here on Friday around 10:15 or so. I have a meeting until ten then we'll see if we can get to the bottom of this situation." Charmaine leaned into him before he opened the door and kissed him very sensuously. Parker was a bit flustered. She said, "I am so glad we talked. Can we have dinner soon?"

Perry saw Charmaine coming out of Parker Clark's office which usually had an open door when a woman was visiting. His closed-door swung open and out walked, Mrs. Sinclair. Perry said to Paul, "Look who Parker was talking to, behind closed doors. We can save ourselves a trip and speak with her now." Paul said, "I will invite her into the conference room. You bring the pictures." Perry walked into the conference room and shut the door. Paul was alone. Perry said, "What happened?" Paul looking very embarrassed said, "She told me her attorney advised her to speak only to Detective Clark so I should either talk to Parker or her lawyer." Perry and Paul looked at each other dumbfounded. Perry said, "Let's go see the Chief."

They walked into Parker's office and closed the door. Parker said, "What do you have for me, gentlemen?" Perry put his hand on Paul's arm as Paul was about to lose his patience and Perry knew it. Perry said, "We have a couple of questions for you Mr. Clark." Parker's eyebrows raised, "Really?" Perry continued, "We want to show you a picture and see if you can identify the person." He put the picture on Parker's desk of the woman in black from the Statler Hotel lobby. Parker looked at it, "This woman's face is obscured. I would not even venture a guess." Perry undaunted said, "Take a look at her jewelry!" Parker looked down and saw the only visible jewelry, "All I see is a fancy ring. No help there I'm afraid." Perry was losing patience as well at this point. Then he took a beat to calm himself and began again.

"Okay Parker, it is the ring we found on Victor Sinclair when he was uncovered in the snow at the marina. Now, who do you think might be in possession of that ring since she buried her ex-husband?" Parker thought a minute to measure his words, "Gentlemen, I have no idea if that is Victor's ring or not. It may not be the only ring of its kind. You are going to need more evidence than that to prove this is Mrs. Sinclair."

Perry responded, "We attempted to speak with her after she left your 'CLOSED DOOR' meeting with her. She said to speak to you or her lawyer. We want to know on whose advisement that was and what were you discussing with her?" Parker replied, "Guys, matters I talk about with anyone who visits my office is NO BUSINESS of yours! Also, I have a question for you both of you, but it will have to wait as I am on my way to a meeting."

Micah was in his home office. He was again looking at each of the pictures he had taken of the woman in black for any identifying clues. He had blown them up. He had printed them and looked at them with a magnifying glass. It was a frustrating process with no good results. He looked at the pictures that were sent to him by the Statler Hotel Manager Dean Coretti. The last one he looked at was a side view of her with her hand blocking her face but her ring visible. As he moved the magnifying glass over the photo, he saw what looked like a shadow on her neck. He got closer and noticed it was not a shadow but something on her neck. He went back to his computer.

He found that same picture and enlarged it. He said out loud to himself, "You have got to be kidding. How could I have missed that? I must have been so focused on the ring, I missed this completely. It was a tattoo. You could just barely make out, it was a part of a crescent moon with a partial diamond covered by make-up. Could he have been looking at it being the wrong blonde?" He dialed Perry's cell phone. It went right to voice mail. Micah left this message, "Perry, Micah here. I identified the shooter. Call me." He hung up.

He readied the picture to send by email to Perry and went into the kitchen to grab a coffee. When he sat back down at his desk, his cell rang. It was Perry. Micah clicked send to Perry's email. He answered the phone, "Hi Perry, what's up?" Perry said, "You called me Micah. What have you got?"

Micah said, "Open your email." Perry sighed. He clicked his email and saw one from Micah. He clicked the attachment. He saw the blonde woman with a tattoo, "Micah, is that Linda Carnello?" Micah replied, "I have been thinking about this since I saw it. I remember looking for that tattoo before and saw it on Linda then when I met her at Jacobi's to interview her, it was gone. She had no sign of it in Key West. Now it reappears on a blonde woman in Buffalo. Could it be an Applique?" Perry looked closer, "It is too bad we can't see more of her figure. Linda and Charmaine do look alike."

"Why would Linda be wearing a ring that belonged to Victor? Once again, we have more questions than answers. Thanks for your work on this Micah. I will let you know if it helps anybody identify the woman." Perry hung up.

Paul and Perry sat in the conference room trying to sort out all the information in the case. Again! Perry said, "I hate to say this. At least we haven't had any more murders with the same M.O. Okay, let's review.

Johnny Galway. We think was murdered in the Hyatt Room 220 and taken to a shallow grave on the 400 Highway until uncovered by Christie Mahern. Had she been the murderer, she would not have unearthed him, would she?

Frank Galway. A womanizer like his brother but with a bit more force and less class. Whoever murdered him would have needed help to move him as I don't think I could have moved him myself. So, no women alone on that one.

Victor Sinclair. A real wheeler-dealer. He liked the ladies as well. Kind of an unscrupulous businessman, it was alleged. Hated Johnny Galway. Had no use for Frank and if one person killed all three; it may have been one of the women they all dumped or mistreated badly at one point or were wronged in business.

Freddy Gilroy. He allegedly told Mel Barstow that he helped a woman get rid of some bodies but wouldn't identify her. He was thought to be connected to the underworld but that was never proven. Then he shows up buried in the snow like the others.

Paul said, "What if it was one of the women? Freddy was helping her move bodies then she had to kill him to keep his mouth permanently shut.

We looked at the love aspect and are nowhere. What if it was purely a business deal? Let's say it was drugs. We have heard that Parker is a supposed owner of the Hyatt. We also know he owns the Santa Maria Suites in Key West. If he was the murderer, he could have moved the bodies himself. If all the three businessmen were in on the drug deals and it went south or they wanted more action, could that have been a motive?"

Perry said, "Well, it could have even been Mel Barstow. She may not have dated them but certainly knew them all. If her boyfriend helped her, she may have been the Snow Villain?" Paul said, "Would she then kill her lover?"

Perry's phone rang. It was Christie. "How are you Counselor?" She said, "I am fine. I want to meet with you tomorrow in your conference room at 10:30 a.m. We have a lot to talk about. See you then. Goodbye." The phone then went dead.

Donna Smith comes into the conference room. "Guys, I have been working on these crazy theories about the murders and looked at all the principals. I have found out some interesting facts. Did you know that Parker Clark is a minority owner of the Hyatt? That would give him access to keys. Did you know that Matt Fogelberg was a partner in Hyatt ownership as well? He would then have access to keys. Micah Blair and I have been working on the Key West Connections as we call it. Parker owns the Santa Maria Suites where all your suspects vacationed. They were driven around by Kirt Leoz, a former Private Investigator that worked closely with Parker Clark on his rise to Chief of Detectives.

Now when the suspects were down in Key West, Catie Fuda overheard Kirt talking to Erik Volsier about drugs and their delivery to Neal's place and then north to Buffalo. She heard the names of Matt somebody and Freddy whose name was obscured as two drunk women came out of the ladies' room making a ruckus. I would like to suggest that the drug connection in Key West is the motive for the murders. I think Johnny, Frank, and Victor, were all in on distribution. Maybe that was unknown to each of them. When they found out, this caused a potential problem for the kingpin of the operation. They were killed off as potential problems to a lucrative illegal business rather than scorned lovers. Any thoughts?"

Perry and Paul, were to say the least, flabbergasted yet again. Paul spoke first, "Donna, you bring up an awful lot of questions. First, who is the kingpin? If the Freddy mentioned was Freddy Gilroy and he was a trafficker, why would he cut off the hands that have been feeding him? Could the Matt be Matt Fogelberg? He has interests in the Hyatt as well. Then…" he stopped. Perry finished his question, "Then could the major owner of the Hyatt be the King Pin? If that were the case, we need to start having these meetings where there is no possibility of being recorded at HQ. Donna held her finger to her lips to shush them. Donna looked at them and collected her papers.

She flipped the papers over and began writing something on the back with her bold black pen. It said, 'Don't say another word. We could meet at my house. I make sure I sweep it for bugs weekly. Let's say 4:00 p.m. The address is: 185 Huntington Ave. off Hertel.

Perry called Christie again after they all left the conference room. He was a bit distracted when she called and they really hadn't discussed in length how she was feeling, when she is going back to work, when she is going home, etc. He wanted to offer his house as a respite as well. Not only for wanting to have the woman he adored with him each night but also out of guilt for not protecting her when she returned from Key West. Her phone went to voicemail, so he left a message, "Hi Christie. I hope you are well and recovering nicely. Sorry, I didn't seem engaged when you called today but I think we may have received a break in the murder case."

"I would also like to offer my home for your extended recovery. When you go back to work, I would feel better if you were not alone out in East Aurora each night. I would also like to know what we are talking about tomorrow because I may be busy so if you have a minute tonight, give me a call. Thanks, Babe."

Christie had decided not to talk to Perry before the Friday meeting. She wanted to believe he had not sent the letters out, but her gut told her he was the author as he was really the lead in the investigation. She waited for the call to go to voicemail before she listened to his message.

Christie had a hunch about Charmaine and Parker being an item. She had told Linda they were meeting in the morning and wondered if she should have told Charmaine who then would have alerted Parker. Oh well, she thought. This was all she could do. She looked at Joni and wondered if they were as close as she thought or not. They shared so much, as friends and she was always there for Christie but still. Joni had a relationship with Kirt Leoz and Kirt is an alleged drug trafficker for the operation out of Florida.

Was she still close to him? She watched them interact when in Florida and she could not see anything but a healthy respectful friendship. Either Joni and Kirt had put on a great act, or there was nothing between them. She wondered.

Parker called Margie Galway but got her machine. "Hello, Ms. Galway. This is Parker. I hope you are doing well. I have not seen you in a while and would like to have dinner with you soon. You have my cell number. If you are interested, Thanks.

Donna let them in saying, "Since I have installed the anti-bugging device, I sleep a lot easier now that none of my conversations here are being broadcast anywhere." They laughed. Perry said, "What spooked you at the office? Donna replied, "Just seeing Charmaine walk out of Parker's closed office door made me think about them planning something. Parker always liked to tape all the interrogations in that room. I do not know who I can trust other than you two" Micah Blair walked in. "and him," she concluded. They could now begin their conversations about Parker without worrying whether he was listening to their conversations. At this point, it seemed like a prudent decision.

Perry began the session as Paul could not resist the chicken wings. Avenue Pizzeria on Hertel was his favorite. Perry said, "Donna, thanks for getting us here to talk. You raised interesting points that we were beginning to put together. Parker owning both majority interest in the Hyatt and the Santa Marie Suites in Key West begs the question, how did the girls find the Santa Marie for their vacation.?"

Donna replied, "After asking the ladies, Joni was the impetus for setting it up." Paul asked after a swallow, "Did Joni and Parker ever date?" Perry said, "When we were looking at each suspect, we skipped over Joni as we had run out of time. She dated Johnny and Frank and maybe, Parker, but we will have to confirm. It could not just be a coincidence that Joni set up a reservation at a place Parker owned, could it? Didn't they also get free transportation around the resort that the hotel provided?

Donna offered, "Let me run that one down. I can call Ronnie Olsen as she is the historian for relationships in the area especially for those in power positions." Perry continued, "Okay, both of you should know that I sent out this letter." He held up a copy for them to read:

'Hello, this is the Buffalo Police Department. You have been our lead suspect since we found Johnny. We have watched you since then but obviously not close enough as you have three additional victims...'

They all looked at Perry in shock. "You did not tell anyone, you just sent this out? Who all received this?" said Donna.

Perry listed them, 'Parker, Linda, Christie, Joni, Margie, Charmaine, Catie, and Matt.' "I suppose that we will have activity at HQ tomorrow before noon as they all should be mad as hornets if they are innocent and absent if they are guilty. Of course, Paul, I am hoping that you will be able to use your expert discernment skills on who is acting and who is not when these folks come in." Paul wiped his hands, took a drink, and said, "Well, I certainly am glad you let us know this information in advance so we could prepare. Why in God's name did you wait so long?" Perry said sheepishly, "I have no good excuse other than wanting to observe everyone during the process."

"Now that we know sort of what to expect tomorrow, let us further discuss the things that Donna brought up earlier. We know that Kirt Leoz had the task of driving the ladies around Key West. Kirt was heard, talking to Erik Volsier about a drug trafficking operation which means he is a runner for the operation through Neal Seagle's place. Jodi, Neal's bar manager is the contact there. If Parker owns the Santa Maria Suite, then he ordered Kirt to provide transportation. Kirt being a longtime friend of Joni Wilsco would indicate that she may be a part of the drug ring as well." Donna added, "I have seen her wearing a blonde wig before and she has tattoos. It would not be that far-fetched if she were our female suspect working with Parker who orchestrated things. She and Linda are close so she could have enlisted her to pose as a man asking for the Key at the Hyatt for Room 220."

Paul being the voice of reason at times said, "That's fine folks but do we have any proof?" Perry said, "I know. Paul, check with the clothing issue on when Parker got new gloves. Colello's found one under Christie's car when she uncovered Johnny. Joni dated both Johnny and Frank receiving poor treatment by both. In fact, all their women reported that as well. I will check on how often Kirt flies out of Key West to Buffalo. We need to get more information on Jodi Petrissi from the Buffalo Café. I will research that as well. Donna, follow up on Charmaine. See if she has been involved in drugs or any unlawful activities. Paul, check on Linda and Margie's attachment to either Kirt or Erik Volsier. We'll meet here at 7:30 a.m. tomorrow if that's ok with you Donna." She gave him the thumbs up as she ate a wing. Then Paul and Perry left to return to HQ.

Paul, Perry, Micah, and Donna appeared at Donna's on Huntington at 7:30 a.m. sharp. Micah was the last to arrive and started, "Wait until you hear this. Linda was once married to Erik Volsier. They stayed together for three years until she and Erik differed on a major deal. We guess it was a woman or drugs. She likes women and so does he. Margie has written checks to Erik for large sums of money over the past ten years.

Erik has been a contributor to all of Johnny Galway's campaigns. Also, I found out that Kirt dated Joni, Linda, and Charmaine. Kim Volsier worked as a stewardess on Eastern Airlines."

Perry said, "Great work, Micah. Paul what did you find out?" Paul brought Danish and had just finished one, "Good grief. Parker ordered three sets of winter gloves in November. As Micah filled you in on Linda and Margie, I further researched the Volsiers. They were from Syracuse but broke up when Kim found Erik with Linda his ex. They rekindled the relationship and moved to Reno where they met Parker Clark on a gambling vacation and what turned out to be a search for a Cuban connection for drugs. They formed a partnership, it would appear. This is from a reliable source in Reno."

Donna went next, "Charmaine owned a coffee company with her ex-husband in Syracuse. They split because her ex-husband went to jail for drug trafficking from Venezuela. They bought coffee beans from there and the shipment went through Aruba then Cuba before they arrived in Key West. She got off Scot-free." Our initial investigation of her indicated, she allegedly ran a cocaine operation but there was no evidence to indict. That would not be a large leap to trafficking drugs from Venezuela and Cuba as she may still be in contact with her former suppliers." Perry was furiously writing notes and shuffling papers, "Great job everyone! What I found out after contacting four major airlines is that Mr. Leoz has travelled to Key West 24 times in the past 12 months on those airlines alone.

I also found out that Jodi Petrissi used to work for Charmaine in Syracuse. She left before the CEO went to prison for drug trafficking. Which leads me to conjecture that we have stumbled onto a drug ring of major proportions that led to our four murders at least and quite possibly linked to organizing crime. I connected last night to the FBI here in Buffalo for backup today. I do not know what will go down, but I want them involved and ready later at HQ." Paul, Donna, and Micah were impressed. Donna asked,

"Should we be ready for a shoot-out later?" Perry said, "I considered that, so I have metal detectors set up off the elevator and on the staircase entrances to the second floor. I have a detail of swat there as well.

Matt drove to Christie's office Friday morning and picked her up. She had been there early to sort through mail and catch up with Wendy. Wendy was ecstatic that she was back to work. Christie said she was only in for the morning and would only work half the day. Matt texted that he was out front at 10:15 a.m. Christie was waiting and ready. She jumped into the elevator and went out front to Matt's car. They walked into Police HQ at 10:25.

Margie was there at the door, Catie and Linda were walking across Franklin Street toward them as they entered. As they all greeted each other, Joni walked in. They went upstairs to the second floor.

As the group exited the elevator, they saw Charmaine walking toward the conference room ahead of them. Inside were, Paul, Perry, Donna, and Parker already seated at the conference table. Perry stood up and said, "Well Ms. Mahern, you have brought a small crowd with you this morning. Please, all of you, help yourself to the coffee and Danish. We will wait for everyone to sit. Matt was the only one who grabbed a coffee. The rest of the ladies sat around the conference table.

Perry began, "Thank you all for coming. I assume you are here to confess to the murders, but I will let each of you have your chance to speak. I imagine the first question for all of you may be, why was the letter sent. The truth is, after our long investigation and research, there was no clear suspect.

I had hoped that the true Snow Villain, as we have nicknamed the murderer, would have reacted to the letter, and come to us for a complete confession. Now which one of you would like to begin?"

Christie stood. She had spoken briefly to everyone except Charmaine. She wanted to express everyone else's concerns, "Mr. Kline, if I may, all the recipients of the letter had a range of emotions. From anger and disgust to fear, trepidation, and confusion. I too received a letter. I want to clearly assert that I committed none of these crimes, except uncovering Johnny Galway's body buried in the snow. I will allow others to speak for themselves."

The tension in the room was palpable. Parker stood. Everyone held their breath. He began, "During the investigation, I asked my Detectives to include me on the list of suspects. They completed their investigations and I was no longer on the suspect list. I have had a relationship of some kind with most of you here both inside my job as Chief of Detectives as well as in my personal life. If anyone here has any questions about the allegations made toward me, I would like them voiced in front of this group as I am sure you will then have an opportunity to get these questions answered."

Donna Smith spoke next as she sat next to Perry, "Chief, I have questions that we need answers to. Is not your majority ownership of not one but two hotels, a conflict of interest? Why did you as the owner of the Santa Maria Suites in Key West provide transportation free of charge to the six ladies in the room who traveled there for vacation.?" Parker replied, "Donna, I have owned portions of both of those hotels since before I came onto the force. There was no impropriety around my owning property. I provided transportation to the group in Key West for two reasons. First, they were all listed as suspects in this case. I wanted to keep as close an eye on them as possible. Second and most importantly, as we do not know who the murderer is, I wanted people the ladies did not know to be as close as possible to them so nothing untoward would occur without protection from anyone or each other."

Donna continued, "Chief, you assigned Kirt Leoz, a former investigator you used here in Buffalo years ago to provide that transportation. Were you aware that he is a mule who transports drugs out of Venezuela and Cuba through Key West to Buffalo and all points north?"

Parker remained seated when he spoke this time but responded firmly, "Detective Smith, as I have asserted to others who have alleged my criminal involvement, I have done nothing illegal and would never involve myself in this type of activity to jeopardize my career and reputation."

Donna was not convinced, "Well Chief, did you know that FBI Agent in charge, Michael Donavan has been following the drug activities with his team from Key West. Agent Donavan, come in please."

Five gentlemen entered the conference room. One, Michael Donavan stood at the door. Another two walked behind Parker Clark. The last two stood behind Charmaine Sinclair. Agent Donavan said, "Mr. Clark, put your hands, on the table. You are under arrest for drug trafficking. We are charging you with the murders of Freddy Gilroy, Frank Galway, and Victor Sinclair. You have the right to remain silent. Anything you say, can and will be used against you in a court of law." The two Agents, behind Parker, grabbed his arms and place handcuffs on his wristed behind his back. They also removed his .32 caliber handgun from his shoulder holster.

At that moment, Charmaine panicked and ran. The two Agents behind her held her and handcuffed her. Agent Donavan continued, "Charmaine Sinclair. You are also under arrest for drug trafficking as well as the murder of Johnny Galway. We are also charging you with the attempted murder of Christine Mahern in the bank parking garage. We are also charging you as being complicit in the murders of Freddy Gilroy, Frank Galway, and Vincent Sinclair. He read her the Miranda rights. Gentlemen. Please remove the suspects. Everyone stay seated as we are charging two more of you.

Four new well-dressed agents in dark blue suits entered the room. Two of them stood behind two additional suspects. Agent Donavan continued, "Joni Wilsco. You are under arrest for bank fraud and conspiracy to traffic illegal substances. You have the right to remain silent… (He recited her the Miranda Rights). The officers placed her in handcuffs, then and removed her. Donavan continued, "Matthew Fogelberg. You are under arrest for violation of the court order to not leave the city of Buffalo. We are charging you with conspiracy to traffic illegal substance. You have a right to remain silent… (He was Mirandized as well.) Officers place Christie's brother in handcuffs and escorted him out of the room.

Donavan spoke again, "Ladies and Gentlemen, you are all free to go. The proceedings in this room are under Federal Rule. You are not to discuss this outside of this room with anyone who has not been in this room. Detectives Kline and Gorci, the FBI appreciates all your efforts in the case, and you are to receive a Commendation from the Bureau. I have my assistant coming in now to answer any questions you might have regarding the events that have taken place today."

EPILOGUE

Micah Blair walked into the conference room as Agent Donavan walked out. Micah began, "As I look at your faces, I see that you may be in shock at what just happened." I am here to debrief everyone. Let me formally introduce myself. I am Micah Blair. My official title is Assistant Agent in Charge, FBI-Buffalo Region. This case has a long history of investigation. There have been hundreds of police agents from all divisions of law enforcement assigned to bring to justice the following players so I will take them one at a time.

Johnny Galway. Johnny was a very, ambitious man starting in his high school sports. When he and his brothers played sports, they ruled the events they were in. Whether it was sports, politics, or women, the Galway family sought only to win at any cost. Margie, you know better than most that John was charismatic but needed significant guidance and support which you provided for years. He unfortunately got involved with the wrong crowd in the mayoral elections to raise lots of money and influence. Margie, you also provided a great deal of monies to Erik Volsier for the campaigns for your late husband. All that money went to the criminals for illegal operations.

You may not have helped as much as John thought he needed. He sacrificed his integrity to master the game without your continued support and got involved in the drug business. Johnny was murdered because he challenged the kingpin for power, thinking he could hold the threat of divulging their identity over them. He lost. He was a major distributor of cocaine and other illicit drugs coming from South America through Aruba and Cuba to Key West then north to Buffalo. His greed is what killed him.

Frank Galway was a much simpler case. He always wanted to win but his only victory was fist fights, dominating women, and working for the unscrupulous element of society thinking he was beyond the law. He too, was a major distributor of illicit drugs.

He double-crossed not only the kingpin of the drug operation but mistreated the wrong female who was unfortunately for him connected to the South American drug lord. He was killed by the same person as his brother.

Victor Sinclair (real name Victor Volsier) has a rap sheet, as long, as I am tall. He and his first wife ran a drug operation in Reno Nevada. She took the hit for that as he framed her. He left Reno.

Victor came to Syracuse New York. He met Charmaine and they were of the same mind and formed a very, strong partnership. She managed the legal aspect of things. He was the mastermind of everything illegal. She got jealous of him and his philandering with women which angered her. He was a major player in the drug distribution organization, and he tried to squeeze his wife out of the operation which led to his demise. Which of course brings us to Charmaine.

Charmaine Sinclair came from a rich family. They imported coffee from Cuba and Venezuela and were not making the kind of money they needed so she began to augment their riches by the addition of drugs in the shipments. The smell of coffee was throwing off all the dogs used to detect drugs. It was successful for years. We eventually charged and imprisoned them. Charmaine's first husband took the fall, or I should say, he is now serving time for that one as she went free. She and Victor partnered initially due to their romantic attraction then developed the dual-focused company. Victor, as I mentioned, wanted to control all the business and every woman he met. This led to Charmaine's anger. They split up but kept an image in public of solidarity. She dated Johnny Galway and financed his campaigns. He owed Charmaine a great deal of money for the drugs Johnny received. He never did pay her back then he dumped her.

She then dated Frank Galway to upset Johnny. He made the mistake of mistreating her. She held a grudge. She no longer needed any of them, so she killed them.

She had worked for the Hyatt Corporation in New York City and still had access to all the hotels because she oversaw the Hyatt corporation's security. She made all the keys for the rooms used to kill Johnny, Frank, and Victor. She also manipulated the computer room registration. She was the one who posed as the man from Room 220. She dressed like a man on many occasions. For example, asking for the key to Room 220 at the Hyatt Hotel, while shooting Ms. Mahern as well as driving the white Cadillac that tried to run Ms. Mahern over at the marina. You were lucky both times." Micah said to Christie.

"We were not sure you were even going to make it out of Key West. That is why we had three different surveillance teams down there.

Matthew Fogelberg was a political leader in Buffalo on the rise. He fell short of victory. He was unable to tolerate that. He got into the drug game through Frank Galway. In an effort, to make enough money to win the election as well as irk Johnny Galway, he got further and further in trouble with the underground. They almost got to him when he had the ski accident but was miraculously saved and nursed back to health by Linda Carnello. She knew he was in over his head because in her efforts to write a column for a magazine, she became a confidant to Charmaine and did not want to be involved with him past their encounter at Kissing Bridge. Not only did Matthew violate his court order about leaving the city, but also went to Paris to follow Ms. Carnello.

While in Paris, he contacted an FBI agent we had planted there under the guise that the money he needed to pay back what he had stolen from the Hyatt would appear when he returned to Buffalo. His stalking of Ms. Carnello really angered Ms. Sinclair as she and Ms. Carnello had developed a deep bond and we believe Matt was her next target after his sister Christie. We also believe her plan was to kill Ms. Carnello as Linda's dating the same men as Ms. Sinclair was what really angered Ms. Sinclair and did not fit into the controlling relationship that she sought with Ms. Carnello.

Freddy Gilroy was in and out of trouble since his teens. He got involved in the Syndicate years ago and it was lucrative for him. He became a very, good hitman. Parker and Charmaine used him for the hits on Johnny Galway, Frank Galway, and Victor Sinclair. Charmaine called him to meet her in Delaware Park off Parkside to pay him for the job he did. She called from Florida. Parker drove up on the snowmobile. He entered his car from the right rear door, handing the money to Freddy. When Freddy turned around to count it, Parker shot him. He had come on a snowmobile, tried to clean the car, and drove him to the zoo parking lot.

Mel Barstow brought us the book Freddy kept in his safe. The last page had Charmaine named as his last business deal and the deal before that was with Parker Clark.

Just so you all know; we have arrested Erik Volsier who is Victor's son. He is also Linda Carnello's ex-husband. He was the drug czar financed by Victor and his wife Kris Volsier, who was embezzling money from VASCO as their accountant out of an office in Reno, Nevada. Linda had left Erik as she realized he was using her as a mule to unknowingly transport drugs. Early this morning, we also arrested Kirt Leoz. He was playing both sides. The police as an investigator and the drug cartel as a carrier. Jodi Petrissi in Key West is in custody as well as she ran the entire smuggling operation out of the Buffalo Café. Ms. Petrissi, as well as the members of her team must have served you there.

Micah took a long drink of coffee. He looked around the room. Those that remained seemed to have looks of disbelief wash over them as he made his remarks.

He went on, "Finally, we come to Parker Clark. The Kingpin as he was known by our organization. He worked so long to develop the power and influence he obtained. Mr. Clark began to need more power and control. This need went seriously out of control. The number of women he dated exceeded all the characters mentioned put together. I would name them all again but most of you are quite familiar with Mr. Clark.

Suffice it to say, he went bad very, early in his career. His aim was to be Chief of Police then Mayor then Governor of New York. He found, however, that he could amass more power by setting his goals a bit lower and using the crime syndicates.

These syndicates he worked against as a police officer, served his need for power and control. He was also a land baron. He owned three hotels. The Hyatt in Buffalo, Santa Maria Suites in Key West, and the Eldorado Hotel and Casino in Reno, Nevada. He has been running a drug organization out of Venezuela for the past twenty years. He visited Aruba and bought condominiums there when they were first building high-rise hotels. He used these to store his drugs from Venezuela.

Aruba is 90 miles from Venezuela and as everything is shipped into the small 'Happy Island', it was a short leap to smuggling drugs there. There are flights to the U.S. twice daily so that was convenient as well. Kris Volsier, for example, was a stewardess on Eastern Airlines and moved the drugs on her flights.

Parker focused on building an empire because he thought the criminals made so many missteps that he found he could improve on them. In his dealings, he found it better to eliminate people rather than try to persuade them to follow his plan. Once he killed Johnny Galway, the other murders became easy for him and his partner, Charmaine Sinclair. No one would dare stand in his way. Charmaine registered herself in the Hyatt system as M. Keen. This we assume was a joke between her and Parker. He strategically dated the women he did to assess them as potential foes. He shrewdly made you investigate him knowing that it would send you off the track. If you discovered any evidence of his illegal activities, he would have eliminated you. He became ruthless and even coined his own nickname, The Snow Villain.

Micah sat next to Christie. "Are there any questions?" said Micah. I went through the information I just recited to you because I want each of you to know how close you were to being another statistic of this crime syndicate. We provided, around-the-clock protection and surveillance to all of you.

It was our suggestion that Perry send a letter so that we could have you all together with the perpetrators."

Perry was the first to speak, "Micah, how long have you been with the FBI? Micah responded, "I just got my twenty-year pin last week. I have worked with Michael Donavan for that long both indirectly and directly on this specific case."

Paul asked, "Perry, how long have you been working with the FBI on this?" Perry said, "Sorry, Paul. I could not give anyone notice the FBI was involved but it was the day Christie uncovered Johnny Galway.

Margie said, "Perry, Paul, and Micah. I guess, we all owe you a great debt of gratitude as you not only solved the case but kept us all safe during the process. Thank you for doing such an outstanding job."

They all began to get up to leave. Micah said, "You all have a great weekend. You will receive a subpoena to appear in court. Please know, we will notify each of you, well in advance. If you have any questions, please do not hesitate to contact me." He handed them each a card as they left the room.

Christie walked over to Perry. He stood as she approached. "Detective Kline, now that you have put this case to bed, could I interest you in having dinner at my place tonight? We have things to discuss of a personal nature."

Perry replied, "Counselor, I have already packed an overnight bag as I plan to provide protection for you this weekend. This protection may be longer, but we will start with the weekend. I just want you to know that I love you very much. I want to be with you forever if you will have me." As always, Christie gave him her biggest smile. He shut the lights out in the conference room as they were the last to leave.

THE END

CPSIA information can be obtained
at www.ICGtesting.com
Printed in the USA
BVHW080050031222
653304BV00009B/869

9 781088 072011